FLESH OF THE BLOOD

GODS OF WAR

To

LISA

MOTHER
SAYS
THANK YOU!

CHEERS

Books by E A. Channon:

Ballad of a Bagpiper - Whatever Blows Up Your Kilt

Flesh of the Blood

Flesh of the Blood - Devastation

Flesh of the Blood - A Call to Arms

To Mother Earth

Prologue

The hunter pulled his heavy fur hood tightly around his face so only his eyes could be seen. With each step he could feel the wind slamming against his body, pushing him back and making it harder to track the animal.

He squinted left and then right quickly as he tried to find out where he was, for suddenly, the landscape disappeared in the white wind. Moving a fur-gloved hand across his face to remove the ice forming by the moment, he stopped quickly, for he caught movement ahead.

He knelt slightly, pulling his pack tighter as he attempted to see through the snow. But try as he might, the frozen landscape revealed nothing as he stared in the direction in which he thought he had seen something.

"Curse the gods!" the hunter said, his breath quickly turning to ice as soon as it left the warmth of his hood, only to be swept away in the wind.

Every hunter had hunted among these mountains for generations. Past hunts had yielded furs from the wolves and bears that roamed the lands, including the impressive white and gray fur coat, boots and gloves that he currently wore. But as the hunter had hiked for days, now the cold was getting inside, making him shiver more than once. Tracking his prey, he considered how far he had come. He had traveled farther into the lands than ever before, and since leaving the valley where his people had lived for generations three days earlier, Viahan Methnorick had used every trick he knew to try catch this prey, but this wolf was the most cunning one he had ever tracked. It had even been able to get out of two of his traps, which he found destroyed like they were toys. In his frustration, he continued to track the animal across the tundra in hopes of finding its lair and cornering it there, but today, he wondered if the creature was playing a game with him instead.

A hunter standing over six feet in height with a powerful muscular frame made from moving stones and hunting animals for many cycles, he remembered when he had seen the wolf he was following for the first time, its massive body almost as big as himself. He paused for a moment.

Closing his eyes quickly to wipe away the thoughts, he remembered something his father once taught him about how to hear even the sound of a mouse's movement. He slowed his breathing and listened for only a moment longer when he finally caught the sounds of his prey.

"WRRRRAAAAAAA!!!"

Methnorick turned his head slightly to determine where the sound was coming from when the howl echoed again. *There you are!* Methnorick thought when he heard the howling echo drift past him through the wind. *Not far away either … good!* Methnorick opened his eyes, pulling his hunting spear from his pack.

I am close now, he thought again, listening to the howling a bit longer.

Gripping his prized spear, he moved as fast as he could through the deep, loose snow, smiling under the fur as he approached the howling. As he moved closer, he flipped back his hood, revealing long dark hair that whipped out behind him.

Methnorick stopped suddenly as he glimpsed his target standing at the top of a hill.

He smiled, believing the snow was covering his scent as he started to approach his prey once again. *Just a bit closer!* he thought as he made his way closer to the creature.

When he got within about 20 feet of the wolf, he quickly took in both its massive size and the beauty of its muscular body as it leaned over an animal it had just killed.

Hoping it didn't get a whiff of his body scent, Methnorick pulled his arm back, and in one quick movement, the spear left his hand and shot across the bright white landscape. Methnorick's smile faded as the creature suddenly turned its head to look directly into Methnorick's eyes.

Everything slowed as Methnorick saw the beast spring back just enough for the spear to pass it by. Methnorick cursed loudly as the wolf turned away from Methnorick and galloped off, disappearing over the crest of the hill, leaving Methnorick standing in the high wind.

"Bastarddddd!!!!" he screamed. "Not again!" he roared as he jumped forward, struggling to move through the thick snow.

Climbing up onto the crest of the hill where moments before the beast had been standing, he looked across the tundra, scanning for any sign of the wolf.

"Where have you gone, beast!" he mumbled. As anger took Methnorick over, he screamed when suddenly the ground gave way under him. Methnorick's screams of anger turned to ones of panic as he disappeared into the dark. For a moment he felt as if he was flying like a bird. Then everything went dark.

Opening his eyes slowly, Methnorick groaned as pain shot through his body. His mind raced as he attempted to look around. As his eyes slowly began to adjust to the darkness, he thought of the legends of his people and what waited beyond, for he wondered if he had entered the realm of the gods at Valu'um! But then he remembered that the first thing you are to find is that the stars above are white and silverish in color. As he considered this and realized he saw no silverish stars, he moved on to considering other options.

As he considered were he might be, he moved to push himself up, but instead of feeling icy rock or dirt ground like he expected, his hands slipped on what felt like the metal his people used for battle. Looking down at his hand, he saw that he was right. He was lying on what felt like metal ... armor. "I am in Valu'um," he stated with wonderment, thinking of the place where the dead roamed above the clouds.

Suddenly, a loud, familiar growl made the warrior jump to his feet and look around.

"You survived as well, beast … Then I am not in Valu'um, for no beast is allowed there … I am alive … alive enough to end your life!" Methnorick grumbled as he reached into his fur coat to pull out the small sword that had belonged to his grandfather.

Gripping his small sword handle, he knew he only had one chance to kill the beast. If he failed, he knew that its muscular arms and claws could ripe him apart blink of an eye. Pulling quiet, slow breaths, Methnorick stepped forward. He quickly stopped when his eyes picked up movement just ahead and above him.

As his eyes adjusted to the dimness, he quickly surmised that the wolf was in some kind of trouble. Slowly stepping forward, prepping himself to move quickly if necessary, he saw that his prey had gotten tangled up in large vine-like ropes near cavern floor.

Smiling at his luck, Methnorick looked around for a way to reach the trapped wolf when a glint of metal caught his eye. Hoping it was his prized spear, he leaned down, using his other hand to steady himself against what he thought was a wall, only to realize his mistake when it suddenly gave way, making him fall hard to his knees. Suddenly, a sound echoed throughout the area, causing him to look everywhere quickly.

"Xitong, yi zuiziao gonglu kaishi chongqi," the unknown voices erupted. A thought quickly crossed his mind that the gods were speaking to him.

Suddenly, the cavern exploded with bright lights, sending sparks of fire everywhere as Methnorick covered his face to protect his eyes.

Another explosion near him made him scream. "The gods are here!"

If Methnorick had been able to look up through the flashes of light and explosions, he would have also seen glass-like cases lining the walls, and where the wolf remained tangled lay two tables — one with a man in a glass case. But, for now, all he cared about was protecting himself from the exploding fire as the wolf roared.

Taking a deep breath, Methnorick lifted his head and looked up just as bolts of light shot through the wolf's body, slamming it hard against the empty table behind it. Finally, the sparks subsided enough for Methnorick to risk lifting his head. As he looked around, he saw an opening. Methnorick stood up and shook the glass off of his hair and cloak, grateful and somewhat amazed to have escaped harm. Looking up, he saw that the wolf wasn't as lucky.

Bolts of light continued to shoot around and through its body, making it shake and spasm. It appeared trapped, which suited Methnorick fine. Damned wolf had caused him more trouble than it was worth. He still needed to find a way out of the cursed cavern when he noticed the table beside the wolf with a coffin on top. *There is a man inside!* His thought was cut off suddenly. A massive stream of bright light flew across the room to wrap around his body, rocketing Methnorick back into a wall and trapping him in the same bolts of light that were holding the wolf on the table.

Around him, bright lights of red, blue and yellow flickered everywhere as he screamed from an unbelievable amount of pain. Suddenly, the bolts of light holding him disappeared, releasing him suddenly so that he hit his head on the side of one of the cases and passed out.

Methnorick awoke with a groan and a throbbing headache as he very slowly opened his eyes to find that he was surrounded by tiny lights that flickered on and off along the walls like fire bugs of the forests.

Pushing himself up fully, he felt his headache immediately subside, and something else. Something … different. Straightening himself, he looked down at his hands and slowly opened them to see sparks of light snake along his fingers and move up his arms.

"What's happening to me?" Methnorick whispered as he looked up, seeing that lining the walls on both sides of the chamber were hundreds of glass cases filled with what looked like men and women sleeping. Then he noticed the coffin on the table top was smashed to pieces and the man inside was gone. The wolf before it was now transforming into something else before his eyes. Slowly, the wolf was becoming a man.

He steeled himself and stepped closer to find himself staring down at a man, not the wolf he had been chasing.

The man lay still as Methnorick observed him. He was about the same height, dressed in robes of some kind, but it wasn't those that made Methnorick curious. It was the fact that the man's hands were slowly going from large claws like those of a wolf to hands like his, and his face … It was doing the same, going from what resembled that of a wolf to …a man.

In all the lands, what is this place? Is this truly Valu'um? Methnorick raised his hands up to his face as he thought about his situation. Suddenly, anger flowed through him and sparks of light shot out of his hands, slamming against the glass cases closest to him, making him jump back in shock.

He gasped at the fire he had produced.

He could feel the heat within his hands as he stared at both palms. What he couldn't feel was the madness filling his mind and soul as he leaned his head back and threw out the loudest laugh he had ever produced.

"The gods have given me their power!" He laughed loudly as he opened his right hand and welcomed the burning feeling in his palm as another stream of fire shot out to quickly cover another wall in flames.

Methnorick danced around the chamber, laughing as the entire chamber was in flames.

"I have your power and now I am free of you!" he screamed out. "I can do anything!"

But if I am ever going to show the world what I can now do, I had better find a way to get out of here, he thought quickly as an explosion erupted not far behind him. His eyes moved to the opening he had fallen through as snow drifted down.

How? he wondered as he closed his eyes, thinking of it.

Suddenly, Methnorick felt cold snow and wind slam into his body. As he opened his eyes to find himself standing on the surface, Methnorick laughed in delight.

"I AM A GOD!" Methnorick screamed loudly as he raised his hands, sending out more bright-white fire into the sky. He turned himself around a few times as he let the fire race high into the air when he saw the pack he had dropped earlier falling into the hole. Kneeling down to lift up his pack, Methnorick began walking back towards where his people lived, no longer caring that he had no furs to protect him again the cold winds.

As Methnorick's form slowly disappeared into the snow drifts, below, within the chamber, the man that Methnorick had left lying unconscious awoke with a loud gasp of air to find himself surrounded by flames and smoke.

The man looked around with wonderment, trying to discover where he was and what had happened. Lifting his palms, he looked at them, trying to figure out what the strange feeling was as he blinked his eyes. He attempted to think of a place just on the edge of his mind … maybe the place he must be from …

"What was it called?" the man mumbled as he looked around the chamber, taking in the lights that flickered on and off around him and the spreading flames as a memory flashed across his mind. He saw himself tied or strapped to this table near him … a man looking down at him … laughing.

Voices in a strange language erupted in the air around him, causing him to jump. Or maybe not so strange. He felt he knew the words. As he listened, he looked around for a means of escape. "Xitang chongxin quidong, xitong you huozai weixian … Xuyao gangzhu."

However, the smoke was too thick. He couldn't even see the lights anymore. He began to cough. His body was failing. His existence was going to end here, just as it had begun.

As he sat down and wrapped his arms around his body, ready to accept his fate, he thought about how he didn't want to end; he just wanted to be away from the fire.

Suddenly, the man felt a gust of frigid air nearly knock him over. His hands instinctively reached out to balance his body and sank into a soft white substance.

As he pulled himself up, hand over hand, he took a moment and found himself staring at one of the broken glass chambers with some writing along the bottom.

Whelor ... My name is Whelor! He blinked a few times as the word rang through his mind and he attempted to think of why he would have been behind that glass. *Why ... Who am I?* he considered as a small explosion below made his thoughts return to where he was, and he grabbed the slick, weird rope. He pulled himself to the opening and slowly clawed his way out through the hole and into the terrible, cold wind and snow.

Nothing moved around him — no life, nothing except whiteness. Pulling in a deep breath, Whelor shook his head, not knowing what to do, when he noticed what looked like footprints in the snow. *Life!* he thought.

Putting one foot in front of the other, Whelor walked slowly to disappear into the snowy wind, unknowingly following Methnorick.

Chapter One

Within the forest, on the western side of the battle field, the elves were engaged in a fierce battle. The surprise appearance of the trolls made it very hard for the elves to get any advantage over them.

Screams of pain and yells to fight rang through the trees as trolls tore into the elven defenses. Kalion arrived to find himself deep in the lines, fighting, ducking and moving quickly, attempting not to get scratched by the dirty creatures. He had heard that one scratch could cause a man to get sick, eventually turning him into one of those creatures.

He already had a nasty gash on his arm from an orc's blade that had gotten by his sword earlier, but as he had told the cleric who tended his wound, nothing short of death itself would keep him out of the battle.

"We need to move NOW!" a cleric cried out. "Trolls are getting close to the wounded, and the general doesn't have any other warriors to protect them." Kalion turned to observe clerics lifting the wounded to their feet and moving those that could walk to another area as the threat from the trolls grew.

Blowing out a breath, Kalion heard a deep growl behind him and instinctively dropped and spun around just in time to duck under the claw that had been aimed at his head. Seeing the still-smoldering arrow within reach, he rolled away from the troll to hide it from the sight of the troll still pursuing him. Just as the troll reached him, Kalion flipped around and stabbed the burning arrow he'd been hiding hard into its face. The troll screamed in pain as fire burst out of its face to envelope its body. Kalion turned and ran over to the fatally injured elf.

"Let me help." Kalion smiled down at the warrior, who was sweating heavily. Both knew that the wound on his leg was one of death. Neither mentioned the fact.

He pulled the elf to the rear as Niallee ran up, dropping her bag hard on the ground to look at the warrior for a moment and then at Kalion.

"Do you feel well enough to move?" she asked the injured elf. "Do you want some potion to help you?" she continued as she opened up her pack.

"Give it to ones that need it, my friend … I'm doing well enough to fight trolls," the elven warrior teased with a weak smile. Niallee winked and smiled back at him before pouring a small amount of liquid into the elf's mouth. Standing up, she turned to see Kalion's eyes boring into hers.

"It won't be long now. He will soon feel no more pain," Niallee whispered sadly.

Kalion stared at her a moment longer and then nodded, turned and ran back into the thick of battle.

* * *

Kikor fought with Holan at her side, who was keeping up his end of fighting, for around the dwarven warrior lay as many as 20 dead orcs. Holan was grinning from under his beard, now thick with orcish blood as he sliced his axe through their armor. He stood there for a few moments, breathing heavily as he looked around to see his results.

"I do na think they are retreating this time, my friend," he moaned up at Kikor, who lowered her bow after killing an orc who raised its head above the shield wall. She nodded to herself as she looked around, taking in the battle before her. She could see orcs falling to the ground everywhere, but when one fell, two took its place. Then something, or the absence of something, caught her eye: arrows being released from the cliffs had almost stopped, and she could see this was causing a difference on the field. Around her she could see her fellow elves dropping as orcish arrows flew into them, but their own archers were only causing a small amount of damage to their enemy.

The lines were holding, though, even pushing the orcs back as she spied Whelor swinging his weapon, cutting through everything he hit. She saw that they were using the rock face as a defense of their left flank, and using it well. Hearing a cry from Holan, she turned her head just in time to raise her bow up, killing an orc that got close to her.

She scanned the field, watching banners rise and fall, as arrows flew overhead, but it was the figure in the middle that caught her attention: Methnorick.

* * *

"TROLLLLS!" The screams echoed through the battlefield as elves scrambled to form a defensive. Just as General Summ ordered his elves over to battle, the trolls came out of the tree line. One of the mages released bolt after bolt of flames at the trolls, which had little effect on them.

Summ considered the progress of the trolls as they pushed further towards the center of the battlefield when suddenly a burst of bright light erupted amongst the trolls, making those closest to the light instantly evaporate and others a bit farther away burst into fire. As Summ looked around, he noticed not a single elf was affected by the light. Those elves fighting the trolls stopped, looking at the light as it dissipated to reveal a man standing there.

"When you battle a Budador, always bring the power of the gods with you!" the figure said as it pulled back its hood, revealing the smiling face of Meradoth.

As Meradoth looked around, he saw a team of elven arrows now trained on him. An elven officer walked over, looking at Meradoth with confusion. "While we appreciate what you just did, who are you?"

Smiling at the question, Meradoth looked around at the scene before him and saw that all the trolls that had broken out of the forest line were now just dust. He looked at the elven guards with weapons trained on him.

"Meradoth, my friend ..." He looked around, waiting for them to lower their weapons. When nothing changed, he reminded them, "I am with Kikor and Kalion's group." This seemed to work, for the elves around him lowered their weapons. Meradoth, looking around once more and making sure all the creatures were dead, then stated, "We have to deal with the Budadors quickly."

"Budadors?" the elven captain asked.

"Trolls!" Meradoth stated. "There are still more of them nearby that we will need to deal with. My magic would not have reached into the tree line."

Nodding, the warriors gathered around the mage. Summ watched as his elven troops turned and disappeared into the forest with Meradoth.

* * *

Methnorick watched the battle from his horse.

"My lord ... the Budadors are causing the desired chaos in the elven ranks, sir," the mage next to him said, speaking loudly enough to be heard over the noise of the battle. "They have drawn a good number of the elves into the forest."

"Good, now Chansor can continue his attack," Methnorick stated under his breath. Methnorick looked up towards the sky, signaling Chansor flying overhead with his mind: *Continue attacking the southern elven ranks to break them.* He still needed to get out of this valley, and that was the only way.

"As you wish!" Chansor returned, heading towards the southern ranks to make another run.

"My lord," Methnorick's slave said a number of times to get his attention before Methnorick looked down, seeing the dark elf standing below him, looking up with a question.

"My lord ... scouts have found Sunorak," the dark elf said, swallowing.

"Where ... where, elf?" Methnorick's voice made the elf shake more.

"On the high cliffs to the east, my lord, where we are trying encircle the elves." The elf swallowed.

"Then why has he not answered me?!" Methnorick's face showed his anger.

The servant quickly finished what he started. "Sir, that is ... We found his body, my lord."

Methnorick's anger grew as the news of the mindslayer's death sunk in. But to the slave's surprise, Methnorick slowly let the anger leave as he looked down, telling the elf, "Go and make sure to hold the cliffs at all costs."

Methnorick remembered the message he received several days back from Sunorak, telling him that all was well. Without the mindslayer, he knew that his numbers, even with the trolls, wouldn't hold long. Chansor was his only hope.

* * *

As the fighting continued in the northern section of the battlefield, in the southern lines General Vana and General Auliic were keeping the orcs back. Each time they charged in, their quick reactions confused the orcs, allowing them to make headway.

As Vana directed a few of his men to move to the western edge of the line to keep the orcs from flanking them, he saw an elven messenger running up.

"What news do you have?" he called down as the elf ran up.

"Sir, the northern army is being devastated by trolls that have entered the battle, but they are holding the line, sir." The messenger paused to take a breath and then continued, "General Summ believes they need reinforcements!"

"Our original mission was to block Methnorick from getting south into the mountains ... It seems he's having a hard time moving his troops from the north to the south and is pushing harder against us!" Vana paused and looked at each of the leaders. "If we attack using a quick, hard movement from the south, it could throw them off balance … giving Summ what he needs without sending actual troops. Sending troops from our ranks would give Methnorick an opening south, and we can't have that."

"Actually, that would be three equal fronts, then, with the Pegasi fighting from the air," Auliic piped in as he looked up in the air. Vana and the others turned their eyes to look up and observe that coming out of the clouds were scores of flying horses.

Vana turned to the messenger. "Let Summ know what is planned." Vana then whispered, "The battle has turned against Methnorick!"

Chapter Two

Summ turned to see fires now glowing upon the fields, making those fighting near him turn into shadows. He looked high above to observe the battle now raging in the skies. A huge dragon was fighting the Pegasi that had come from the south. This was keeping the dragon in the clouds away from the field. He turned to see Kikor and Holan fighting when an explosion to their right made both look quickly to where they saw a huge ball of fire rise up from the ground as screams erupted.

Both looked at the other, knowing that the shield wall would fall apart and collapse. Elves everywhere turned and ran away while the elven sergeants that were still alive tried to control their retreat.

Kikor released the few arrows she found into the now-charging hordes of orcs that were taking advantage of the elven confusion. Her arrows made many burst into the now-familiar flames, which, for the moment, stopped the charge before it could really start.

"Come on, Kikor!" Holan screamed as he could see orcs charging through the opening of the shield wall. The dwarf's feet ran hard over the ground as he stumbled over bodies of wounded and dead elves. Kikor stood for a moment, and then, shaking her head, she ran to catch up to the dwarf.

As the two retreated, they noticed many elves were forming another wall in the hopes of holding off Methnorick's troops even longer. Enough had gathered to hold the orcs back from moving any farther north.

As word moved through the orcs ranks of the elven resurgence of strength, a moment of reprieve from the onslaught occurred as the orcs paused to consider retreating. This gave the elves the confidence that they might win this battle, charging back into the battle, driving the orcs back once again.

Kikor looked about and saw General Summ off in the distance. General Summ had been wounded by the axe of a large orc who had tried to cut his head off, only to be deflected by Summ's shoulder armor, but in doing so, Summ lost the ability to use his left arm. Throwing the shield to the ground, Summ fought the large orc for a few more moments until he was able to move around the creature and surprise it when his sword erupted out of its back, cutting the spine of the orc in half.

As the orc fell to the ground, blood gurgled out of its mouth as he tried to say something to Summ. Just then, Summ heard yells from his troops. Looking around the area, Summ was as confused as many others near him.

"Find out what is happening!" he yelled at one of his guards. Meanwhile, Summ's guards were finishing off the orcs that had tried to attack the elven general.

Taking a moment, Summ pulled out his water pouch and took a deep drink, closing his eyes for a moment. Then he looked around, trying to see if there was a cleric nearby. He saw a few, but all were busy taking care of his wounded warriors. The pain from his shoulder started to move through his body, but it was not bad enough to take one of them away from his men.

Holding his arm with his hand, he tried to massage the area to determine if the arm was broken. He felt a tremendous, sharp pain, and he still couldn't move it. This caused him to rethink the move of sending his guards away or getting one of the clerics.

Instead, he turned back to the battle, asking the captain nearby, "Do we have any mages left?" The captain's face told him the answer. "Find any still alive quickly and move them to join the battle here and here," he stated as he pointed to the right and left lines. "We have to move up the middle of the field with the rest of the warriors we have and push ... and I mean push hard ... to get the orcs to panic." The captain looked at Summ and then at Summ's arm but then ran off to carry out his orders, leaving the elven general.

"I'm sure we do not have enough warriors to finish this battle, but by the gods, I'm going to make sure that every orc and Methnorick know who tried to stop them this night!" Summ's voice made the elves around him nod. "Take your blade and put it through the heart of every orc you find!"

As he lifted his own blade, still covered in orcish blood, every voice around him cheered.

"Let this be a night of song and legend!" Summ called out as he ran forward.

* * *

Meradoth was joined by Kalion once he entered the trees. After a brief acknowledgment, they continued together farther into the forest, watching for trolls, with elves that had followed Meradoth spreading out through the trees.

Kalion was the first to catch sight of one. He motioned to Meradoth that the creature was just ahead and to the left of their position. Once Meradoth acknowledged back, Kalion moved slowly farther into the trees, with Meradoth following just behind him. They came up to a clearing, where they saw a number of trolls gathered around.

Meradoth whispered in to Kalion's ear, "That must be the Budadors' leader in the center there. The tall one with the strange horns on his head."

Kalion whispered back, "What would you call those horns?"

"They look to me like the horns of a sheep." They both looked at each other with raised brows.

"How do we kill it? And, if I recall, if we kill the Budadors' leader, the others will turn tail and run, right?"

"Correct. They are unusual creatures that do not work together without a leader, and they will have to wait for a new one to be born. The only way to kill the leader is to take his head."

Kalion motioned to the other elves and laid out a plan. The other elves were to move around to the far side to distract the other trolls while Meradoth blinded them all with fire, leaving him to come from behind to attack the leader.

As the elves moved into position, everything occurred just as Kalion had planned. However, when he attacked the leader, he found that it was a bit harder to just cut his head off than he originally thought. For he hung on to his sword, which was wedged into the creature's throat, as he gargled and tried to scream for what seemed like ages. Slowly, the blade worked its way through the creature until, eventually, Kalion was able to jump to the ground as the creature's head rolled to land at his feet. The death of their leader made the rest of the trolls retreat back to the swamps to the west, just they had thought.

Kalion watched them run away for a moment. Then the ranger moved to assist a wounded young elf, helping him to an area where the clerics were treating the wounded. Kalion smiled down as he handed the elf off to the clerics and then turned to review the battle before him. Breathing in a deep breath, he could see the entire battlefield from where he stood and saw that something had changed.

The sounds of screams echoed, for the hard push that the troops to the north had been receiving from Methnorick looked to be redirected towards the south. He could just see that the orcs were gathering more of their troops to make a push in that direction.

Looking around the field, he tried to determine where he would be needed most. Nodding to himself, he jogged up the field quickly. As he moved around a group of elves fighting, he came face to face with an ugly-looking giant of a creature holding a blood-covered longsword. Lifting the weapon up, the creature screamed as it swung it down at Kalion.

"Wow … big boy there!" Kalion ducked under it just as it cut across the air. Feeling the pressure of the blade just pass his ear, Kalion was able to look up and smile as it flew past.

Lifting his body slightly, he struck his own sword forward, hoping that in doing so it would knock the creature off balance, but seeing the sword coming, the creature stepped back.

As it did, though, its left foot stepped on a dead orc, and as Kalion watched, it stumbled back slightly, losing its balance and giving Kalion the chance to move in and dig his sword into the creature's stomach.

The motion of Kalion's sword digging in finally pushed the creature over to fall back and slam into the ground with a loud grunt. As it fell backwards, Kalion used the momentum of his sword in its stomach to fling himself up, making it easier to jump up onto its chest. Seeing it struggle for a moment, Kalion pulled his sword out of the stomach and stepped forward quickly to swing it across the creature's exposed throat, killing it.

Kalion leapt off the creature to continue further into the battle when he came upon a dwarf lying on a dead body of one of the large creatures that it must have killed. Instantly seeing that it was his friend Holan, Kalion ran over and fell to his knees next to his friend.

"Holan!" he yelled while shaking the dwarf.

The dwarf's eyes were closed, but, hearing the familiar voice, they slowly opened. Looking up to see Kalion's blood-caked face looking back, Holan opened his mouth for a moment, but all that came out was a was massive cough that made the dwarf bend slightly over as his body squirmed from the cough.

"Aye … I am alive, my friend … Are you taking a break, then?" Holan's voice was scratchy and rough, but at least the humor was there.

"I am taking a break from saving the elves to assist you," Kalion said, smiling back and almost laughing himself as he tried to keep up the conversation. When he pulled his hand away from his friend's shoulder, it was covered in dwarven blood. "What happened?" Kalion asked quickly as he looked at his hand covered in blood.

Holan leaned his head back slightly and indicated the blue-black armored creature that was lying behind him. Kalion looked the creature over and saw that the blood coming from the wounds was different from anything he had ever seen, but similar to the green of an orc.

"Did he … The ugly thing surprised me as I was fighting those orcs behind you …" He coughed a few times and then slowly continued. "I was able to get its knee hard with my axe, but … but it got my helmet off with a blow of its sword." Holan's face showed Kalion that the dwarf had fought a hard battle.

"Have you seen the others? … Kikor?" Kalion whispered as he looked up, hearing a yell off to his left and seeing an orc run by.

Holan thought for a moment at the ranger's question and then looked up as Kalion saw some blood leaking out of the dwarf's mouth now. Holan swallowed slowly as he tried to answer the question.

"Kikor … She and I were keeping those orcs from flanking us. She saved us from those orcs getting behind us … but somewhere she and I got separated.

"Kalion … we need to end this battle … I'm getting hungry." Kalion looked over, seeing that Holan was looking at him, smiling now. Holan's smile made Kalion almost laugh as he looked from his friend to a group of elves running past, charging into the battle.

"Let's get you to into the care of the clerics. Can you stand?"

"No. Just let me be. I'll be battle-ready in just a moment." But Kalion could see that wasn't true.

"Is there anything I can do? Anyone I can give a message to?"

"Just kill Methnorick for me."

Seeing two elven clerics helping a wounded elf, Kalion called them over to assist his friend. They looked into each other's eyes, and he said, "Do what you can. Just stay with him, please." Kalion looked down at his friend.

"Give Methnorick my regards. It has been a great adventure."

Reaching down for his sword, he stood up to continue moving

through the battlefield. He needed to find Kikor and Methnorick, but first he looked back at his friend one final time.

He was scanning the battle around him when bright flashes of something erupted. He heard screams, which got his attention, so he ran to stand on top of a dead giant in order to see what the screams were and where they were coming from. As he looked around, he caught sight of the one he was looking for not far away from where he stood.

"Methnorick!" he gasped. The figure sat on top of his black horse, swinging a fire chain. When the chain hit anything, it would burst into flames. Kalion watched the scene for a moment longer as he considered what to do.

Not even taking a breath, Kalion gripped his sword, looking around for a way to get within reach of Methnorick and seeing a path open up when some elves were able to knock a group of orcs back. His only goal was to try to get to Methnorick, no matter what the cost.

* * *

Methnorick could see the battle through the flames as he reduced each elf to ashes. Things to the north with General Summ were not going in his favor. The Trolls had failed, and now, to the south, he saw a whole detachment of orcs fall backwards like they were toys, so he leveled a few blasts at the elven monks trying to stop them. Even Chansor had failed him, for after he sent him to continue dives on the southern lines, it seemed he ended up engaged in battle with those flying horses. As he gripped his reins tightly with one hand and swung his fiery chain with the other, using its flames to ignite those elves around him, he saw through an opening in the battle a man standing on top of a dead giant. A fire raged behind the man, making his silhouette look darker, causing him to stop laughing and stare at him. Looking over him, his long hair whipped across his face as a high wind moved through. Methnorick could see the two blades he held to his sides were covered in blood.

His mouth curled slightly as he studied the man, quickly taking in the flowing clothing that moved with the wind and noticing that he was not as covered in armor like all the others. Recognition started to show on Methnorick's face.

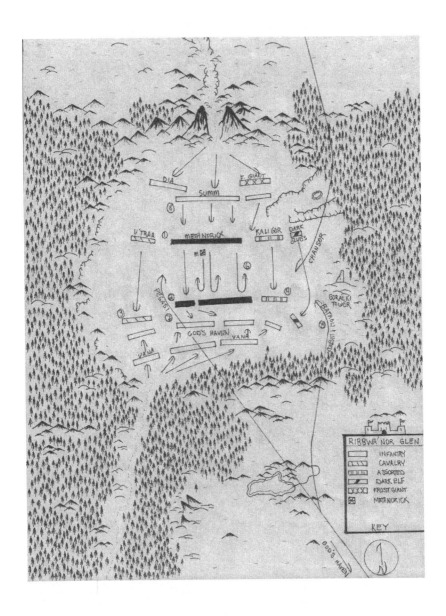

Chapter Three

Battle raged all around Kalion as he stood watching Methnorick move closer on his black horse until he suddenly jumped from the back of the horse, charging towards Kalion. It seemed like a dream, for everything to Kalion moved in slow motion as he squinted his eyes, waiting.

Even with fighting raging around him, he kept his eyes on the black-armored man as he got closer by the moment, but Kalion did not care — he had to finish this. Gripping the handles of the swords in his hands, he readied himself, moving his feet slightly to spring into the air when Methnorick got close enough. Over the sound of battle, he heard a familiar voice ask him a question.

At first he thought it was his imagination. Then he heard Kikor's voice again as he felt a hand touch his right arm. Looking over, he saw a blood-stained face looking back at him with a tiny smile and bright eyes.

"Are you ready?" she asked him, making him blink a few times until he realized it was his friend Kikor and this was real. She was beside him.

"Yes, my friend," he answered as he looked back up at the evil quickly bearing down on them.

"Let's finish this," Kikor said as Kalion heard the familiar sound of a bow being pulled tight, knowing that the elf was aiming an arrow as he gripped his swords again.

* * *

Whelor, in the meantime, had been doing his best to kill as many orcs as possible. He fought to stay in human form to ensure that he only killed those that were not among his own, even after he received a deep wound on his left thigh.

His vision started to cloud, his arms felt like stones, and his mouth was so dry it was like he was eating sand, but he fought on. Turning and stepping back as an orc fell forward from the deadly blow he had just delivered, he realized that only three of his people were left, so he looked around, trying to find a way out of the mess they were in. Then he saw it. The shield wall behind them had created an opening for them and was motioning for them to retreat behind its protection. He yelled at the three men, pushing them towards the opening while keeping a group of orcs back that tried to kill the retreating men.

Finally reaching the shield wall of the elves, he stumbled through the opening and past the elves, who quickly closed the wall back up and released a few arrows against the ever-large numbers of orcs pushing towards them.

Whelor saw with relief that the men made it behind the shield wall. He turned to start to run towards the wall himself when he noticed familiar shapes not far away in the middle of the battle. Blinking again, he finally recognized who he was looking at, shaking his head at what he saw.

"Kalion … Kikor … By the gods!" he gasped with a dry, raspy throat, seeing the ranger and the elven maiden about to take on … *Wait, is that … Methnorick? …* Whelor squinted a little more as he saw Methnorick move closer towards his friends.

"Methnorick … you …" Whelor turned and looked at the men now kneeling behind the shield wall, being cared for by Niallee.

"Niallee will care for them!" Whelor said under his breath. "I must fight to end this battle!"

Niallee was wrapping one of the arms of the man, so she didn't hear Whelor's words, but she looked up just as the big man turned and moved deeper into the middle of the battle.

Peering over the elven wall, she watched her friend disappear into the dust, wishing she had heard what he said, not knowing if she would see him again.

"Care for yourself, my friend!" she whispered as she watched for a moment longer and then returned to caring for the groaning man lying next to her.

As Methnorick got closer to his prey, he saw that the man was joined by another man and an elf maiden. Suddenly, he realized that his fiery chains had fallen out of his hand, so he quickly scanned the ground for this weapon. He was now only a few hundred yards away from the three standing in front of him, and since he still had his sword and his magic, he figured they were no match for him.

Whelor, Kalion and Kikor looked at each other for only a moment longer when Whelor held up his hand to the other two.

"He is mine!" Whelor stated.

"I have been looking for you!" Methnorick looked straight into Whelor's eyes.

"NOW!" Whelor yelled. All three ran forward, Whelor keeping his eyes directly on the face of Methnorick as Kikor, hearing the word of action, made her way to the left of Methnorick, while Kalion did the same to his right.

Methnorick raised one of his hands. Suddenly, they saw his hand start to glow as he pointed his fingers at Kalion. As the words passed his lips, his hand erupted in a bright blueish glow that streaked out and shot across the open ground at the ranger.

Kalion's instincts took over, and he dove off to the side. Kikor jumped behind a small broken cart just as Methnorick moved his hand towards her.

Whelor roared, "METHNORICK ... THIS ENDS NOW!" only to hear a deep, almost haunting laugh from Methnorick as an answer.

"You are no match for me."

Whelor quickly closed the distance between himself and Methnorick, bringing up his massive sword, when he heard Methnorick release a spell.

"Fann ser lu ko!"

Instantly, bright light erupted out of his hand, shooting across the distance and slamming into the chest of Whelor, causing the warrior to fly backwards through the air to slam onto the ground.

Kikor, not waiting, grabbed her bow and arrow, quickly releasing arrows one after another. Methnorick's eyes were on Whelor as he slowly pushed himself off the ground, while Kalion brought himself up on one elbow and tried to reach for his sword that was lying not far away. When one of Kikor's arrows slammed into Methnorick, it pushed him back slightly from the momentum. However, he reached down, grabbing the arrow and pulling it from his body as if it didn't even affect him. Both Kalion and Kikor gasped in surprise.

Kalion watched Kikor release another arrow, but this time, instead of hitting Methnorick, she hit the Blingo'oblin that was trying to catch up to its master, causing it to fall dead at Methnorick's feet. She released another arrow and then dropped her bow to grab her sword. Running after the arrow, she used a goblin corpse to launch herself at Methnorick. With her sword over her head, she screamed at the last moment, hoping to cut Methnorick down, but Methnorick shot blue flames, igniting Kikor's sword and causing her to tumble onto the ground behind Methnorick.

"Is that you have, elf? … All those cycles of killing and fighting … That is all?!" Methnorick laughed loudly as he watched her get up on one hand, looking up at him as he stepped up and grabbed her by the neck. Methnorick grunted slightly as he picked her off her feet to stare directly into her eyes. "Are you one Dia's people … one of those looking for that spoiled daughter of his?" Methnorick's breath made Kikor almost throw up as she struggled to get out of his grip.

Out of the corner of his eye, he saw the ranger running up with his sword. He could see the man screaming as he got closer by the second.

"And I suppose he's also with you, hmmmm?" Methnorick turned to look at Kalion as he approached. Kalion got within a few feet as Methnorick lifted his right arm up, encasing Kalion in a blue fire from his hand. As Kalion watched, unable to move, Methnorick maneuvered his sword to come down hard onto the man's head when, suddenly, a large piece of wood slammed hard into his arm, just below the elbow.

Screaming out in pain, Methnorick stepped back, dropping Kikor and releasing Kalion as he turned to face Whelor.

"Methnorick … I come for you!" Whelor snarled as he flexed his arms and fists, breathing so hard that he was actually growling.

Suddenly, a look of recognition crossed Methnorick's face. "No, I've been looking for you. I was sure we would meet again!" Methnorick hissed as he let out a scream. "Chansor …"

"Never mind that thing … It is just you and I!" Whelor snarled loudly. As Methnorick watched, Whelor leaned his head back, and within a few moments, he had transformed himself into the wolf creature his friends had seen back in the elven kingdom, giving Methnorick no time to react. Whelor roared one last time and jumped at him.

Methnorick ignited his hands with the bluish fire, attempting to push the beast back. However, this only enraged Whelor more. Getting desperate, Methnorick pulled out his sword, slashing at Whelor's face.

Both Kikor and Kalion lay on the ground next to each other, watching as Methnorick's blade cut through his now-furry skin, causing blood to flow. Kikor rubbed her throat as Kalion's clothes smoldered from the blue flames.

Whelor's anger grew as he turned his face to look back at Methnorick, his jaw tightened and releasing saliva that dripped off his teeth, now long and sharp.

Methnorick moved himself to take another slash at the creature, but Whelor jumped directly at him, grabbing both arms as they tumbled back hard onto the ground. Kikor gasped, stepping forward, only to be stopped by Kalion's hand holding her back.

"I think this is between them, Kikor," Kalion spoke calmly as they both watched the two tumble around in front of them. "Remember what Whelor said about Methnorick before the battle: he could feel him close by like he was being drawn to him. I think Methnorick has a lot to do with his condition. I think Whelor needs this."

"He needs our help!" Kikor answered back, looking at Kalion and then back at Whelor.

"No ... I think he's got this!" Kalion smiled as both saw Whelor's claws slash back and forth at Methnorick's chest armor, slowly cutting through it. "Besides, if you step in now, Whelor could hurt you as well. We can step in if we need to, but give Whelor a chance."

Chapter Four

At the far eastern side of the elven left flank stood Harbin fighting with two other mages. Each time the giant kind was about to break the elven lines, Harbin or one of his companions was able to take them down with fire or by opening a hole in the ground that quickly closed up after they disappeared.

Harbin was able, during a pause in the fighting, to help a few elves that had been wounded when Chansor flew overhead, igniting the battlefield in flames. Harbin released several spells at the beast, but all failed.

When Chansor turned around to come for another run, Harbin rubbed his hands together, quickly making a ball of blueish fire glow in between as he waited for the creature to get closer.

"If this doesn't kill you … then nothing will!" Harbin whispered as he moved his right arm back to get ready to throw the ball of light when, out of the corner of his eye, he saw something huge moving towards him.

It was like life slowed down for the mage as he turned his face just a bit to see what it was that caught his sight. He turned to see an ugly giant coming towards him.

Knowing it could kill him, Harbin turned his hand around and flung the ball at the creature coming at him instead of the creature in the sky. A moment later, Harbin's face and body were covered in blood, guts and clothing as the ball erupted inside the giant's body. Harbin instantly regretted throwing the blue flame at the giant as the huge body fell over and landed directly on top of the mage.

Oh damn! was all Harbin could think.

After battle with the Pegasus, Chansor took a moment to rest. The battle high in the sky had taken its toll on him, for there were too many. Chansor landed on the cliff to look down on the field of battle, quickly turning himself back into his human form, hoping to escape being seen. As his eyes scanned the field, he saw a flash of white light. He squinted, catching sight of Kalion and Kikor standing off to the side of Methnorick, who he could see was having trouble, but against whom?

Chansor stepped to the edge of the cliff, gasping loudly when his eyes saw Methnorick thrown back by ...

"Whelor!" he gasped loudly. *Nooooooo,* he thought. *How ... where ... impossible!*

Chansor started arguing with himself about what to do, help his master or rest, for he needed rest, but his master was battling the one he was supposed to have killed.

As he watched a moment longer, something flew across his vision as he blinked to see what it was: the Pegasi swooping down to take orc after orc high into the sky to drop them. He continued to consider his next step when he heard whispering within his mind. At first, thinking it was that inner voice of his, he shook his head for a moment. Then he heard the words again.

"Hello, Brother." He turned to see his sister Elesha standing behind him.

"Methnorick is losing, Sister, and the Pegasi are destroying the orc battle lines," Chansor stated as he turned back to the battle.

"Interesting ... The masters will not be pleased with that." Elesha's voice sounded angry to Chansor. "Kaligor ... U'Traa ... What of them, my brother?"

"I can't find them within the fray, Sister ... and the elves ... They have recruited Pegasi to combat me!" Chansor's eyes continued to watch the horses lift screaming orcs as the sky soon filled with their bodies falling.

"Forget them, Brother ... The masters are coming!"

"No, I will continue to destroy these ... these Pegasi. I just to rest a bit. The masters will see us win this battle."

"It is too late, Brother. Save your strength. The masters know this battle is lost, and they have a plan for Methnorick. Let what will happen, happen. There is nothing else you can do. Come, we must go now."

As the fighting continued, Chansor decided to listen to his sister and leave the scene to return to Blath 'Na.

* * *

Dust clouds had formed around Whelor and Methnorick, making it difficult for Kikor or Kalion to see anything, but as the dust disappeared, Kalion, along with Kikor, could see Methnorick lying on the ground with Whelor breathing heavily, standing over him. Kikor looked Whelor over as he stood covered in blood but back in human form.

Kalion looked down at Methnorick. He could see Whelor had used his claws to cut through the armor that Methnorick so prized, ripping Methnorick's chest, stomach and face open. His insides had spilled out from his chest. One arm had been ripped cleanly off and was lying not far away. It was the face, though, that made even Kalion wince for a moment as he stood looking down at the man that had caused misery to all on the lands. His left eye had been pulled out and was only hanging on by the tendons inside, and the ranger could see the man's teeth through the gaping wound in his cheek.

Leaning down, Kalion didn't say a word as he moved closer to check the body. Kalion continued to check the body, moving his hands slowly over what was left of Methnorick. The ranger found something in one of Methnorick's pouches and pulled out a box. He noticed that it was heavy for its small size.

The sudden gurgling, coughing sound coming from Methnorick made Kalion fall back slightly, falling into Kikor and Whelor, who were right behind him. Kalion could see the other eye open up to stare at him and the chest squirm slightly as blood squirted out as Methnorick attempted to breathe.

"You ... you think you have killed me?" the raspy, whizzed words spoke as Methnorick was struggling to speak to him. "You ... of all think you have won this ... You think you won?" Methnorick's voice sounded weaker by the moment as his one eye looked at each of them. Kalion pushed himself up to stand over the body now.

Kalion's anger shot up then as he looked at the face, knowing he had to ask sooner than later. "Why did you kidnap the princess?" Kalion yelled angrily. The man before him coughed a few times, almost laughing.

"Your princess ..." He coughed as his body spasmed again. "She left long ago," he whispered.

"Left ... What do you mean, Methnorick?" Kalion yelled directly into Methnorick's face, making his one eye close slightly. Methnorick nodded his head slowly, not answering the ranger's angry question.

"Know this ... I will deny you the world, ranger. This is only the beginning ... and your princess ..." A few coughs caused blood to leak from the gaping hole in the side his mouth.

"Beginning ... beginning of what?" Kalion asked quickly, wondering what Methnorick meant, but his question was only answered by a smile. Kalion knew Methnorick had finally died before him.

With Kikor and Whelor to his left, Kalion suddenly felt someone standing to his right. He Turned his head quickly, lifting his sword to defend against an attack.

"Meradoth?" Kalion gasped, seeing the mage standing before him not looking at him but at the man before them, smiling slightly as he did.

"Meradoth ... By all the gods ... I am glad you're alive, my friend." Kalion repeated, "Where did you come from?" as he lowered his sword slightly, getting the attention of the mage, who smiled back at Kalion.

"I felt something occur and had to come see for myself. My friend … you killed him?" The mage's words were ones of surprise as he looked from Methnorick to Kalion, who still stared at him with large, wide eyes.

Kalion shook his head slightly and stared at the mage. "Sorry … No … Whelor did." Kalion's answer caused a look of surprise to cross Meradoth's face as he looked back down at the body of the man that had caused all the death on the lands.

"Whelor … great job." Meradoth looked up at Whelor, who was standing behind Kalion.

Smiling and tilting his head slightly, Meradoth moved over and knelt down next to Methnorick and repeated the same thing that Kalion had just done, moving his hands like he was looking for something.

"Is this what you are looking for, my friend?" Kalion asked, kneeling down next to Meradoth and looking at the mage, holding the small chest in his hand up.

Meradoth looked over, and seeing the chest, he began to mumble, making Kalion lift an eyebrow as he listened, for it sounded like some form of chanting. When Meradoth realized that Kalion was staring at him, he explained, "When we were in the tower back in Blath 'Na, I was told that Methnorick was looking for artifacts around the land that had been hidden many cycles ago. These artifacts, if put together, could bring some ancient power back. These objects are dangerous. Hence the spell I was just chanting. Where did you find that?" Meradoth asked, reaching out to take it from Kalion's hand quickly.

"I searched Methnorick before you arrived." Kalion leaned closer and had to yell as horns erupted again behind them.

"You did not try to open this, did you?" Meradoth asked Kalion. Taking the box, Meradoth stood up as he stared at it. He placed it within his robes and looked at the elves around them and then back at Kalion. He could see that the ranger had been hurt during the battle as he groaned standing up.

"No, I was just about to when you showed up. So, you believe these artifacts are within the box, Meradoth?" he asked the mage.

Smiling at his question, Meradoth replied, "Yes, but we dare not look, for they are far too powerful for our eyes." Meradoth smiled again, not looking at Kalion, who was about to ask another question when he caught the sight of his friend smiling back at him.

"Kikor … shall we?" Meradoth made the elf nod her head and smile back as the three turned to join what was left of the battle that had raged around them.

* * *

The light caught the eye of the huge creature cutting his way through the bodies that were between him and his lord. When he got within arm's reach of his lord, he suddenly stopped, for in front of him lay the body of his master. "Orkani … Orkani … Methnorick … He's dead … Our lord be dead!" the Blingo'oblin screamed.

Instantly, in panic, orcish horns erupted everywhere, which was followed quickly by screams. As if a dam had exploded, Methnorick's army began to run everywhere, trying to get away. The elves on the field erupted in cheers as they watched the thousands of orcs dropping their weapons to run quickly to get away.

Chapter Five

*A*fter hearing orc after orc run by him screaming "Methnorick is dead," Kaligor couldn't believe how quickly the army fell apart, when he saw Chansor fly over the battlefield. Waving his hands, he saw the beast look his way and swing around to circle over him.

"METHNORICK'S DEAD ... GET THE BODY!" he yelled upwards at the creature.

Chansor considered continuing on his journey to Blath 'Na and the masters, but then nodded back to Kaligor and slowly turned himself around to look for the man who had been responsible for who he was now.

Slowly drifting over the field, he caught sight of many bodies, making it hard to locate the one he was looking for, when his keen eye sighted the one thing that distinguished Methnorick from the other black-cloaked figures lying dead on the field of battle: his amour. As Chansor moved to land by Methnorick's body, he saw standing nearby three people he used to call friends. He readied himself for the confrontation, flapping his giant wings to slow down as he transformed himself back into his human form of Chansor the thief. As he walked out of the grayish dust, Chansor found himself face to face with the three people he had seen moments ago.

"CHANSOR!" He watched Kikor swing herself around to stand firmly, lifting her orc blood-covered sword and getting ready to pounce on him as he stepped over to kneel down next to Methnorick. He shook his head as he saw that Methnorick's body had almost been ripped apart, parts of his insides were lying on the ground as his blood covered the trampled grass everywhere.

"You deserve to die with him!" Kalion stated, looking Chansor in the eye.

"Maybe, but not today. My masters will have their revenge!" Chansor hissed through his teeth, staring at the ranger, who tilted his head slightly at the words.

"He's dead, you moron!" Kikor angrily moaned at him as she cautiously stepped forward.

Chansor's mouth lifted from the side as he smiled at the elf. "We will see." He leaned down and picked up the body when he caught sight of Niallee pushing through the chaos, staring back at him.

Giving her a gentle smile, he looked back at Kalion, Kikor and Whelor. He could almost feel their anger from where he stood. "My master will have his revenge!" he repeated as he burst into now-familiar body of the massive dragon and reappeared carrying Methnorick in his claws.

Chansor flapped his wings hard and slowly rose up into the sky, pushing those that stood watching back as he slowly circled around and then took off to the north as Kikor, Kalion, Whelor and now Niallee watched him.

"What do we do?" Niallee asked, knowing that none had the answer, but Kalion smiled at the druid as he watched a score of the Pegasi fly over in pursuit of Chansor. He watched the dragon out-distance the Pegasi.

"Nothing we can do," Kalion replied. Quickly, the group moved to wrap bandages on those that were in need as clerics moved in and pulled the wounded, placing them on wagons and carts.

* * *

As clean up continued, small skirmishes continued, mostly among those trapped in the fringes of the battle that were not able to escape.

Amlora and Niallee continued caring for the wounded when they were told that Harbin had been found. Not speaking, they followed the two warriors to the huge giant that the mage had killed.

"How do you … ohhh!" Amlora asked, catching herself when one of the warriors pointed to show a foot and leg sticking out from underneath the giant.

"It does look like his boot!" Niallee whispered, bending down to examine it further. "Any other sign that it was him?" She looked at the warrior, who nodded yes and stepped over to the other side, showing her the large pouch that their friend was given during the march south.

Nodding, Niallee blew out a breath, reaching out for it. "That's his. I remember when it was given to him." Taking the pouch, the druid turned to Amlora, who, she saw, had a tear in her eye. She moved up to place a hand on the woman's shoulder to console her, whispering that there was nothing they could do now.

Turning, they returned quietly to help the critically wounded being transferred to the wagons, as the field itself was quiet. Friends found friends, weapons were gathered and placed in wagons, and the dead were moved to the western edge of the field, where the sun's final rays were hitting. A group of clerics said their goodbyes to those that had perished fighting against Methnorick.

Meradoth was helping move the orcs and other creatures into piles when he was told of his friend Harbin's death. Turning his hand, the mage, without a word, sent a burst of fire at each pile of decaying corpses, and quickly, the night sky turned red and black as the bodies slowly burned under the stars. When he finished, the mage quietly walked off the field onto the road, following the hundreds of warriors that traveled south to get to God's Haven, which had been turned into a makeshift hospital.

Once they entered the city, Meradoth soon disappeared into the city to console himself about the loss of Harbin while Amlora finally collapsed once she reached the city. She was carried in to be cared for by other clerics.

Kalion found King Dia receiving care for a wound he received in the first cavalry charge when an orc spear dug deep into his thigh, killing his horse at the same time. Luckily for the king, when they both fell forward, he had been able to get himself off the saddle before he was rolled over on by the horse.

"What will you do now, my friend?" Dia whispered as the ranger knelt next to him.

Looking at his king, Kalion swallowed and thought for a moment. "Methnorick is dead, but your daughter is missing, my king … She is still out there!" Kalion's voice quieted lightly as Dia placed his hand on Kalion's forearm.

"Son … if she is out there … maybe lost but …" Dia smiled as the pain shot through his leg, making him wince slightly.

"We know she is in the south …"

"Well, wherever you go, we will venture forward together."

Kalion smiled, looking down at his king, the man that felt more like a father to him than his king, and said, changing the subject, "The clerics are saying you should be up and about soon, sir … That is good to hear!"

"Clerics … What do they know?!" Dia laughed until the pain hit him again, which made Kalion smile back at him as they quietly talked about the good times back in Brigin'i.

* * *

Kikor tightened her grip on the reins of the horse she had been riding. The cold morning wind hit her face softly, making her smile as she remembered the times when she was younger, sitting on a cliff edge and watching the morning sun rise up, wondering what was beyond it — if indeed the gods lived on the bright ball that rose each day.

The memories were bringing back lovely thoughts of her family when the grunt to her left brought her back to where she was at the moment. Turning her face slightly, she saw one of three riders that were with her as they all rode north through the crisp morning air.

Kirian, one elven warrior who had fought near her during the fierce battle with Methnorick, had quickly come to respect after seeing him charge three orc warriors, dispatching them with one swipe of his blade and dropping their heads before he even landed on the ground. Now, on their mission north, his eyes pierced through the dark.

Kirian's hair was whiter then most elves' due to the unusual circumstances of his birth, for his mother had been raped by roving bands of dark elves.

Just behind Kikor rode Guala, an elven warrior from the northern tribes that had journeyed down with King Dia to join General Summ. Her features were opposite those of Kikor, and instead of an outspoken manner Guala was quiet, too quiet for Kikor's liking, but her skills in battle were excellent, for she had killed a hill giant during the battle earlier. Guala also had hair shaved on both sides of her head, leaving a long tail of hair that hung down past her shoulders.

Kikor's ear quickly picked up the grunt and snap of the last rider that was with her on this mission, Barcla. This was one warrior she had wanted to join on this mission when she was ordered to scout the north. Barcla's people had lived in the same forest as her people had. The Eagle people thought he was born into the Light Feather clan while she was of the Bright Spear clan, but it made him family of a sort.

Barcla was muscular, even for an elven warrior, and very quick. His clan would smile at him as he almost flew by them, seemingly dancing like a butterfly or bird. Barcla was different in one way from Kikor: he had decided long ago to keep his long elvish ears always tied back using a silverish chain. His long silverish hair almost hid the chain, but Kikor saw it as it bounced while he rode, making her smile. It was a memory of his clan, a clan that had been slaughtered many cycles ago by a group of a mountain giants that had tried to move into their forest.

Kikor turned her head slightly to look forward again as, together, the group rode across the field. Since waking up a few hours earlier and leaving their camp, the elven warriors had taken it easy. The night earlier had been quiet, almost too quiet for all of them, but it was a rest they needed after the fierce battle.

Kikor bounced lightly in her saddle as she thought of the words that General Summ had given her earlier: "Go north and see the happenings." Since leaving the Ribbwa'nor Glen, where the armies were recovering from their wounds, General Summ had received orders that bands of elven warriors were still willing to move out and track escaping orcs and to dispatch them quickly. Over 500 warriors volunteered for the job and quickly rode out, tracking hundreds of orcs that had escaped the final battle.

Kikor and her group had themselves killed at least 30 orcs that were making their way north. Barcla asked over a camp fire the night before why any orc would try to make it north when their own people were seen gathering in strength just south near the base of the Sernga Mountains.

Kikor had been wondering the same thing for a while as the group rode closer by the moment to the massive forests of Fuunidor, when she and the others started to see dark clouds to the northeast of where the forest lay.

"Any ideas?" she asked pointing to the dark clouds, not really speaking to anyone, just thinking out loud.

Guala squinted hard as she bounced on her horse, trying to understand the cloud formations. "No ideas!" she answered back, still wondering, when she heard the others answer back the same thing.

"The city of Blath 'Na is in that direction, I believe," Kirian called out, making Kikor nod as she came to the same thought.

"Could just be storm clouds coming off the oceans, you know!" Guala called over.

"Maybe, but would storm clouds just sit there?" Kirian mentioned quickly. "Storms move … It looks like that one is just sitting there." Kirian's words made the rest of the group quiet.

Kikor reflected on her last visit to Blath 'Na. *The creatures we saw were contained within Blath 'Na*, she considered, but she wondered.

Could it be that they got out? What does this storm cloud have to do with anything? "Something is wrong!" Kikor finally spoke out loud, and the rest slowly nodded back when she looked at them for answers. They could all finally feel the same thing. Something was in the air as they got closer to Blath 'Na.

Guala was the first that saw the patch of trees to their northeast as they moved across the field and up a hill, quickly kicking their mounts and riding over, jumping off as they moved into the trees. Tying their reins to trees and then kneeling down slightly, they approached the edge of the tree line to look north over the plains towards Blath 'Na before them, each quietly gasping with wide eyes at what was before them.

Chapter Six

"Sir, we need to make sure that your people are taken care of … Methnorick might be dead, but his armies are still roaming around and could counterattack us at any time … even attack your city here!" Kalion quietly spoke to the group sitting around the great table as he and Meradoth now sat with other elven leaders in the elven chamber that stood proudly in the middle of God's Haven. Both General Summ and King Dia, who sat propped on a chair, listened intently.

The stone building they were in had been the first building raised within God's Haven. First as the sole temple to the gods, but then, as time went on, the monks decided to build individual temples to each of the gods worshipped on Marn — all twenty-five of them. Only the elven temples seemed to be used on a regular basis.

Within the chamber, General Vana who had led his troops from the Empire north, sat with his arms tightly crossed and a stern look on his face. Since entering the city, many of the elven monks celebrated, believing that this battle was the last of the orcish problem, but his instincts told him this was not over.

Since his first skirmish with the orcs south of the Father Gate, he knew that the orcs would be back. Methnorick's other servants had lived, as he had seen one or two get away. He tried to explain this earlier, but the monks didn't want to hear it, so for now, he waited.

Auliic, the head monk and leader of God's Haven, stood at the end of the large table. His tall frame overshadowed the rest as he stood, trying to calm the disagreements.

"Please, please, calm yourselves … This is a place of peace, and you all will calm yourselves!" Auliic waved his hands slowly until everyone had stopping trying to speak over others as they argued.

"My people here in God's Haven have for many cycles believed only in peace and secrecy, even when the elves fought against you, General Vana ..." He moved his hand and head in the direction of General Vana. "My people stayed here within the borders of God's Haven ... Even during the wars against our cousins of the dark, we stayed quiet. Only during the dark cycles when the plague came to these shores did my people venture outside these walls to care for the sick and dying ... Now I must defend my people and not extend us any more." Auliic's voice seemed to calm many in the chamber, but he could see that both Generals Summ and Vana were not happy.

"We will, of course, care for all wounded, and you may stay to rest and feed your army, generals, as long as you care to ... but when you leave ... you will leave without my people, and you will not come back!" Auliic's stern answer made General Summ finally stand up, placing his hands on the wooden table. He had been told the table was a gift to the monks by the gods themselves so many cycles ago that none knew how long it had been there.

"Councilor Auliic ... thank you for taking care of the warriors that have been wounded, but Kalion here is right ... The orcs by themselves are not a threat to this city ... even if a few hundred are able to gather ... But, though Lord Methnorick might be dead, information brought to me states that two of his lieutenants were seen escaping north along with that creature that fought against Lord Lugtrix and his flying horses ... This is not over, sir!" Summ stared directly into the councilor's eyes, but he could see that the peaceful monk wasn't going to change his mind.

Summ lowered his head to look at the table for a moment, gathering his thoughts. Then he looked at each face around the table. "Our king — King Mass-Lorak — was killed by one of Methnorick's minions, and since he had no living children, now I command all of the elven tribes that live north of the Sernga Mountains, and all I can do, sir, is ask you ... if the call comes once the battle starts again,

I hope you will let your people hear the call for help!"

"General, but what could my people really do to help you? ... March north — or is it south? — to the empire? ... You have many choices, sir ... but I have one choice ... to stay here and make sure that any evil that might come knows not of my city." Auliic sat down, crossing his arms as another monk stood up, raising a hand just as Summ opened his mouth to speak.

"Combined, we were able to stop and destroy Methnorick and the threat he posed on these lands, sir ... So saying, what could our people do? ... They have done a lot already to stop the evil." Summ could be seen slowly clinching his fists.

"That is true, but now we must protect our city. Never have our borders been broken. The secrecy of our city is our defense. The two towers that stand in the mist guard the great tunnel ... never has anything passed them meaning harm to us ... So, General ... we are safe here within the city. We have done all that we can do." The monk moved his hands to clasp behind his back as Summ looked over at Vana, who returned a look of not believing what he was hearing.

"Sir ... you are?" Summ leaned back to stare at the monk, who smiled back, nodding as he did.

"Sorry, General, my name is Finnor ... I am what you would call the captain of the guard for God's Haven ... I am in charge of all defenses of our lovely city, and I work with Captain Bataoli." He smiled, lowering his head slightly to acknowledge the general, who returned the same nod.

"Then, Finnor ... they will find your city and your people. I hope you understand this."

Finnor smiled and looked down to the end of the table at Auliic, who nodded in return. "We understand, General ... but after your warriors are cared for, they can march from our borders, which will close and never be seen again."

"I am sure the people of my city and those of both Bru Edin and

Blath 'Na were saying the same things days before the orcs broke through their walls." Kalion's quiet voice carried through the room.

"True, I'm sure. However, those cities did not have the same protection that we do here in God's Haven, of which isolation and secrecy are key."

Vana, not being able to take it anymore, stood up and walked out of the chamber, grabbing Kalion on the shoulder as he did. Quickly, the two warriors walked out into the large marble hallway, leaving only Meradoth to sit and listen to the arguments that began after Kalion's words.

As they got outside, the general coughed once to clear his throat as Kalion looked around to see if there was anyone listening to them, for he understood the general's frustration.

"What do you plan on doing, General?" Kalion quietly asked, knowing that elves had incredible hearing. If they wanted to really hear something, they would — something he learned from Kikor a while back.

Thinking of Kikor, since she left for the north, he felt … empty. A similar feeling to the one he had had since Shermee's absence, but now … it was stronger for the elven warrior, and it surprised him.

"I plan on marching out of here as quickly as possible and, depending on Summ, I think we should march back to the empire and gather ourselves there."

Kalion raised his eyebrows at the General's comment, looking at the populace as they walked by. Slowly, a smile appeared on the big man's face.

"How can I help you, sir?" the ranger whispered.

* * *

Back at the tree-covered knoll, the elves quietly kept their eyes north as they watched the activity before them. They looked out over the fields that once lay between Blath 'Na and the elven forest that were once green with high grass but now were burnt and smoking. The once-proud elven forest kingdom that lay just east was burning

52

bright, the flames so big and hot Kikor and the others could feel the heat from where they lay watching, over five miles away.

She could just see the hill that just a few days earlier she and the others had used to escape the city of Blath 'Na. Now covering the field were the creatures that covered Blath 'Na, moving slowly, acting like they were lost or dazed.

"I saw those creatures within Blath 'Na ... They are men but not alive ... This was Methnorick's work. Somehow, magic has turned the dead into that," she whispered. Then she went on to explain what she had seen them do when they attacked.

"How many do you think are down there?" Guala whispered as she tried to count the numbers but got lost in trying.

"I saw a few groups of them within the city ... It seems they have made more ... so only the gods would know." Kikor looked at the other maiden who tightened her lips, understanding. "We have to get this information to Summ right away. Who will ride now?"

"I will," Barcla piped in quickly.

"Make sure you ride hard and don't stop for anything ... This must get to Summ as quickly as possible!" Kikor whispered in the shadows of the trees as she completed her note and handed it to him. Barcla rolled the message she had written up, pushing it deep into the pouch he had wrapped around his thigh.

"Do not stay too long ... If you're seen ..." Barcla whispered when he was done preparing himself.

"Never!" Kikor smiled from the corner of her mouth as the elf stood up, grabbing the reins from his horse and swinging himself up in one move as he looked at the others, who nodded back.

"See you all soon!" Barcla whispered as he pulled the horse around, kicking its hind and shooting off south as hard as the horse could gallop.

Kikor watched her friend ride off for a moment longer. Then, turning, she and the others moved quickly to peer north over the edge of a cliff they found a bit earlier to watch and listen.

All three pairs of eyes looked from the elven forest to the city of men and tried to understand what was before them. Black smoke rose out from behind the walls … Flames could be seen snapping back and forth, as well as a dark red glow that came from deep within the city.

"Methnorick is dead, right?" Guala whispered, not looking at the others as she asked the question. "So, who is in charge now?" Both Kirian and Kikor looked at each other, wondering the same thing. Kikor was sure he had died under the claws of Whelor … but …

"Whoever is leading this seems determined to continue this battle, and soon," Kikor whispered as she moved her eyes west. "I see what looks like battalions of orcs and other creatures as well." She pointed as the others groaned.

"Looks like hundreds of them there." Kirian looked at Kikor, both showing looks of concern and not wanting to believe the battle they had just won was just the beginning.

"I would even say thousands!" Guala whispered back. "And look above them … Isn't that the creature that fought Lord Lugtrix?" His words made the others groan again when they saw the creature fly out of the smoke and circle around the army being assembled below it.

"No, that is another one!" Kikor clenched her teeth as she reflected back on Chansor and how he had been a traitor all along, and now there were two of them!

"That one is big …" All three instantly stopped thinking and breathing when they heard the snap of a branch as Kikor tightened her grip on her bow that she had placed next to her on the ground.

Kirian nodded and flipped a few fingers, indicating where the noise was coming from, causing Guala to grip her bow stave and place an arrow between her fingers. As she watched Kirian point to his eyes, indicating that he could see something walking towards them, she nodded slowly that she understood, knowing that Guala would first shoot at whatever was moving behind them.

She could just make out Kirian quietly telling Guala what to do as she watched the other elf lying on her stomach to get herself ready to release her arrow as she heard movement getting closer behind them.

"Now!" Kirian whispered as Guala flipped herself onto her back, in the same moment pulling the bow string back and snapping her arrow out at the head of the creature moving up behind them.

All three watched her arrow fly and burst out of the back of the skull of the creature, watching it collapse before them. Kikor looked from the creature farther into the trees, seeing that it wasn't alone.

No one had to say a word. All three jumped up onto their horses. Kirian cursed as he saw that Guala had just killed one of those dead creatures, smiling at her as he knelt over it. "Good shot there!" he whispered, making her smile and nod back.

"We need to get out of here now!" Kikor pointed through the trees, and all three could see large groups of the creatures slowly moving closer.

Kirian pulled out a blade and in one movement cut the head off of one of the creatures that came up on his left trying to grab at his leg.

"MOVE!" he called out, not caring if his voice carried now as he turned his horse around and galloped south out of the tree grove as he heard both Kikor and Guala order their horses to follow just behind him.

The three elves burst out of the wooded knoll, looking back when they found themselves in the midst of hundreds of those dead beings slowly moving through the forest. Their moans began to echo through the morning, many trying to grab the elves as they rode past a few that were stumbling on the field.

Kikor cursed herself for not checking their surroundings better after seeing the situation north in the port city and their elven homeland. She began to wonder what was going on … Had Methnorick planned for the city to be used for something, or had someone or something else moved in, she wondered.

Chapter Seven

Kaligor finally approached Blath 'Na with the news that Methnorick was dead and that his armies were scattered. He was quickly put into chains by the Blingo'oblins that were standing guard and thrown into the dungeon without warning. Any orc that had retreated with Kaligor had been put in a temporary camp built in the north of the city.

After a few hours in chains and having been whipped by Blingo'oblins for his retreat, the cyclops was brought out of the dark, along with a few orcs, with his hands tied together. Three Blingo'oblins pushed him out into the light of a large yard, where he saw three poles standing in the middle, each burnt black with what looked like a charred body tied to it.

Kaligor's anger had been high since being put into chains, and he was yelling that he did what had been told and that Methnorick had been a fool. Now, seeing death before him, he regretted his decision to not fight being put in chains, or even fight Methnorick for his decision to fight on two fronts.

When an orc pushed him a bit too much, the cyclops turned quickly, grabbing the head of the creature and throwing his tied arms around the creature's neck. He hoisted the creature onto his back, and then, with a quick snap, the orc's neck was broken. He would have killed another that tried to attack him with a spear if not for a Blingo'oblin that got between the two.

"Calm yourself, General ... Death is a just a release that all should be happy to have!" The crooked smile from the giant creature made Kaligor snarl at the comment.

"Death will not happen to me but to you if you touch me again!"

The cyclops' powerful frame made even the elite beast step back, seeing the intense sense of anger in his eye.

"Tie him up!" the Blingo'oblin yelled, pointing to the pole and turning around to store his embarrassment away for a later time. Quickly, the muscular general was brought up to the poles, only having to wait as a few orcs cut the ropes, making the burnt corpses fall to the ground. Fighting the hands that had been dragging him, the cyclops was quickly tied to the pole with his arms tied behind him tightly as he looked with his one red eye at his jailers standing silently.

The Blingo'oblin ordered the orcs to leave the yard, leaving him to look at the snarling figure of Kaligor as he grunted through clenched teeth, cursing each creature and Methnorick for his stupidity as he stared at each with his red eye.

Waiting until the cyclops was done with the curses, the Blingo'oblin unrolled a parchment he had been holding and began to read as the prisoner listened quietly.

"I hereby order Kaligor, General to Lord Methnorick, to be put to death for his weakness in not taking the sword to those they were to conquer. For abandoning your orders and returning to Blath 'Na unsuccessful." The Blingo'oblin lowered the parchment and looked up at the prisoner that had returned.

Each Blingo'oblin turned and left the yard as Kaligor snarled more curses at them until the gate door was closed, making a loud metallic bang as the bolt was pushed down, leaving the general alone.

When the loud echo of metal erupted a few moments later, Kaligor turned his head slowly over, wondering if it was his punisher, only to see that it was instead something else. "Lord U'Traa!" he gasped quietly.

The death creature was brought out roughly, being pushed to the ground a few times as a Blingo'oblin pushed him to the pole that stood next to Kaligor's.

Neither spoke a word to the other, as Kaligor couldn't understand this whole situation. He should be out there fighting and not in these chains.

"Why are you not fighting this? … I know your kind … You could easily release those binds and get out!" his voice echoed as he yelled.

U'Traa lowered his head, looking at the chains that crossed his robes, and then turned to look at the cyclops that still struggled within his bonds.

"Why fight when there is nowhere to go? … The masters know all and will find me … I failed them! My failure was not killing Methnorick before the enemy could! The masters knew he would fail in this task and sent me to end him," U'Traa's familiar voice whispered to Kaligor.

"You failed nothing, my friend … We were under the command of a fool." Kaligor looked at the door, knowing that whatever was going to kill them would be coming through it any moment.

"A fool, yes … just misunderstood!" The voice made both look around. Even U'Traa couldn't find where the voice was coming from.

"Who is that?!" Kaligor yelled out, looking around where he could as they both heard what sounded like a slight snicker, almost a laugh. "Show yourself!" he yelled again.

"For so many cycles, I have seen creatures rise and fall. The powerful become weak, and the weak become powerful … and I have seen the strong become fools!" Kaligor blinked his eye as he saw a shadow figure that slowly stepped out to stare at them both.

"Who … who are you?!" Kaligor asked, trying to calm himself down, wondering who it was.

The figure snickered a little more as it stepped forward so both could finally see the man. Wearing grayish clothing that lay loosely over his body, the man had very short hair chopped closely to his skull, with only a belt to hold his clothes against his body — a man-creature that did not seem dangerous to Kaligor.

"Who are you?" Kaligor hissed through his teeth as he struggled with the heavy ropes.

"Never think that way, my friend … This creature is dangerous!" U'Traa's words whispered in his ears as his eye continued looking over the creature that stepped up, smiling with a wide smile.

"Who am I? … Well, that, my friend, is a long, long story … one that I might tell you someday, but for now, I am here for you both You both failed in achieving the plan that you had been given … to destroy all the creatures of Marn, including your current mission, the elves … Really, how hard can that be? … Instead, they destroyed you!" the man spoke, giving Kaligor an odd feeling that he was about to do something dreadful.

Turning slightly, the man held both hands behind his back as he stepped away, speaking quietly, "How hard is it to destroy those creatures, really? … They're … In the end, you were weak … weak for not standing up to Methnorick the instant you knew that he was taking on two fronts and that he was trapped … weak for not destroying the elves!" At that, the man turned sharply around to stare back at the two as they were held by the poles.

"You have Methnorick's body?" Kaligor asked quickly, remembering that Chansor had flown off with the Dark One's body. *I never liked that man-creature, so why ask?* he thought quickly.

The man sent out a quick laugh, twisting around to look at the two and then slowly walking around them as he spoke. "Methnorick … You worry about him … Interesting, but he's not dead … Well, he won't be soon … I have plans … plans on top of plans."

Kaligor's face moved from being angry to confused as he looked over at U'Traa.

"His body was brought here a few days ago … or what was left of his body. He was killed by that wolf creature … I saw it!" Kaligor gasped, wondering what magic this man had.

"Ohhhh, nooo. He is dead … sort of, really … His body is in the dungeon, waiting for me to decide what to do with it!" The man laughed again as he clapped his hands together like he had come up with an idea just then.

"Methnorick believed he had the strength ..." U'Traa's voice was cut off as a bright flame of light exploded, making Kaligor shut his eye as his mind heard a scream and then nothing. As Kaligor felt the heat of the light disappear, he opened his eye to look over and gasped as he saw the figure of the death knight on the pole, completely burnt.

Whipping his hand like it was burnt, the man jumped slightly like in celebration and then looked up at Kaligor and stopped himself. "I am sorry ... It just happened ... Sometimes I have that problem ... I do something terrible ... Well, that creature ... never liked it, really ... hated that Methnorick wanted it in his council!" The man jumped up and slapped Kaligor's surprised face.

"Should I do the same thing and kill you? ... Well ... but we have plans for you, my friend!" Wrapping an arm around Kaligor's head lightly, the man smiled wildly, blowing a breath out like he was relaxing from a hard run.

Kaligor looked at the little man, unsure how to respond.

Chapter Eight

The city was enjoying the bright, crisp morning as birds flew lazily over the sky and the river rushed like it did every day, but like it was being gentle this morning as well. The populace was feeling excited and rejuvenated by the activities of the last few days. Rebellion was in the air.

Many woke excited to get out and join the crowds of people that were gathering everywhere. All wanted to see the woman that was proclaiming herself empress, a word none dared to say out loud, for under the current leadership, there were stories of people disappearing, but this woman was saying it. Saying it loudly so all could hear. For so long now, they had lived in fear that they would be the next to disappear. Now there was hope. This girl was giving them hope. A number even believed she would save them not only from the high minister but from the evil in the land.

The only person that woke up that morning feeling dread was the high minister of Manhattoria, Minister Halashii. He walked out onto the balcony like he did each morning. Except, this morning, instead of the regular amount of people lazily walking around, setting up their stalls and shops at the market, he saw what perhaps could be hundreds of people all moving down the street, talking and cheering loudly.

Gripping the rail tightly, Halashii for the first time in a while felt alone. The sickness and headaches he had been feeling had suddenly disappeared a few days ago, but so had the voice, and in its place was a large nothingness. It was new to him, and he was scared now. He considered what he was feeling, and he thought back to the voice in his head and how it helped him make decisions, but now that voice was gone.

Just then, a knock made him turn around. "Come in!" he called out, watching the door open and one of the elven generals that commanded the cavalry corps for the city-state walk in. Looking around, the elf saw that the minster was outside.

"General!" Halashii calmly turned around to look back out upon the city and the activity below.

"Sir ... the city is gathering outside in very large numbers, and the city guard is informing me that if it gets out of control, they won't be able to do much to stop them." The elf raised an eyebrow when the minister didn't respond for a few minutes, making him wonder if the man had heard him....

"Sir?" he asked, stepping closer, about to speak again, when the minister turned around, nodding slightly.

"What are they demanding ... to let that woman just walk in here and become this empress? To just walk in here without my say-so?" Halashii walked by the elf, who stepped back and turned, looking at the minster as he walked into the chamber.

"So far, sir, they are not demanding anything except to meet this young woman but there are rumors, sir." The general swallowed, wondering if the rumors were true, when the minster turned quickly to stare at him.

"General Malaa ... what rumors are moving around?" Halashii quickly snapped.

Lowering his head slightly, the elf looked up at the map of the empire then back to his minister. "That the girl might be the answer to save us from the evil that is coming."

Halashii smiled, turning back to look at the massive map of the empire and the lands beyond. He pulled his hands behind his back as he stood there, pretending to look at the map, but his mind was racing.

What have I done? he thought.

* * *

Shermee walked out of the room she had used as a sleeping

chamber to confront three men that had been waiting since the crack of the morning for her to wake and come out so they could go over the activities for the day.

Nodding to each man and smiling when her eyes laid on Quinor, who stood up as she walked in, she stated, "Morning everyone … Looks like a lovely day out there!" Her voice made each man smile back at her.

"My lady … the city has heard your voice … Talking this morning, we believe that more than 75 percent of the populace is out there, gathering to see you!" the man to the right of her spoke calmly.

"That is good to hear, Jacoob … That means one thing, then, do you not think?" She looked at each of the men.

"I believe this is the day, my lady … The high minister knows of you … my spies tell me that he just hides in the tower of ministries, scared and confused!" When he finished, the group laughed quietly.

Shermee smiled at their laughter. When she heard the rumor last night she couldn't believe it. This city was hiding something so huge that if they heard, the council might fall apart.

"Ethaan … you need to explain to Quinor what you told me last night … It is surprising that this city is such a happy place." Shermee sat as the older man rose and cleared his throat. Quinor, who had ridden out into the mountains near the city to bring in reinforcements, had missed the news. Now, he looked at Ethaan with a face of both expectation and excitement as the older man explained.

"Our high minister has been ruling this empire for many, many cycles … so long that many cannot even remember when he was voted in. At first, he seemed to bring peace, and people believed every word he said. In the last five cycles, he seemed to disappear from walking the streets of the city, something he was known for when he first took office. You could see him at a cafe with the populace … but …" Ethaan looked over at Jacoob, who tightened his mouth and nodded for the man to continue. "I used to be part of the city guard ... but when I heard what I'm about to tell you, I had to leave ... Our high minister has for the last five cycles been making citizens that disagree with him disappear. Also, what he tells the people is not true. The prosperity he tells people we have is not true. He inflates the numbers so that people think that Manhattoria is wealthy, but we are broke. He hordes the money in his own coffers, raising taxes to pay for this or that."

Quinor, confused, lifted an eyebrow. "Disappear ... to where?"

Ethaan tilted his head back to face Quinor in order to answer him, but Shermee started talking before he could answer. "That's ... that's incredible ... Do you know why? And how?" Quinor crossed his arms, not believing what he was hearing now.

"He has a special team or division that he uses. They report directly to him and produce no written reports, unlike all other departments in the city. He would say he was sending them to live in the farthest southern reaches of the empire where land is open and ripe for growing food. A few other guards like myself questioned this and actually investigated. They came back to report that none of the people that disappeared were there and that it was a frozen wasteland. We have not been able to find where he sends the people!"

Quinor's mouth dropped in shock at what he was hearing. The empire was supposed to be a place of peace and equal justice, but this made him shake his head in disbelief. "Has he been confronted about it?" Quinor looked Shermee when he asked the question.

"He refuses to answer to the council or the people ... and when anyone questions him, they disappear by the next day. When you showed up, my lady, the prophecy of a girl from the north coming here to become empress brought those that knew prophecy together quickly. I'm afraid the truth about the high minster is starting to move quickly."

"First, Ethaan, there is more to the prophecy, and we must deal with that. Second, do you have any proof that it is him doing this? I do not want his blood running down the street ... If I am to become empress, this will be done peacefully, you understand ... no killing! Do we expect opposition from anyone on the high minister's side?" Shermee's voice sounded strong as she cut in, making Ethaan smile slightly. "But we also must have some proof, not just rumor."

Bowing his head, Ethaan replied, "Of course, my lady ... We will bring you the proof in the morning, and the word will be sent out as soon as we leave this building ... no blood ... no killing!" Shermee smiled back, nodding. Ethaan turned to Jacoob next to answer the rest of the questions.

"My lady, we have no reason to suspect that anyone will oppose us. However, there is always a chance. The high minister has been isolating himself for the last few cycles, so I doubt that he has many true supporters."

"Then let us get this going ... I want to meet the high minister to inform him that the people would like him to step down!" Shermee stood up as the men stepped back, all smiling at her words.

After a few words, Ethaan and Jacoob turned and walked out, leaving Shermee and Quinor alone. "There are a few things that bother me about this, Quinor. Am I helping create a coup, or am I really the one?" He smiled at the woman as he lifted his hands, and quickly she moved in, placing her head on his chest as he wrapped his arms around her, breathing in the smell of her hair. "I want this, Quinor," she said into his chest. "But I also want to do this right."

"Tomorrow, Princess ... you will be Empress of the Empire of Pendore'em and Edlaii," he whispered as he held the woman he was now deeply in love with.

She moaned, wrapping her arms around his torso. She closed her eyes and took in the moment, not knowing what was going to happen as soon as they walked out the door to confront the populace of Manhattoria.

They stood there, quietly holding each other, when they began to hear cheers and loud voices coming from the outside, making them both open their eyes and release each other to look at the door.

"This is it, Shermee … the final day in your journey … This city is yours!" Quinor quietly spoke.

Pulling in a long breath, Shermee grabbed her cloak, wrapped it around her chest, and smiled up at the man. Quinor had become a man she could rely on for advice … and right now, she needed him.

"Let us go and do this then!" she calmly spoke as they walked up and together opened the door to a burst of cheers.

Chapter Nine

*C*oral blocked the view from the two pairs of eyes, so, using a large starfish and a shell from a lobster, both elves slowly lifted their heads up enough to see what was happening. As soon as their eyes adjusted, the sight before them made both look at the other in amazement, for straight ahead were ten huge battle beasts that moved like crabs, using huge legs to cross the sea bed floor. Each was about the size of one giant Mal-mohr, which crossed the seas with armor like that of a lobster. Each time a leg slammed into the loose sand, it sent a vibration through the sea bed.

"We need to get back. Those creatures are heading right towards our city!" the first elf spoke into the mind of the second, who nodded slowly as his eyes moved down the line of the beasts that were now marching by the two elves.

"I count now at least ten and five in number ..." the second whispered back.

Moving themselves slowly back behind the coral, the two elves lifting the shell and starfish off their heads turned to lean back against the rock to think for a moment. *"You go and tell our people what is coming ... I will go and find allies to see who can help."* The second elf pushed his chest out, taking a deep breath and pulling water through the gills that opened up along his throat.

The other elf nodded, turning to leave, but stopped himself. *"You be careful, Volkk ... Those beasts look slow, but ..."*

Volkk smiled, answering that he would, as they swam over to where they left their large kelpies, who still waited patiently for their riders to return. Seeing the two elves move over the cliff, both kelpies flipped their long tails in excitement.

As they pulled themselves into the saddles, Volkk, looking over at his companion, smiled at the younger sea elf's excitement. *"Olen ... be careful yourself ... we might have missed an advanced guard, so make sure you keep clear of their path, yes?"*

"Agreed!" Olen smiled and, kicking his kelpie, pulled the two reins and, like an arrow, shot off into the dark mist of the seas, leaving Volkk by himself. Then he realized there was only one place to start: the fastest and quietest creature of the sea.

Kicking his own kelpie, they shot southeast to find the creatures that since the beginning were his people's greatest allies: the zools.

* * *

Kikor's group rode hard over the grass, leaving the screaming and groans quickly behind them as they made their way south towards where the armies were regrouping themselves at God's Haven.

A few times Kikor was sure she saw movement in the forests that they were passing, but none of them stopped to find out. At the top of a hillcrest, they stopped for a brief rest. They were now within a day's ride of the glen where they left the army.

"Gods ... what were they?" Kirian spoke, looking back and pulling his reins to move his horse around. Kikor shook her head when Guala chirped quietly, getting their attention. They looked at her covering her eyes to block out the sunlight for a moment, getting a sharper look at something far ahead of the three.

"Looks like some type of wolf ... but it is huge," Guala whispered, lowering her hand to look at the others. "You know of such wolves, Kikor?" Her question made the other shake her head slightly.

"Are there riders or anything near them?" Kikor asked, raising a hand to cover her eyes from the light as Guala and Kirian did the same.

"No ... just the beasts!" Guala squinted a bit harder as Kirian looked to the hills that lay just west of the road when he saw movement on top of them. However, the shadows from the clouds and sun could have been playing tricks on his eyes.

"Wait ... I think I see movement on the hilltop — there!" Kirian whispered, pointing. Everyone turned to look in the direction of his finger. "They might be riders."

"Whatever they are ... I count at least six of those beasts standing on the road ... like they were waiting or watching for something," Kikor answered her comrades calmly.

"We need to get south!" Guala looked over to her friend.

"You think Barcla encountered them?" Kirian voiced what they all were thinking.

Kikor suddenly saw movement on the road and looked slightly east. "Wait, are those elves on the road? It looks like ... no ... Those could be from Fuunidor. We are south of the forest, and we saw it ablaze. They must have escaped the fire." She looked at the others.

Kirian said, "If we ride hard ... and if that is indeed riders along the hilltop, we could get through before they organize themselves." Kirian knew the plan was dangerous, but all three knew they had to get past this obstacle.

"But what of those on the road from Fuunidor? We must help get them to God's Haven," Kikor stated.

"They could and probably will chase us. That will pull them away from the refugees," Guala said, reminding Kikor what could happen.

"Won't that then put them between God's Haven and the elves down there?" Kikor asked.

"They must be a patrol sent out to check the roads and passes for whatever is running Blath 'Na now!" Kirian whispered again.

"Maybe ... we should distract them from the refugees pulling them away and then attack. Those elves don't stand a chance otherwise. I say let's go for it!" Kirian smiled at Kikor, who laughed gently, shaking her head. Kirian wanted a fight, unlike Guala, who wanted a sound plan of attack.

"I say first we connect with the elves and let them know the plan so they can hurry everyone along," Guala said.

"You are right. No matter the risk, we must move them along. I'll ride down. You try to distract those riders. I will catch up with you. Tie down everything tight … This is going to be a hard ride." Kikor smiled, knowing her words were a joke to the others … This whole ride was hard for them.

Nodding, they kicked their horses, galloping towards the road and the elves on it.

Kikor was the first to reach one of the few elven guards that were protecting the refugees. She explained what was going on and encouraged them to hurry everyone one towards God's Haven.

Hearing the words *God's Haven*, the elves' guard looked at Kikor with a questioning look.

"What is wrong?" she asked.

"God's Haven is a myth, isn't it?"

Kikor then explained how to get there. "There is not much time — hurry. We will do what we can." Then Kikor joined Kirian and Guala on the field as they moved themselves to be on either side of Kikor. Like an arrow point, they rode hard southwest, ensuring the riders on the hilltop saw them.

Kikor saw that not only were there more of those beasts but they were larger wolves than normal wolves. However, they were turning to follow them just as they planned.

Howls echoed as the wolf beasts lifted their large front paws and flapped their heads hard back and forth, challenging the elves and roaring loudly as Kikor caught sight of figures running down the hill.

Kikor smiled from the corner of her mouth. They were going to make it before any of the beasts could get down from the hill. Kikor thought quickly, *No beast shall stop me now!* Her anger rose again as a flash of Birkita moved past her eyes.

They closed the distance every second until each could clearly see that each wolf was about the size of a medium-sized horse and their fangs looked like gigantic swords. Kikor pulled her sword pulled it out quickly and gripped it tightly, knowing she had one shot to wound and maybe kill one as she rode past.

The others pulled their blades out as well, together screaming battle cries as Kikor brought her blade down hard on the first wolf. She felt it strike bone, hearing the beast scream in pain as it fell away.

She heard two more howling screams as both Guala and Kirian's swords did the same and more wolves quickly moved to give chase.

* * *

The riders came on the first dead wolf, blood seeping into the dirt from the wound on its head. The figures approached the wolf, whispering words quietly to the beast and holding the fur of the wolf, calming the beast down as he watched the three elves ride off, disappearing into a small gully.

Another rider with the same long blackish robes moved up to stand next to the one comforting the animal.

"Your orders, Master?" The words almost sounded like a hissing snake from under the hood. This rider wore black robes like the others, but lying upon his chest lay a small round emblem with sharp points along the edges.

"Inform the others that the road has been broken by an elven patrol riding south!" it whispered from under its hood, only moving slightly to look at other, who nodded under its hood. "The trap has been set!" the master spoke as he turned back to comfort the animal in his arms. The other turned to jump upon their wolves and rode off hard towards the city.

The rider stood alone, looking south as the others galloped off. From under the hood, a smile broke from the pale-skinned mouth, showing off a pair of sharp pointed teeth as it snarled slightly, watching the elves disappear in the distance.

"Welcome to the last days of your life, elves!"

* * *

Not far away, lying in the thick of the grasses, were two beings that observed the black riders shoot off north.

"What do you think?" Bennak calmly whispered as his companion, Ame-tora, the frost giant, did his best in trying to stay in the bushes and not be seen. "Mmmm, from the sky over that man's city to those creatures there, I think Methnorick plans for something." Ame-tora's response made Bennak nod in agreement. Methnorick was planning on cutting off the roads and maybe cutting off the south totally.

"With those wolf beasts roaming around, it's going to be hard to get through, me think!" Ame-tora spoke again, bringing a smile to Bennak as he looked over, seeing the giants face looking back at him seriously through the grass.

"If they got through hill giants, then we should be able to get through two or three wolves, my friend!" Bennak and Ame-tora, in their journey trying to catch up to the elven army marching south, had run into groups of orcs and even two pairs of dark elven scouts, but the giants made the loudest noise out of their encounters. Each time they were able to dispatch them all with no sign of being found out.

Bennak saw the three riders burst out of the woods to ride south. He was sure one looked like Kikor. Her long blondish hair was hard to miss … It had to be her. The thought brought another smile to his face. He hoped she would forgive him for leaving the group earlier.

Looking south, he saw what looked like a deer trail moving along the top of the hill they were hiding on, so he pointed to it. "If we move along that trail, we could get past those creatures without being seen." Ame-tora followed Bennak's finger, nodding that he agreed that would work.

"Now or when the sun above is gone?" Ame-tora whispered.

"I would think now … Are you ready?" Bennak slid himself closer to his friend, wanting to get out of these bushes himself as they were cutting slightly into his skin.

As he got close, he could see the giant's right hand grip his weapon tightly as the half-orc moved his eyes up to look at the smiling frost giant, nodding down at him. "I have been ready to

74

fight those that are trying to slaughter my people, my friend … Methnorick might not be below … but they fight for him … and they will die for him!"

"Then let's move!" Bennak pushed himself. Still bent over, he moved past the giant, whom he could hear struggling to get up himself.

Without saying a word, the two hiked down the trail, avoiding being seen. So far, their movement was not noticed. Ame-tora nodded down at Bennak.

Bennak's thoughts drifted to thoughts of Jebba. *If I had just worked with the others, we might have found the princess by now, and even if the king is dead … The jewels and more might be ours!*

The half-orc was deep in thought as they both stepped over rocks and branches that lay along the trail, not noticing the two scouts that came around the corner as the pair moved up the side of a hill. Both groups stopped instantly, surprised upon seeing the other, as Bennak reacted upon seeing the two black-robed figures. The wolves roared and reached out to try to rip at Bennak's face, but quickly he stepped to the side as the claw flew past.

"Ame-tora!" he screamed as he brought his sword up, moving to defend himself as another claw came out of nowhere to try for his head again. He felt a massive cold wind fly past as Ame-tora pushed his left palm out towards the beast and rider. A loud rush moved past Bennak's head as he ducked down, knowing that, at that moment, a stream of freezing cold ice was enveloping both rider and wolf.

Bennak, not stopping to see the results, turned his attention to the wolf and rider moving past their now-frozen comrade as the half-orc could see the rider pull out a curved sword with sharp points along the curved edge like nothing he had ever seen in his life. He didn't have time to think as he had to swipe his own sword across from left to right as the wolf creature clawed at him, only to have the wolf scream as his blade cut the wolf's paw completely off.

Bennak had to twist himself slightly to get his sword up and deflect a blade moving down on him from the rider. As the two blades slammed into the other, all Bennak felt was a burning, fiery pain that shot up from his hand into his shoulder.

Hearing the rider speaking words to its mount, Bennak stepped back as the wolf tried to use its other front claw to swipe at his head, barely missing. He heard a grunt just behind him as he could just spy Ame-tora moving up along the trail to join him.

Without thinking, he brought his sword up as another strike came down at him. Bennak gasped silently as he watched the black-robed figure's blade almost ignite like it was on fire, but without the flames that a fire makes. Crying out in pain as the two blades cracked and sparked against the others, Bennak pulled himself back as the wolf lunged at him one more time.

Turning himself completely around, Bennak cut his blade across his front. Then, turning himself, he lifted his sword up for another blow. He spotted for a moment his friend, who was not fighting the wolf, which was a statue, but its rider, who had somehow survived the ice. Standing between Bennak and Ame-tora, it was fighting with the similar-looking sword to the one that he was facing as he moved back to face his own threat.

Before either its rider or the wolf itself could think for a moment longer, Bennak turned himself in a circle and stabbed up, bringing his sword up and cutting through the fur into the wolf's stomach. The movement made the wolf land just to the side of the warrior, who jumped back as the wolf fell to its side, bringing the rider down with it.

As Bennak watched for a moment, the wolf beast let out a final burst of air and died as its rider, now stuck under its beast, struggled to get its leg out as Bennak moved around the fallen beast to finish the rider. Bennak stepped right next to it, pointing his sword point directly at the chest of the rider.

"Who are you?" Bennak spoke harshly as he saw from the corner of his eye Ame-tora pick up and toss the other rider over the edge of the hill to disappear from sight.

Looking at the struggling creature, Bennak noticed that its robe still covered his face, so he moved his blade up and with a quick flick moved the hood off the creature's face.

"Who are …?" Bennak asked again as he stepped back, for what he saw shocked him. The creature was so pale, but it was his ears that really surprised Bennak, for they were pointed like an elf's. As Bennak looked at the rider's face that was now completely exposed to the light from the sun, the creature suddenly burst into bright flames.

The scream sent a shiver down the warrior's back as Ame-tora stepped up, grabbing his friend's shoulders and tried not to look as the creature squirmed while its whole body burst into flames now. "We have to move … There may be others!" The frost giant stepped past the warrior, who moved to follow, but instead he turned back, remembering that sword it had used against him. He wanted it.

Seeing it lying just next to what had been the rider, Bennak reached down. As Ame-tora once again called for him to hurry, he grasped the handle of the blade. Suddenly, he felt something move through his body like he could fight evil moving through the land all by himself. His smile didn't last a moment longer as a pain of fire shot through his arm. This time Bennak screamed as he was thrown back to land about ten feet down the hill.

Ame-tora, seeing his friend fly into the air, saw for a moment that the rider was no longer there — only smoking robes. Not knowing what it did to his friend, he jumped over to find his friend lying on his back, smoke rising from his body with a look of total surprise on his face.

"Bennak … of all the gods, are you well, my friend?" Ame-tora leaned down to look at his friend, wondering if he was dead, only to lean back when Bennak blinked quickly a few times to look over at the frost giant staring back down at him.

"Well, that was a mistake!"

"What happened?" Ame-tora leaned over, using his strength to help the warrior up to his feet. "Never mind, my friend. We need to move!"

Bennak blinked again as he coughed and then he began to giggle under his breath as both made their way back up to the trail. "Stupid me to think that I could hold one of those swords of theirs!"

"Mmmm!" Ame-tora could only answer, shaking his head slightly as Bennak looked between Ame-tora's legs to see that the rider was no more. Before either could say another word, their ears began to catch the sounds of wolves howling in the far distance.

"MOVE!" Ame-tora almost screamed as Bennak got up, still coughing slightly. They both ran as hard as they could south along the deer trail, leaving the scene.

Chapter Ten

The sound of chains being dragged along the stones echoed through the dungeon that lay under the city of Blath 'Na as the echo rang again. Then the sound of hinges moving as the large door swung open, bringing in a bit more light to the chamber, showing a man kneeling on the floor. His arms were held up by chains, making it impossible for him to get any rest. His clothing was ripped and covered in dried blood, and his black hair was covered in mud and dirt.

The man tried to raise his head up, but the light made him quickly close his one good eye from the pain it caused. He used his ears to locate whoever was walking around as he shook from the cold.

"Soooooo, what shall I dooo with youuu?" a voice echoed through the room. He heard footsteps slowly step around him to stop just to his right. "You failed me … You failed usss … You lost it all." The feet again moved to step around him as he tried to swallow, but his throat was too dry. The pain that shot through his head and neck didn't make this any better when a hand slapped hard across the back of his head as the voice continued. "Your death would be the answer … but I spent so much energy bringing you back from death that I think … Yessss, first torture is the answer!" the voice stated from behind as the man struggled to speak.

"Ohhh, you have something to say, do you? … Come on, speak!" The voice sounded a bit angry as it spoke again. "SPEAK!" The word echoed throughout the dungeon so that even the Blingo'oblins that guarded the other prisoners shifted in their boots.

"I … I did not … fail …" His voice came out almost like a whisper, making the shadow bend down to grab the jaw of the prisoner, bringing the being into the light as the man opened his one eye slightly as his head was made to look up.

"'Masssterrrr' … You call me 'Masssterrrr'!" A loud spark erupted from its hand, bringing pain to shoot through the man's head, causing him to scream.

"Pain is the only relief for you!" Another spark shot out, answered by another scream from the kneeling man.

"Our armies are gathering for the final destruction of the elven scum … And you will have your part in it, but first I want you to understand that you will do as we command and not take liberties again." The being stepped away, letting go of the man's face as it continued to speak quietly. Turning around, the master moved an arm out like it was swatting a fly, but instead, another spark came from its hand, which slammed into the man, lifting him up to slam hard against the stone wall behind him where he stayed.

He screamed from the very depths of his body as the being whipped his arm back and forth. Each time the man screamed louder and in more pain.

"Yessss … yesss … Let me hear your screams, Methnorick!" The voice almost sounded like it was laughing as the chains held Methnorick up as he screamed and struggled to get away from the pain.

Moving its other arm around in a circle, it opened each hand up like it was shoving something away as a burst of light ignited from it to slam hard into Methnorick's body, making him respond in a gurgling scream of pain that made the Blingo'oblins look at each other down the hall.

His body felt the massive burning pain like it was fire being punched into his skin as he screamed. It quickly overwhelmed everything he had in his mind as he struggled and squirmed in the chains as the being watched Methnorick erupt in flames. Through his one eye, for a moment, he could see what looked like a smile under the hood of the master, but then his eye noticed what looked like stars flying faster and faster towards him until the whole of the room began to shine so brightly from the fire that he had to close his eye.

His screams echoed throughout the dungeon so that the other prisoners whimpered, all knowing that they would be getting the same pain. They began to hear Methnorick begging for mercy as his body did a dance of sorts as the fire continued to cover his body until, all at once, the flames disappeared, leaving Methnorick hanging in the chains, smoking but alive.

"Now, Methnorick, how many pieces of the secret engine were you able to gather? And where are they?" The being laughed as it spoke from down the hallway as it left the dungeon. "I resurrected you just for this. We need those pieces."

One of the Blingo'oblins, knowing he had to find out what happened, swallowed deeply as he slowly stepped down the hall to find the heavy door ripped off one of its hinges, tilting outward. Looking at it carefully, the guard stepped past it, looking into the chamber quickly for the sign of the man held within it.

"Well?" the other guard called out, wondering why his companion was taking so long to tell him what was going on. "What happened to the man?" he repeated.

"He's there ... just hanging!" the answer echoed back out of the chamber.

"Is he alive?" the first Blingo'oblin whispered.

"I'm not about to find out ... You go find out!" The other guard shook its head quickly and turned to return to where it was supposed to be.

"No way ... The masters will kill us!" the guard said. The dungeon went silent.

* * *

Volkk was maneuvering the kelpie when he caught movement to his right. Motioning the kelpie in that direction, he whispered for it to hurry. Quickly, both moved up and over the last barrier of coral that was between him and the school of zool that were chasing something that looked like a shark.

As he approached, he got the attention of the leader of the group, Cruen, who turned himself around and swam over, flipping its fin up and down until both were looking at each other. Volkk rose his hand to give his greetings.

"Hello, my friend … I see you're having fun today!" Volkk said.

"We always have fun, Volkk. You know that … Why you here? … You want to play too … We have lots to play with!" Cruen clicked a few times.

Volkk understood that, for the zool, everything was a game, and if it was not fun, they were less likely to participate, so he chose his words carefully. "Thanks, my friend … I cannot … I need your help in a different game, though … You want to play?" The zool, hearing that a game was at hand, clicked and whistled, bringing a smile to the sea elf's face as Cruen called his friends over.

"What is game? … Game is here … me need to know!" Clicks rang out, as did a few whistles, as Volkk could see in the distance the shapes of his companions swimming their way.

"I need you to follow some unusual creatures to find out what might they are up to … whether they are dangerous or playful." Volkk knew that sending the zool in might be dangerous, but he needed to know, and the zool could get close without raising to much alarm. "You have to be careful, though. The creatures could be dangerous."

The zool flipped its tail, flipping itself around in circles as others swam up, whistling and clicking to each other as Cruen told the others about the game. Then it turned and looked back at Volkk.

"We go. We go … Where we go, Volkk?" Cruen looked directly into the elf's face, who smiled back.

"I'll show, my friend … but, Cruen … please be careful with this … they might be dangerous!" Volkk gripped the reins, about to turn his kelpie around as other zool, hearing his comment, quickly whistled and clicked something to Cruen, who quickly answered back to them.

"They say nothing can harm us ... Me agree!" Cruen smiled as he spoke into Volkk's mind, who then nodded, not wanting to argue with that. Volkk could not remember a time when he had seen one of them injured. Their kind were just too fast for other creatures of the ocean to catch. However, in his lifetime, there had been no serious battles under the seas of Marn.

Pulling the reins, the kelpie kicked out its long tail, and together the group shot through the water, back to where both he and Olen first spied the massive battle beasts walking along the ocean floor.

As they moved through the water, he thought of Vigaluna, the city of sea elves, a massive city with high spires of polished rock that reached through the coral where it was built. Using the natural cover of high cliffs on both sides of the abyssal plain, the city had expanded into a place of beauty over the cycles. His people had lived under the sea throughout the ages. Only a few had ventured out to explore the land, but Vigaluna was the home of the sea elven people, the Sawa Amnach.

Volkk and the zool swam quickly through the water along the seabed to follow the creatures and determine their direction and intention. As he did, he saw other ocean animals making their way towards the creatures, as if they could feel that something was amiss.

* * *

Meradoth listened as the council continued to argue for another hour, finally deciding to get up and leave the chamber for some fresh air. He had neither seen nor heard of this massive city that the elvish monks called home, and he wanted to explore it before they had to leave.

Stepping onto a set of stairs that rose up from the building he had been in to the next, he bent his back slightly, hearing it crack from sitting for so long. He looked around at the city. His eyes moved across the buildings interconnected by staircases.

Temple spires rose high into the air, causing him to raise an eyebrow at how beautiful each was, but wondering how the city could have remained so hidden. Seeing one temple not far away, he stepped down the steps and onto the stone road that wound its way through the main parts of the city. Many elven monks walked here and there, all in quiet conversion that he couldn't hear. All bowed slightly as he walked past. Pausing, he returned the gesture.

As he got closer to the temple, he could see lining the edges of the wall small statues, each painted in wonderful colors. The massive doors were open and also lined with metal figures. Looking up, he could see writing lining the top of the door, making him stop for a moment as he read it.

"Here the followers of Uusha be in peace!" Meradoth's eyes grew a bit larger when he read the words again.

"Uusha … interesting that the dwarven god has a temple within an elvish city!" Meradoth whispered. A shuffling behind him just at that moment caused Meradoth to jump in his boots.

"May I help thee, sir?" the voice whispered as the mage turned around to see one of the elvish monks smiling up at him.

"Mmm, well, no … Well, yes … I think … This city is elvish in making … but you have dwarven temples, temples of man, and even one for the Orkani — an enemy — within your walls?" Meradoth placed his hands before him, grasping them together as he spoke.

The monk smiled a gentle smile and almost seemed to be laughing at his question as Meradoth tilted his head in confusion.

"This city is called, my friend, 'Gods Haven' … That means all gods are welcome within it … Gusfana, Vaca'nor … even the Orkani. All were built within this city, waiting for the day when we believe peace will win out and all could join us." The monk quietly spoke of all the races on Marn that had been battling for space for so many cycles. Meradoth wondered how they could ever think there would be peace.

Meradoth turned and looked within the doors, seeing in the

foyer a table which held up flowers and a parchment.

"Are they all open like this one?" he asked, turning around to look at the elf who nodded yes to him.

"All are open for those wanting to go within … Peace begins with an open door, my friend!" the monk spoke as he stepped closer to the temple. "You are most welcome to enter any, of course!"

Meradoth quickly smiled. "Thank you … I was just looking at the beauty … It is amazing!" The monk bowed slightly, turning to enter the temple. Meradoth returned the bow and then turned. Clasping his hands behind his back, he walked farther down the road. He could see farther along the road three temples to each of the gods of the elven people.

There was Anda, the god of the earth and animals. His temple was covered in green plants and vines hung everywhere. Quiet music came out of the temple as he walked past. The music was beautiful, like the world should be, Meradoth thought as he peeked in, seeing monks in green and brown smiling at each other as they held conversations. Seeing the mage, two bowed slightly waving for him to join in, but Meradoth just smiled, nodded thank you and continued on.

Walking down, passing stalls filled with food and more, the mage walked up to the next elven temple, the center for the god Cava'nu, god of the sky. He was the mightiest of all the elven gods. He represented life and death to their people. Meradoth knew that many worshipped him before going into battle.

Meradoth stopped and looked at this temple, the largest of all temples within the city. Each spire shot up into the sky, each with a bell at the top to inform the city the time of day Everywhere he saw food being laid on the ground along the walls of the temple. He asked one on the monks why this was being done. The monk explained, "It is a way we show respect for the god and ask that he bring a strong harvest to make more food." Music came from many kneeling on the ground as they quietly sang words that drifted across the square that the temple stood in front of.

Beautiful! Meradoth thought as he looked at the monk, thanked him and then looked around, watching many warriors that had been within the battle, all probably saying their thank yous to the gods for letting them all live. Many, he could see, were wounded. Bandages covered shoulders, chests and legs. Many had their heads covered and were being escorted by others to give their prayers to the god.

As the mage stood, taking in the sounds and smells of the temple, he caught the movement of a horse rushing not far away, which got his attention, so he turned to look fully at the rider, who was jumping off and rushing into one of council buildings that stood at the edge of the square.

As he looked on, three warriors that stood speaking to the rider turned and rushed up the few steps that led into a building as the rider rushed behind them, all disappearing through the door, sparking his curiosity about what was going on.

Meradoth moved around the fountain that was quietly splashing in the middle of the square to slowly walk up to the building, where he now fully could hear the commotion and excitement.

"What is happening, my friend?" he asked a warrior that was making his way out of the building, looking like he was trying to find someone.

"A messenger from the north has arrived, sir … Methnorick's army is on the move again!" The elf spoke quickly. Seeing the person he wanted to talk to, he excused himself and rushed past Meradoth, who gasped slightly.

"Methnorick's army … but he's … he's dead, and his … his army was destroyed on top of that!" Meradoth wanted to know more, so he jumped up the last few steps and made his way past elven warriors and monks who were now scrambling until he was in the main chamber, looking around for someone he knew until he spied Kalion speaking to one of the elven monk leaders.

"Kalion!" Hearing his name made the ranger look up and wave the mage over. Meradoth pushed himself through a group of warriors, who rushed in from the outside as he finally got to the side of his friend.

"What is going on, my friend?" Meradoth asked quickly.

Kalion put a hand up to stop Meradoth from speaking for a moment until he was done telling the monk what to do. Bowing, the monk thanked Kalion and rushed off as the ranger turned, placing a hand upon the mage's shoulder, giving him a serious look.

"Well … there is good news, my friend, and bad … Which would you like?!" Kalion's sense of humor made Meradoth return a look that made Kalion smile from the corner of his mouth.

"The good news is that we have time to prepare … The bad news is that, even though you and I both saw it when Whelor ripped him apart … it seems that Methnorick's army has regrouped and is heading this way … and it seems the undead things from Blath 'Na are part of what is heading toward us."

"The gods help us!" Meradoth whispered.

Chapter Eleven

The crowds were loud as people yelled back and forth. Almost everyone had a weapon of some sort in their hand.

Shermee herself walked in the middle of this crowd with Quinor by her side and three strong-looking men that were her guards. None knew what they all might meet as the crowd moved down the streets like a river, slowly approaching the tower where the high minister had stood in power over empire.

Shermee, for the first time, got a good look at the tower as they rounded a corner and shook her head at how it rose in the air and the beauty of the workmanship of it.

Left and right she waved and smiled at people leaning out from windows on either side of the street. She could see children and women of both man and elven kind all leaning out to see her.

"SHERMEE ... SHERMEE ... SHERMEE!" her name rang out.

"The people seem to be taken with you, Shermee," Quinor said as he walked beside her. "It seems the prophecy is coming to pass."

Shermee was amazed at how it happened so quickly since entering the city — what seemed only yesterday. As she walked, he continued to speak to her. "It seems these people really believe this prophecy, and the dark rumors of war continue to help."

"What I am supposed to do with the high minister when we meet? ... I am sure he will not just step down when I ask ... even with the proof we have. Do you think he will fight?!" Shermee kept smiling as she saw a young baby in an elf maiden's arms, even waving at her as she waved back.

"When he and his council see this crowd and see the proof before them … they will listen to you!" Quinor smiled over at her. Both were trying not to show that the encounter to come could turn dark if the council's guards turned against the population.

"Quinor, do you think the proof is really creditable? I mean, it looks like it to me, but …?"

Quinor looked her in the eye. "Yes, I do, and I think that when the council sees it as well, they will have no choice but to side with us."

Neither one spoke to the other then as the crowds moved into the square that opened up before the tower's entrance. Like a river, the people ran into the area and moved quickly up to the gate that had been closed quickly by the guards, fearing that the crowds were going to storm the tower and do harm to those inside.

Still chanting her name, the people stopped just short of the gate and stood, calling out her name as the guards nervously looked at each other and then back at their captain who stood at the tower's giant doorway entrance at the top of the wide steps.

"Hold the gate!" he screamed and then waited for a moment to observe the crowds.

Inside the tower, council members were running everywhere, believing the people of the city were going crazy. Guards were ordered to secure the gates that stood on the four corners as the high minister himself stood looking down from the balcony, watching everything unfold, gripping the rail so tightly his hands were turning white from the loss of blood.

"You will not … You will not … you will not!" he kept mumbling as a few of the council ran in and out of his chamber, trying desperately to find out on why the citizens were suddenly calling for the high minster to appear below.

"Sir … the people are requesting you to come out and speak to them," one of Halashii's assistants stated from behind him, making him groan slightly.

"They bring weapons to kill me!" Halashii whispered, just loud enough that the assistant heard.

"I see no weapons, sir. They do not seem violent." The man's voice told Halashii that something was wrong and he was nervous.

Halashii stood watching the crowd below. He squinted slightly, looking everywhere in the crowd, when he caught sight of the bright blond hair moving through the crowd towards the main gate of the tower. She was surrounded by armed men.

"They are here for her!" He turned, looking at the nervous man from the corner of his eye. "They say they want to speak to me. I'll do more than speak to them, those rats of the empire!" Halashii mumbled as he left the chamber to make his way down the tower's stairs, leaving the assistant, who walked out to look down from the balcony, shaking his head.

"Shermee?" the assistant whispered the name that was being echoed from the crowd.

* * *

The zool swam up and over the beasts, making their way across the ocean floor, acting like they always did in a group, always playing around. As they swam over the first creature, Cruen could see that the beasts were massive in size, even larger than the largest Mal-mohr. As they got closer, he took in that the beast was no living beast like he had ever seen. Along the top, he could see spikes shining like spears pushing out of its hinds, and around its head, he could see dark-looking eyes peering out from under hardened plates that resembled the spear things the sea elves used to catch fish.

Moving their tails up and down to get over one of the creatures quickly, one of his people clicked, informing him that it was seeing more, making him turn his head to his right slightly, where it almost made him stop in the water, if he could.

He couldn't count the number of creatures he was seeing. As they moved around the creatures, none felt like they were currently in any danger from any of the creatures. It seemed as if they weren't paying any attention to the zool, just walking along the ocean floor like a herd slowly marching west towards where he knew the sea elves' home city lay.

Clicking and chirping sounds back and forth, acting like they were still playing, the zool turned themselves around and made their way back to where Volkk was hiding with his mount behind a large bed of coral.

As they got back to the edge of the herd of creatures, the first one they observed suddenly stopped. As Cruen swam over, he heard a loud whistle from one of his kind warning Cruen of danger. He looked down to see a bright blueish light burst through the water towards him.

"Scatter!" he screamed out in loud whistles, and quickly the zool burst out in different directions, just as the light overtook them, just missing one of his friends as it flipped its tail hard at the last moment to escape, but Cruen could feel the strange energy coming from the light as it moved past him.

Swimming hard to where Volkk was watching, he moved himself over the coral and clicked a "hello there" to the elf he saw peering through a small opening of the coral, who waved back at him.

"Beasts are many … Many dangerous beasts!" Cruen chirped and whistled as he swam in a circle around his friend, who swam over, climbing onto his kelpie not far away.

"How many?" Volkk asked as his mount started to move itself to the west, where his people lived, as Cruen himself flipped his tail to keep up with the sea elf.

"Many, many!" Cruen's thoughts were telling more than numbers as Volkk moved himself through small canyons and valleys in the deep, trying to keep out of sight of those beasts.

As the two made their way, Cruen's companions caught up and swam with the elf as he tightly held on to the reins of the kelpie in deep thought. *Where are they from?*

Then the thought came to him. "Cruen … can you track where they come from?" Volkk wondered how creatures that big and powerful hadn't been seen or heard from by the creatures of the oceans.

"Could take long time!" Cruen whistled a few times, and Volkk saw from the corner of his eyes two zool flip their tails and turn quickly around and shoot off towards the east. He knew that the zool were smart and could follow the tracks those things were leaving along the ocean floor.

Not knowing how long it would take, he had to get home to give them enough time to gather and put a defense together. They had lived in the oceans too long to just run.

The elf failed to notice that it had been watched by another as it swam out from hiding and made its way towards the beasts that lumbered along the floor once the elf and the zool moved west. As it approached the first beast, it swam up and over and then around the head a few times. Then it swam down under the legs that were lifting and slamming slowly into the sea bed until it came to land on the back of the beast, lying there like it was resting.

"The Sawa Amnach know of your approach … They are gathering!" The words drifted into the beast as the spy whispered.

Chapter Twelve

When the massive doors opened up, loud cheers erupted from the populace of the empire. They could see the figure of the high minister standing just inside. His name was called out a few times, but it quickly changed as "Shermee" began to be chanted again. He stepped out into the sun's light and stepped down the stone steps, being flanked by guards, all gripping their swords nervously as the minster walked towards the gate.

Shermee herself stood on the other side and watched as the man walked towards her, both staring at the other until he stood only a few feet away.

"Soooo, you are this Shermee ... You're only a girl ... I was told ..." Halashii's voice was interrupted by a loud cough from Quinor, who quickly smiled at the minister as the man looked over to see who stopped him.

"This is no girl, sir!" Quinor was giving him a stern look, which caused Halashii to cross his arms.

"I see ... Well ... what would you like to speak to me about, young lady?" Halashii asked, pulling in a deep breath to show that he wasn't that interested in what she might have to say to him.

"My name is Shermee ... I am Shermee Vaagini, daughter of Dia, King of Brigin'i of the North. I am here, sir, at the request at the people of the empire. They request that you step down." As she spoke, she watched him raise an eyebrow.

"My dear ... whoever you might be ... a princess or a peddler ... you do not, and I repeat ... you do not have the right to ask or demand that of me ... Leave this square, or I will have the tower guards remove you!" Halashii's voice told Shermee he was serious, but she was sure she heard a bit of nervousness in his words.

Voices rumbled around them as his words were repeating through the crowd, who began to chant her name until Shermee raised a hand.

"Sir ... this crowd of your citizens has come here to ask that you step down. We have proof that you have been removing people that oppose you for cycles." Shermee studied Halashii's face and then continued. "You have also stolen from the people of the empire."

Halashii laughed at her words. Shermee was sure it was also a nervous one. "Making my people disappear ... stealing money ... Please, little girl. Where is this proof?" Before Shermee could bring the proof forward, there was a scream from behind Halashii. Everyone turned to look up the steps that led into the tower. A servant, the one whose name Halashii never took the time to remember, stood holding three rolls of parchment in his raised hand.

"YOU LIE!" The man repeated the words again now that he had everyone's attention. "I HOLD HERE PAPERS THAT SHOW THAT YOU, ALONG WITH THREE OF THE COUNCIL, HAVE BEEN FOR MANY CYCLES MAKING MANY OF OUR PEOPLE DISAPPEAR!"

The crowd instantly erupted, with Halashii screaming for the captain of the guards to arrest the man. People pushed forward, grabbing the gate bars and shaking them violently, screaming for the high minster's head on a plate. Quinor reached out and grabbed the princess to protect her from the onslaught of bodies that pushed past them both.

"WHAT DO YOU WANT TO DO?" Quinor shouted as the noise of the angry crowd increased in volume.

"GET INSIDE ... WE'VE GOT TO GET TO THAT MAN AND PROTECT HIM!" Shermee pointed to the man who, at that moment, was being grabbed violently by a group of armed guards inside the tower. Halashii walked up to the top of the steps and turned around. With his hands clasped behind his back, he turned to look directly at Shermee, who returned the hard stare up at him.

The high minister stood for a moment longer when, suddenly, a scream of terror shot across the courtyard. Halashii looked down to where the scream came from, as did Shermee.

Just to the side of the gate had stood three guards, who upon hearing the servant's words telling of the betrayal of their leader, stared at the high minister as he walked away. Quickly, acting on their anger, they jumped forward and reached out, grabbing one of the officers that was trying to hold the gate. One of the guards slit a knife across his throat. An elven woman standing on the far side of the gate saw it and screamed in shock. The three guards turned to fight off other guards who had witnessed the murder.

One of the three men ran towards the gate as some random person from the crowd yelled, "Lift the lever to open the gate!" Shermee pushed her way towards the gate, watching Halashii look back at her. Instead of smiling in defiance, she saw he was frowning. For a moment, their eyes locked before he turned and walked inside calmly. Twenty other guards ran out of the tower to stop the three who had just killed one of their own.

Shermee looked over at the man being dragged back into the tower behind Halashii. She saw a look of panic on the man's face as Quinor was yelling to get the gates open. One of the three rebel guards farthest from the gate reached into his vest and pulled out something, throwing it at the one of his fellow guards that was closest to the gate. Shermee looked the guard in the eye as he produced the key and moved towards the gate.

The gate groaned loudly from the many hands pushing on it as the guard inserted the key to open it. The next moment, the gate flew open to the cheers of everyone.

Shermee herself was pushed through the gate opening with the momentum of the crowd. Moving with the crowd towards the tower and Halashii, Quinor pulled her off to the side just as the crowd started to push on the doors to the tower.

"Let them do the work ..." Quinor started to say but was

interrupted as the door burst open and the crowd moved through the doors. He motioned for her to stay there while he followed the crowd. He followed the crowd into the tower and up the stairs without any further opposition from the guards when they were confronted by another door. He could see the crowd in front of him pounding on the door to no avail. He attempted to push his way to the front of the crowd to get answers when he found Jacoob. Jacoob told him what had occurred so far. Quinor started to move back through the crowd, but as he turned, he found Shermee just behind him.

"I told you to wait there until I came to get you." Shaking his head, he continued, "It seems the people have the high minister trapped within the top chambers along with those of the council!"

"Good ... for the time being. I don't want them harming him."

"What now, my princess?" Quinor turned to look up at the tower.

"We have to convince the minister and the people that the best thing for everyone is for him to face a trial for his crimes. But first we need to find that man who spoke out. With him and the additional evidence he has, the high minister will not get away with anything now ... Plus, it is our duty to protect him." Shermee looked up at her friend. "Did anyone see what direction they took him?"

Jacoob piped up, "I believe the guards pulled him down into the dungeon of the tower."

"Find him and hurry! I will meet you at the top of the tower," she whispered. looking up at his eyes.

"Yes!" Quinor smiled at her.

* * *

The streets were covered in burning trash. This was causing heavy black smoke to rise up as the road was covered in belongings of those that once lived within this beautiful city. Steps echoed through the dark walkways as Chenush observed the destruction that had come to the city once known for its massive ports. Now it was being converted into a staging area for the next stages of the battle for Marn.

When Chenush came around a corner, two of the massive Blingo'oblins were deep in an argument over a richly made cloak. However, when they saw the cloaked figure, they dropped it instantly, kneeling down.

"My lord ... we ... we are sorry ... we leave!" The two bowed a few more times until they had retreated from his sight, leaving the cloak they were fighting over lying on the ground. Chenush reached down, lifting it up. He looked at it and then dropped it. He continued on until he came out into a large square. Here he found many orcs cheering and celebrating.

The figure watched for a long time, eyeing each creature that was in the square when three orcs, each carrying a mug of something, stumbled nearby. Instantly feeling the same as the Blingo'oblins, they quickly squirmed to get away from the creature.

For a moment longer, the figure observed what occurred and then stepped out into the firelight to walk into the middle of the square towards three large orcs, leaders amongst their kind. As he stopped to look down at the now-kneeling orcs, he could hear them whimpering.

"You three stand!" The raspy whisper came from the creature. The three jumped up to stand, nervously looking at Chenush.

"What are you celebrating, orcs?" The words made all three swallow, not wanting to be the first to answer. Then until a cough came from the middle one, making the others look at him.

"My lordddd, weess celebrate ... This our cityy nowww ... not man'sss!" the orc struggled to speak, knowing it could die within a second.

"No, orc ... This is not your city ... This is our master's city!" At that, the figure pulled back the hood, revealing the face that all orcs feared. "The day has come that our masters want ... Tomorrow you march to war!" A smile developed on his white skin, showing off two long fangs as his red eyes looked down at the three orcs.

The one orc on the left finally got the courage to speak. "Yessss ...

We prepare … We fightttt forr masssterrrsss … We fight for youuuu, Lord Chenush!"

The vampire leaned his head slightly back as his hands rose up, opening his mouth as he did, letting out a loud high-pitched scream that could be heard blocks away. Chenush — lord, general, vampire — cried out and celebrated that the day has come, the day when no elf or man walked the lands.

* * *

Bennak and Ame-tora ran as hard as they could, with echoes of screams so terrible that Bennak felt chills down his sweaty back. Finally stopping to rest, they hid behind a boulder as Bennak tried to sort out where they were.

Taking in deep breaths, Bennak peered over the boulder, carefully watching for anything that might be pursuing them. Nothing, so the half-orc leaned back, looking over at his big friend, considering. "I thought your people had the ability to freeze anything," Bennak whispered when he finally could take a breath. Ame-tora blinked a few times as he thought about the encounter with that wolf and its rider. He looked over at the warrior, letting him know he was wondering the same thing.

"Our abilities to do such things is true, my friend … Anything living and breathing will die under my people's hand." Ame-tora's voice told Bennak something was not right.

"Alive … you … wait. You got that thing's beast … It was frozen, but …"

"Yes … but its rider survived and continued charging at me, even at the loss of its mount," Ame-tora interrupted.

Bennak looked at the ground as he thought back. "Wait … I remember something … Yes, when l pulled its hood away, revealing its face …"

"Its face … Why would that matter?" Ame-tora whispered.

"Dead, but not?" Bennak stated.

"I have heard tales of creatures that are killed but then rise up and continue on … but here … and they act like beings that are alive!" Bennak quietly spoke. Looking around for a few moments, he lowered himself back down as Ame-tora leaned closer to him.

"You said that this Methnorick had many different creatures fighting in his army … Could he have also had those creatures fighting for him?" Ame-tora asked.

"That being is pure evil … the feeling I got and I'm sure you got, my friend … but the sight I saw when the light from the sun hit its skin …" Bennak's stated. Then he heard something, making him jump up to peer over the boulder.

"We should be on our way … The closer we get to the elven armies, the better off I believe we might be!" Ame-tora pulled out a pouch, taking a swig of it and handing it to Bennak, who nodded a thank you. He took a drink of the liquid inside. Instantly, he felt heat travel down his throat as the liquid's power ran through his body. He began to shake as if he had run hundreds of miles.

"I forget every time you share that … Power of the gods, is it?"

"Yes, my friend … an ancient power my people were given by a god from above to continue on living."

"I know you use it for long journeys, but you should have given this to us before we encountered those creatures!" Bennak smiled as his joke made the giant smile, shaking his head.

The two got up, feeling no pain in their legs anymore. Bennak looked over the boulder once more. Not seeing a sign of anything moving, they turned, heading south again.

Chapter Thirteen

Meradoth stood in the corner watching and listening to the crowd of elves and men talking about the news that the scout had brought. Methnorick's army was regrouping. Word spread of another army assembling within Blath 'Na and of the undead creatures.

"Have you heard any news about Kikor?" Kalion's voice interrupted Meradoth's thoughts. Looking over at his friend, he shook his head.

"No … but that scout over there was with her, so I presume she had him return with this news … I am sure she is making her way back. Do not worry, Kalion. I am sure she is well. She can take care of herself." Meradoth placed a hand on Kalion's shoulder.

Kalion smiled. "Oh, I know she can, Meradoth … I just want to be sure she made it back."

Meradoth shook his head, smiling wide as he gripped the ranger's shoulder. "There is no need to worry, my friend … I am sure she will make the enemy know who she is if there is any trouble."

They both started laughing until they heard something from the crowd gathering. They both leaned in a bit closer to make sure they heard it right.

"Did he say 'dead'?" Meradoth whispered. Kalion nodded, attempting to hear better. Neither spoke as the scout continued.

"Yes … Blath 'Na is still not only burning, but the fields around it are covered in beings that were alive but not," Barcla spoke as he drenched his throat with water from the hard ride south.

"How many did you see, my brother?" a monk that was standing nearby asked.

Lifting his eyebrows as he thought back quickly to what he saw, he tilted his head slightly as he spoke. "I saw at least a hundred, but … that is only what I saw. They seemed to be coming out of Blath 'Na, so I am not sure how many more there were."

"Well, that is not many to worry about then!" The monk smiled, wondering why everyone in the room was worried.

"Sir … the fields were beginning to fill from what I saw … and they are moving this way!" Hearing that, whispers erupted as everyone began to speak. Both Meradoth and Kalion shook their heads.

"It's worse than we could ever think," Meradoth whispered as the ranger nodded in agreement.

"Hold on!" Kalion whispered as he stepped forward, raising his hands up. "Excuse me … Excuse me …" Kalion's voice made the room quiet when they saw the ranger step up to Barcla, who nodded back at the ranger.

"My friend, Meradoth over there and I believe we met those very creatures that Barcla here speaks of within Blath 'Na … They are — or once were — the populace of Blath 'Na … Somehow, Methnorick was able to turn them into something that is … undead, I guess you can call them … but they are or were once alive."

The room again turned into whispers as people discussed what Kalion suddenly said. One monk, that the ranger could see was many cycles old, raised his hands to quiet the room down enough that he could asked Kalion a question.

"Sir … did you fight these creatures that Barcla speaks of?" The monk smiled as he spoke.

"A few, yes … Enough to know that they are very dangerous in large groups … and if they are moving this way … you must prepare … for their bites or scratches are deadly," Kalion stated. "And if I am correct, there are more then 100, for like I said, the whole of the

104

populace of Blath 'Na has been transformed."

"This city is very unique. Do you not believe this city can stop creatures such as those, brother?" The monk confidently smiled as he looked around the room. "God's Haven has protections that no army ever in the history of these lands has been able to breach!" the monk spoke proudly.

"The power of the gods will protect us like it always has!" another monk spoke up as Kalion shook his head, not believing what he was hearing suddenly.

"The protections in place hide God's Haven from outside view, so unless you know we are here, you would not even know to look for us," the original monk stated directly to Kalion.

"Sir, they are dead. Do you expect them understand or care that the city is hidden? If there is a way, they will find it. It will only take one to fall from the cliff walls into the city." Meradoth lifted his head to look at the monk whose smile was making him irritated.

The room erupted in arguments suddenly as the monks argued that the city could not be breached, and the warriors argued they needed to form a defense and fight.

"If we get their attention to move another way, we need not worry about the creatures. We will just need to worry about what is behind them," a loud voice stated, making the room quiet down. Kalion moved back and forth, trying to see who it was, until many of the people in the room sat back down, allowing him to see Kikor and her two companions flanking her as they stood at the chamber's entrance.

"Behind those undead creatures is something even more dangerous ... Methnorick's army. We do not know who leads them, but they have gathered more orcs and other dark creatures and could be marching very soon." Her voice made many look at each other as she made her way up, hugging Meradoth quickly, who smiled widely, whispering how glad he was to see her.

"My lady, Kikor ... speak please?" the older monk asked as she walked closer to the front, where both Kalion and Barcla were also smiling.

"My companions and I rode back not long after my friend Barcla left us … we observed hundreds upon hundreds of those dead creatures moving south … and there are more!"

Bowing her head in recognition of the monk's status that allowed her to speak, she continued, "We observed movement in and around the city by the undead. We also saw movement by other creatures, including the beast that flies. In fact, we saw two of those creatures." She looked at Kalion as she mentioned how many of the flying creatures there were. Kalion understood and looked away to pull in a deep breath, knowing that one was Chansor.

"Like our friend Lugtrix and his Pegasi?" one monk asked, wondering what the warrior was talking about, confused.

"No, like the one that attacked and slaughtered hundreds of our people during the battle, sir … Now there seem to be two of them."

Hearing that there were more made a few monks and even warriors gasp, shaking their heads until the old monk held his hands up to quiet the room.

"Were there more that you saw, my lady?" he asked.

Kikor nodded. "On the road here, we encountered creatures riding upon the largest wolves I have ever seen. I believe they were scouting the main road."

"Where was this?" Kalion asked. Kikor looked over at the ranger's face.

"About a day's march north of the city," she stated to the ranger, who looked over at Meradoth, who nodded and walked out quietly.

"Let Meradoth see what he can!" Kalion said to his friend as they both looked at the monks.

The old monk walked up, smiling. He placed his hands on Kikor's, thanking her for helping out with the information and being safe. He turned, lifting his hands high in the air, quieting the chamber quickly. "We need to do more than just wait this all out. I believe we need to join in this battle. Those undead creatures and now two of those flying beasts … We have proved that our people will not go dark in the night … We believe in fighting for the light!" He then walked over to the gathered high monks and spoke to them as Kalion and Kikor left the area to catch up on each other's movements.

As the two moved down a small street to get some peace and privacy, they heard the sounds they were both hoping for. Bells started to ring, proclaiming war was coming.

"So, now what?" Kalion smiled as he looked into Kikor's eyes as she returned the gaze.

Chapter Fourteen

"Do you feel it … the silence over the lands? I feel nothing but fear!" one of the masters whispered as he looked across the fields. He was accompanied on the ramparts of the walls of Blath 'Na by two others. The three of them all faced south as they conversed.

"This war could not have gone any better, do you not think?" one asked, still pleased by what he sensed across the land.

"There was more resistance than expected, but now, only the empire remains in our path. We will soon rule these lands."

"Methnorick has played his role perfectly," another interjected as cries echoed from deep within Blath 'Na.

"Perfectly? The man lost two parts of the engine we need!" the first one sneered at other. "Death is all he should have."

"He did give us the ability to find the third part and open the way to the empire. He didn't lose that battle." His whisper trailed off as a familiar beast flew over their heads.

As one, the cloaked figures silently watched the beast land on the wall with so much force that the stone shook under its feet before it was engulfed by mist. A moment later, a beautiful woman with reddish hair stepped out of the mist. With a serene smile, she walked along the ramparts until she approached the trio and sank into a deep bow.

"Masters," the woman said, "your armies are ready and await your word!"

"Bring us Kaligor, Elesha. The cyclops must understand the next move," he ordered. Smiling, she rose and nodded once before turning around and running along the rampart again to disappear into a large cloud of mist before emerging as the winged beast of prey.

* * *

Far in the southern regions of the land, far from Blath 'Na, far from where Queen Shermee now sat on her newly acquired throne, and far from God's Haven, stood heavy skin tents fluttering back and forth in the heavy wind. Steady gusts caused large amounts of snow to build up along the walls of each tent, which, in turn, made its constant removal a priority. Else, one could awaken trapped inside of what could very likely be a snow-covered coffin.

The snow wasn't the only menace; so too was the ice. For miles, large sections of ice would break apart and inch slowly away. Soon after, ice-cold water would appear, making travel very difficult in the area. Finally, there were the constant high winds, which could pierce through most creatures' skin in mere minutes, making life in the Forbidden Lands live up to its name, leaving it a place where only the hardiest of creatures could live.

Like the Hel-tors, a race of giants known as the Keepers of the Frost lived within the Forbidden Lands. Each stood at over fifteen feet in height, with the muscular frame of an animal. They were somewhat like frost giants, but larger and more fearsome in looks and nature due to the long fangs that came out of their mouths and massive claws on their hands and feet. Their white and grayish fur kept each beast warm, and for extra protection, each creature wore leg armor made out of an impenetrable metal found deep inside the Forbidden Lands.

Ten Hel-tors slowly walked the perimeter of the camp, scanning both the inside and outside of the camp as they kept a watch over the orcs sheltered within the tents.

Suddenly, a bright flash of light appeared in the middle of the camp. Three of the Hel-tor guards slowly stepped inside the perimeter, lifting their weapons as they approached the pulsating light, only to watch in amazement as the light dissipated just as suddenly as it had appeared.

Now standing where the light had been was a tiny creature wearing ragged black clothing that flapped in the high wind. For a moment, the Hel-tors all stared in confusion; none had ever seen a man before. And this one stood so still he could have been a statue.

As the Hel-tor closest took another tentative step forward, the man unfolded his arms and emitted a high-pitched scream that made all three giants take a step back.

The scream also alerted the rest of the camp as orcs — fearing they were under attack — ran out of their tents with weapons at the ready, peering through the snow for the source of the scream. Seeing three Hel-tors in the center of camp soon focused everyone's attention and weapons on the black-clad figure now calmly lowering his hood to reveal his bald head, while still showing no effects from the cold, blustery conditions.

A large orc carrying a torch stepped forward to approach the strange man, stopping first to look up at the Hel-tor nearest him, who shrugged in response.

"I am Drimak, general of the southern armies. Who are …?" Before Drimak could even mouth the word "you," the man crossed the distance between them, grabbed Drimak by the neck, and twisted his head until his neck snapped loudly. Even the orcs farthest away heard the general's neck snap and grimaced as they watched the man separate the orc's head from his body before ripping his spine cleanly out of his body, coating the snowy ground with Drimak's blood as his body continued to convulse.

The three giants that had breached the perimeter were quickly joined by the rest of their kind. The closest Hel-tor gripped his ice blade weapon tightly and readied himself to strike if this man now laughing like a madman made another move. One of his kind put his hand on the other's arm.

"He is a master!" he whispered. This caused the other to lower his weapon.

"From this day on, you and your kind will have victories and nothing else! You have been trapped here on this side of the mountains for too long, and we will change that!" the maniacal voice screamed. "I am one of your gods. Those that do not heed my word … will die where they stand!"

The giants stood, watching this man flip the spine in his hand around like it was a whip of some kind. In another blink of an eye, he moved to touch the leg of the closest giant, who instantly screamed out in pain and dropped to his knees. As soon as his knees touched the ground, the man let go and the Hel-tor fell silent. Understanding the unspoken message, each giant slowly dropped to its knees until every creature in the camp was kneeling to him.

The man stepped forward to address the wounded giant. "In time, I will give you a leader that will take you to victory in the east. Send out the word, beast: your gods want every being able to fight the elves to gather here. In a few days, you will march to glory!"

The anger and power of the voice moved through the giant and his companions like the wind that had stopped moving across the ice around them as if time stood still. The Forbidden Lands were waking up finally from the cold.

* * *

Inside the council tower of Manhattoria, chaos had broken out. Some of the rioters had made it to the upper floors before they were stopped by the council's private guards, who had formed an impassable phalanx at the top of the stairwell that blocked everyone from getting past.

Below, the rooms of the tower were being torn apart by rioters still angry at the high minister over friends and family who had disappeared. Council members who had the misfortune to be on the lower floors when the tower was breached had been placed in chains and were in the process of being dragged out for public execution when Shermee entered the tower.

Horrified by the sight before her, Shermee ordered the men dragging the council members to remove the chains immediately. The man at the front eyed her angrily as he shouted, "My son disappeared two months ago, lady. I will know the truth," he finished with another yank on the chain. When his comrades cheered him, Shermee knew that she had to act. Stepping forward, she placed her hand on the leader's arm and rose up to whisper in his ear. When she finished, she stepped back, never taking her eyes off the man.

The man stared at Shermee for what seemed like minutes. By now, everyone on the floor had taken notice of the standoff occurring before them, which, in turn, caught the attention of those on the second floor, and on and on until the stairwells and floor were filled with curious citizens. The tension in the room was so great that Quinor took a step closer to Shermee, only to be halted in his tracks by her raised hand, signaling him to stop without saying a word, all while continuing to maintain eye contact with the upset father.

Which is how she saw his eyes shift away from her to Quinor and then back again before nodding almost imperceptibly. He had come to a decision.

Nodding fully, the man turned and began taking the chains off of the council member he held, silently signaling his comrades to do the same. When the man finished, he hauled the council member to his feet and held his arm tightly before turning back to Shermee.

"Where do you want them … Empress?"

Shermee resisted the desire to smile, fully understanding the magnitude of the moment. She had not only won his acquiescence but also his acceptance of her authority. "Place them in the great room and keep them under guard until I return to speak with them."

With that, Shermee turned towards the staircase with the confident air of a royal who knew that her order would be followed. Quinor seemed to recognize the shift in the room as well as he followed behind Shermee, whose serene presence now compelled the murmuring crowd to part as she and Quinor made their way up to the phalanx still standing guard over the council members. When Shermee reached the top of the staircase, she walked right up to the barrier of shields, putting herself close enough to grab, if they were stupid enough to try.

"Council members," Shermee spoke as if the phalanx weren't there. "You know who I am. I would like to speak to the high minister please." She completely ignored the two guards who had lowered their shields enough to peek back at her.

"My lady," a voice from behind the guards responded, "your followers want us thrown in a dungeon. Or worse! We all saw what happened outside. The people are completely out of control!"

"A momentary outburst of emotion, I assure you," Shermee said soothingly. "In fact, no council members have been harmed in any way, nor will they be, and those responsible for violence will face trial for their misdeeds."

Lowering her voice, she spoke directly to the frightened man. He had not been able to hide the fear in his voice. "Sir, look behind me. These are your people. They will take note of what you do in the next few minutes. Now, do you truly want to attack when all I want to do is talk?"

The sound of whispers from behind the wall of guards told Shermee that there were far more people listening to their conversation, prompting a tiny smile as she remembered the behavior of the council back in Brigin'i. Some things never changed.

"My lady," the voice replied, "I will let you in, but only you. Your followers will need to stay behind."

Shermee lifted one golden eyebrow, but nodded as he finished.

"Quinor ..." she started as she turned to look at him and was momentarily struck by the subtle change in his demeanor. Instead of the somewhat patronizing, indulgent look he usually gave her, his face was deadly serious as he waited for her command, as if he finally believed her to be royalty.

"Stay here and keep the crowd calm," Shermee said aloud before leaning in to whisper to Quinor, "for ten minutes. If I haven't returned by then ... you know what to do." Shermee stepped back and looked at Quinor. She could tell by his tightened mouth that he wanted to argue, but he merely nodded.

114

Turning back, she waited for the wall of soldiers to form an opening. As she stepped into the chamber, she came face to face with a young man no more than fifteen cycles, who looked terrified but still lifted his chin to address her.

"My lady, I am Lord Applori. I am — or was — a member of the high minister's council," he said as he bowed his head slightly.

"Thank you for letting me in. If you would be so good as to direct me to—" she started, only to pause when Applori lifted his hand.

"That is the problem, my lady," Applori interrupted. "Halashii is no longer here." As Shermee's face changed from confusion to shock to anger, Applori hurried to explain.

"Please, my lady, let me show you. This way!" Applori started walking towards a set of chamber doors that had gold trim along the edges. As they approached, another guard standing just inside the opening snapped to attention.

"At ease," Applori said. "This is our new ... empress," he said, as if testing out a new word. Shyly glancing at her, he continued, "She needs to see him."

The guard turned his head and, seeing Shermee, nodded to her with a slight smile as he pushed the door open.

Applori stepped into the chamber then stopped to turn and look at Shermee. "I would have loved to have seen you put the man on trial, but ..." he sighed as he pointed towards the chair.

Shermee had been taking in the large map, plush furnishings and opulent tapestries on the walls when her eyes followed Applori's finger to the large desk, behind which sat the body of the man she had come to bargain with.

Halashii, High Minister of Manhattoria and the Empire of Pendore'em and Edlaii lay slumped back on the plush chair behind his desk. Shermee rushed over to get a closer look at the man and saw the small potion bottle on the floor next to his outstretched hand. She didn't have to touch it to know it contained some kind of poison.

"Why?" she whispered. "You were not going to be harmed ... Why?" Her words were heard by Applori, who stepped closer to look down at the man who had ruled these lands for more cycles than he had been alive.

"I cannot say, but let me say this, my lady. For a long time now I have seen this man change from a man who cared for our empire to a man who many claimed had descended into darkness. Whatever the case, I could see he was struggling with it each day, but ..."

Shermee glanced at Applori when he paused and saw him swallow and stare off into space, as if recalling an unhappy memory. Turning away from Applori while he regained his composure, she quickly calculated how long she had been in the chamber and concluded that it had been no more than two minutes. There was no rush now that there would be no conversation. A second later, Applori took a deep breath and continued his story.

"His orders to send our armies north to attack allies of ours was the final straw for many of us. But Halashii's tentacles ran deeper than we knew. One cannot retain power as long as he did without making connections in all the right places. Soon enough, we discovered that we couldn't do anything without being targeted."

"Did the armies carry out his orders?" Shermee asked, still staring at the body of the former high minister.

"No, my lady. The armies marched north but stopped about ten miles from the city border. As we speak, they are camped on the eastern fields, awaiting further orders." Applori looked over at her with the slightest hint of a smile on his face. Shermee surmised that the idea had been his.

"Well done, Applori. Your quick thinking likely saved the empire."

The young lord beamed with pride, confirming her earlier suspicions. She felt relieved that she hadn't lost her ability to read people. She had a feeling the skill would come in handy, sooner rather than later.

"What are your orders, Empress?" Applori asked, bowing his head.

Shermee didn't answer right away. She continued to stare at Halashii, feeling somewhat ashamed of herself. She had treated this transition like a game and allowed herself to get caught up with the idea of the legend without ever having thought it through. She had certainly given no thought to how Halashii would fare afterwards. After all, Applori wasn't alone in his assessment of the man. She had met several others who had fond memories of Minister Halashii and believed he had been a great leader to the empire. That is, until the rumors moved through the city — rumors that she had recklessly used to confront Halashii. She should have done things differently. These people deserved better.

"Have the minister removed and prepped for burial." She turned to look at Applori. "And remember, he was never found guilty of the crimes he was accused of, so he will have a state funeral as befits his stature."

Applori nodded and ordered the guard standing by to have the body removed immediately. Nodding, the guard left to get help for the task. Shermee walked out to the balcony to get some fresh air and think about her next steps.

"There is a lot of work that needs to be done, Applori. We have to find our missing people before the war comes."

"War, my lady?" Applori frowned, wondering what she meant.

"Before I arrived here, I was told that evil was approaching from far to the east. Considering how everything else has come to pass, I now believe that part of the prophecy to be true as well." Shermee's thoughts returned to her travels under the oceans with the sea elves.

"Are you speaking about this Methnorick, my lady?"

"Yes and no. While Methnorick is a very real threat on his own, he is but a servant, according to the sea elves." Applori stepped back in astonishment and quietly whistled.

"So, they're real. I've only heard of them, but ..."

Applori was interrupted by the sound of cheering. Stepping out on the balcony, he joined Shermee at the railing and looked down at the crowd. Most were pointing and cheering at Shermee, who smiled and acknowledged the crowd before turning back to look at the commander.

"Lord Applori, tomorrow the people must decide if they want me or another to lead the empire, understand?" Applori looked at her quizzically, wondering how she could think the people wanted anyone else after all of this, but merely nodded.

"My lady, I am sure the people will choose you," Applori earnestly insisted.

Shermee smiled at his loyalty. "We will see. Now, find Quinor and send him to me. Then I need you to find that servant who claimed to have proof of the minister's crimes." Applori bowed and left to carry out her orders, but not before noticing that the guards had also replaced the chair Halashii had died in after removing his body.

Now alone, Shermee took a moment to look over the massive city of Manhattoria, a spot of lush green nestled between mountains and the river. It was truly beautiful. And a place that truly deserved to protected, which she silently vowed to do if named empress.

Looking down, she saw the crowd cheer anew as word spread of Halashii's death. *Wherever you took them, Halashii, we will find them!* Shermee promised.

Chapter Fifteen

The clouds above turned black as a thunderstorm rolled across the skies, indicated only by lightning strikes, as the thunder itself was drowned out by the sound of hundreds of thousands of boots stomping towards the gate leading to the southern road.

Spears, shields, helms and more were reflected in the flashes of lightning as orcs and Blingo'oblins marched slowly in rows of six across, each carrying a weapon over his shoulder.

Also accompanying the orcs were scores of muscular, wolf-sized beasts, each carrying a rider wearing black clothing and holding long spears in their gloved hands. These were the masters' elite, beasts and riders that the masters planned to use to counter any elf attack. High above the army flew two dragons that slowly circled the contingent, there to hunt for anything that might watching or hiding in the forests.

Finally, riding just ahead of the army was a small group riding on black horses, which were covered in black armor. Each horse was the height of a hill giant, about nine to ten feet high. Their riders sat in saddles, holding the reins tightly with large swords clanging alongside each saddle, within easy reach for their owners.

At the head of this small group, upon the largest of the horses, rode a grimacing General Kaligor. The cyclops looked around slowly until his eye caught the gaze of the wolf riders, most of whom returned his look, letting him know he was being watched.

He sat up straighter on his horse and pushed his chest out slightly, a task made more difficult due to the heavy armor he now wore. The armor had been made by the masters to be impenetrable, or so they said, even from a mage attack, not that he had any plans to let one get close enough to test. The emblem carved into the metal of the breastplate, an image of a head with its mouth open wide in a permanent scream, made Kaligor smile as he adjusted the weight. He wanted his enemies to see it before they died under his hands and be forever haunted by the sight.

Just behind the general rode two warriors, assigned to be Kaligor's personal guard by the masters, which meant that he couldn't trust them at all. Both riders rode silently behind the general as their cloaks flapped behind them. One wielded a long sword that ordinarily took two hands to hold whilst the other carried a double-edged axe. Both weapons clearly showed signs of having been in battle, along with their silvery-black armor, which bore numerous hammered-out dents from previous battles.

As the massive army slowly marched out of Blath 'Na's gates, it was forced to come to a halt when a flash of light and smoke erupted directly in front of Kaligor. Cursing as he pulled the reins hard to stop the giant horse, four small figures emerged out of the smoke to stand across the southern road.

Recognizing the figures as the masters, Kaligor and his guards quickly bowed deeply in their saddles and waited for their orders.

"Kaligorrrrr … youuuu have beeen given a tassskkk … Youuuu must succeeeed." The haunting voice echoed across the field, sending a small chill down the cyclops' back as he looked up to see that all four of the masters were staring at him from under their hoods.

"Masters, I am and will always be your servant. I will take your hand and wrap it around the elven throat until they all die!" Kaligor boasted.

"If youuu fail …" the voice continued. Kaligor narrowed his eye as he dared to look directly at the masters.

"I won't," Kaligor replied, fully aware of the implicit threat. He would not be spared again. If he failed to defeat the elves, he would die. This was a fight for his life, literally. Turning to his lead orc standing about twenty feet behind the general, he gestured for the creature to lift the black banner high.

"We ride!" he yelled.

In response, the whole of the army lifted their weapons high in a wave as screams and cheers erupted down the line, until the ground under their feet shook from the tremendous sound.

Bowing once more, Kaligor lifted his right hand and pointed forward. Quickly, the masters disappeared in a puff of smoke, leaving the road open for the orcs to march past. Kaligor and his guards trotted forward until they reached a small knoll where the three moved themselves to the side until the storm passed.

While they waited, Kaligor thought of the battle plan given to him personally by the masters. How could he know for sure that it was designed for his success? This could be a total charade, a suicide mission to divert attention from the real target.

Suddenly, one of the dragons flew low, flapping its wings and causing the dirt along the road to cover the area as it flew over and away.

Blinking as the dust got into his eye for a moment, the general looked to the west, where just a while earlier he had fought and destroyed both Brigin'i and Bru Edin, both massive places of power, now both destroyed thanks to him. Now he was being tasked with doing the same once again. With someone else's plan. Never.

As he waited, he watched patiently as the army broke into two halves. The narrowness of the North Road slowed the progress of the first half, forcing the dragon to drop again and again to keep the second half of the contingent at bay.

He sent this second half down the road as his own diversion came to him as soon as the masters told him the plan. Why should he lead the first wave? He would allow the second group to confuse and, hopefully, break any elven resistance that might be waiting near the glen. However, if they failed — and, frankly, he expected them to — the elves would still find themselves surrounded, with no avenue of retreat, once he surprised them from the south, with a fearsome force of his own by his side.

It was the second half of the army he waited for as the dust settled. On his nod, Blingo'oblin lieutenants screamed out the order to about-face.

Seeing the orc army turn around, one of the riders approached Kaligor. "What are you doing, cyclops?"

Kaligor gave the creature his most menacing glare. "You forget your place." Before the creature could react, the cyclops grabbed him by the throat and held him high over his beast.

The rider cried out. "I have my orders ..."

"As do I," Kaligor growled. "And I will not be questioned by the likes of you. Do we understand each other?" The rider nodded almost imperceptibly. Kaligor narrowed his eye once more before dropping the rider back onto his beast, which objected to the unexpected mounting by bolting forward until the rider got the animal back under control.

One of the masters' spies had informed them that the elves were still loosely assembled, but surprisingly not camped at the glen where they had destroyed Methnorick. Instead, they were just south along the road about halfway from the glen to the Sernga Mountains.

According to the masters, there were over ten thousand orc warriors in those mountains, ready to join Kaligor's forces, but not until Kaligor was close enough. Their leader had explained that, as far back as anyone could remember, no Sernga orc had ever made it to the glen. All who tried had been found on the road, killed by elven arrows. Yet no sign of elves had ever been found. Kaligor planned to change that legend.

Kicking his horse, Kaligor reined his horse around and followed the battalions of orcs back into the city as his guards followed without saying a word. As he approached the massive gate of the city, a red dragon descended, landing hard on the ground, blocking his entrance.

"*I await your orders, sir,*" the red dragon communicated

telepathically as Kaligor quieted his horse. Kaligor looked up at the creature's massive head and smiled.

"I have many plans, Elesha," he said aloud. "You and your brother will join me and finish this once and for all!"

"*You have plans for us?*" The black dragon flew overheard, slowly flapping his wings as he, too, spoke to Kaligor's mind.

"Oh yes, Chansor." Kaligor nodded. "The two of you together will devastate them, forever!" Kaligor smiled as his mind formed a picture of the two massive beasts laying waste to every elvish army on the field.

With a cry of excitement, Elesha shot into the air to join her brother. "Isn't that what you want? Revenge, destruction, death?" Kaligor spoke with a cheerfulness in his voice as he watched both dragons circling over him.

"*What do you think?*" Elesha whispered back in the cyclops' mind.

"*I want the lands to burn!*" Chansor added. Kaligor smiled widely upon hearing Chansor's thoughts.

"And they will, my friend … They will!" the general whispered as he followed the last of the orcs back into the mighty city.

* * *

The scream echoed loudly throughout the dungeon.

"You don't seem to realize your failure in ending their reign, do you, Methnorick?" The only answer was yet another scream as the man hanging from the chains shook uncontrollably, if one could still call him a man. His skin had all but melted off his face, leaving only his skull underneath to stare back at the master torturing him.

"We all hoped this war would be over quickly, but you had other ideas, didn't you? EMPEROR!!" A flash of fire from the master's hand struck Methnorick's frail form, igniting more of his skin and again evoking an unholy scream of pain that could be heard throughout the city. Unsurprisingly, a few of the orc guards shook in their boots upon hearing the screams.

"Answer me!! Are you my slave? My servant? Tell me ...
Emperor," the master taunted as he walked around the chamber with
his hands behind him while staring up at Methnorick's skinless face.

"This pain can stop if you give me what I want. Just give me what
I want!" the voice needled. Methnorick shook from the pain moving
through his body. He couldn't have answered even if he knew what
the insane master wanted. He had taken his tongue early on.

Methnorick saw a smile appear on the master's face as he opened
his mouth uselessly.

"Ahhh, yes. Sorry about that. I was having some fun earlier!" The
master snapped his fingers. Methnorick felt the familiar weight of
his tongue within his mouth again.

"Speak, slave, and give me what I want!" the master ordered as
Methnorick stared down from his skinless eyes.

"M-m-m-master. I am ... y-y-y-your s-s-s-slave!" Methnorick
stuttered, screaming the last word desperately, and was rewarded by
the sight of the master's mouth curving into a smile.

* * *

Olen and Volkk waited in the Hall of Memories while the elven
council convened. Olen had always enjoyed this place, where statues
had been carved into the rock to resemble the ancestors who built
this beautiful city. Volkk barely noticed, so preoccupied he was with
the danger approaching the city.

Luckily, it didn't take the council long to reach their decision.
Soon, chamber guards quickly floated past with instructions to
assemble and move the population of the city to an area where they
could be guarded. Volkk was called in and quickly placed in charge
of a detachment of warriors. His orders were to lead the first wave
of defense against the beasts moving towards the city. Olen was
assigned the rear guard that would defend the city if the beasts got
past Volkk's forces.

Within minutes, hundreds of armed riders on kelpies were ready
to move. Each rider held a spear tipped with a gem that not only

shined brightly in the sea light but was also capable of puncturing the hardest known armor. Speaking of armor, sea elves had no use for metal in the seas. Most wore barbs of coral and starfish called living armor, as it constantly moved and gathered information around the wearer, giving elves an extra source of protection by alerting them to unseen dangers.

The kelpies themselves were already covered in a shell-like armor taken from creatures of the deep to give them an extra amount of security as their riders led them eastward through the water, forming themselves in a stingray formation.

As his army gathered at a massive rock formation, miles outside of the city, Volkk was accompanied by hundreds of massive turtles that had come to join them as reinforcements. They weren't alone. Volkk looked toward the south, where a school of Mal-mohrs was heading his way, along with hundreds of zool, all following Cruen's lead.

Soon the ocean waters outside Vigaluna were crowded with hundreds of thousands of sea creatures, including crabs, stingrays and eels, all brought together to stop the oncoming threat that was moving along the sea bed.

Unlike their surface cousins, sea elves worked in cooperation with most of the creatures of the deep. They had literally spent centuries strengthening their relationships amongst their allies, mainly for defensive purposes. Instead of arrows, which would be useless in water, their "archers" worked with electric eels, training them to shoot out of a tube to hit their victims with a massive charge strong enough to thoroughly shock, or even kill if needed.

While the group was assembling, Volkk sent two scouts out to confirm the path of the beasts. Other elves met with their allies' commanders to pass on the plan, which was simplicity itself: do not let the beasts pass. When Volkk saw the grim face of the first scout racing towards him, he didn't even need to hear the report to know that the beasts were still on the same path. So be it. This is where the beasts' march forward would end.

It didn't take long for the group to get their first sight of the beasts marching towards them. The slight glint of their "eyes" could be seen more than a mile away.

"They look like giant crabs of some type!" a nearby warrior cried out.

Volkk nodded in agreement and motioned to three elves he knew to be elite warriors. "I need to know what kind of defenses they have. The beasts seem unwieldy, but still … be careful!"

The elves nodded and shot through the water towards their targets.

Volkk watched the three elves close in on the front beast, which, surprisingly, did not initially respond to them. This might be easier than he had first thought if they could simply disable the creatures. The elves continued their approach, careful to avoid the light of its eyes. The lead elf advanced to within a spear's throw of the beast when, suddenly, a bright blue beam of light shot out from just above its eyes.

Volkk watched his elves maneuver themselves away from the beam with relief, until he saw what happened next. The red light that missed his elves slammed into the rock bed, where it flashed and blew the rock apart as easily as a mallet hitting an egg. Volkk frowned and turned to the elf beside him. "Pass the word. The beasts shoot out red spears of light that smash rock. I have no doubt that they are powerful enough to kill many of us, so try to avoid them at all costs!"

Looking back, he observed his warriors now swimming up and over the beasts, staying as close to their bodies as possible to avoid more red bolts from more and more beasts as they emerged out of the dark. Soon, the entire area began to shake under the tremendous amount of fire.

It was time to begin the assault.

"Send in the archers," Volkk ordered, still watching the elves furiously trying to avoid the bolts being aimed at them. The beasts had stopped caring about missing each other.

Moments later, the first of the large crabs moved forward carrying the elven archers. Just behind them, a few heavy catapults were being carried on top of the crabs as well.

Good, we're going to need them, Volkk thought, just as one of his elves got hit by one of the red bolts.

Volkk watched in shock and horror as the flash dissipated. Having expected to see no sign of his warrior, he was surprised by the sight of both the elf and his mount. Then he noticed that they weren't moving. Hoping they were knocked out, he started to order a rescue until the elf and his mount began to shine brightly. Still, they did not explode but, instead, fell to the sea bed, where they were instantly trampled by other beasts.

Volkk had no time to process the why of the matter, as the crab archers and catapults were now in position. Their assault gave the two elf scouts enough cover to escape the red bolts and return to the army, where they found Volkk immediately.

"They never even stopped to engage us, sir. And their shells are like nothing I have ever seen. Our spears were completely useless. When other bolts hit them, their shells were merely scorched." Volkk could sense the nervousness of the sea elf as he nodded and dismissed him.

Volkk turned back to the assault being waged by the archers and catapults. *Give me something!* Volkk pleaded silently, only to find his hope waning as eel bolts slammed against the beasts and fell away, leaving no mark or even slowing them down. Same for the catapult. Rocks slammed into the beasts, some striking so hard that a few beasts seemed to shudder under the tremendous force, but still, the beasts continued to march on.

Volkk leaned back in his saddle, knowing that he was running out of options. Thus far, spears, archers and even the catapult had proved to be useless to stop the beasts. His allies would have to save the day. Suddenly, a red bolt hit one of the crabs that had been carrying the archers. Luckily, all had jumped off the crab before the bolt hit. Expecting the crab to die like the elf and kelpie, he was almost giddy with delight when the crab appeared unaffected beyond a scorch mark. *Finally!*

"Have the Mal-mohr move to the southern edge. Send a contingent of crabs with them to set up a diversion while the whales gather enough speed to hit them hard and fast. Take out the legs!" Volkk ordered. "The shell of the turtle is even stronger than that of the crab, so have them move to assemble a shield wall. I need the zool to gather ropes of seaweed to tie around the legs of the beasts. Quickly! They are getting closer. Let's see if we can trip those beasts up!"

Elves and sea creatures scrambled to quickly get into position. The turtles moved ahead of the crabs and began to line up side by side to create a protective wall that hid the army from sight while the crabs repositioned themselves to provide cover for the Mal-mohr.

Meanwhile, young zool with mouths full of seaweed rope began swimming towards the beasts, flipping their tails hard to fly under and over the red bolts fired at them. They had seen the range of the bolts when the beasts attacked the elves earlier. Now they knew how to avoid them.

With remarkable speed and agility, they swam around the first beast's legs, tying the legs up. The beast slowly fell forward to slam its head hard into the sea bed, scattering the sand into a cloud.

As warriors behind him cheered the success of the zool, Volkk watched the head of the beast closely. He could have sworn that he saw something escape the head of the beast as it blew open. Seconds later, his suspicion was confirmed.

"How?" he whispered to himself. Having no time to ponder the matter further, as the men escaped to the rear of their formation, Volkk motioned the closest warrior over. Placing his hand on the elf's shoulder, Volkk leaned in to speak to him over the cheers.

"Get back to the city and inform the council that these beasts are not beasts at all. They are machines, controlled by man, who have created machines to breathe!" The elf swam, giving Volkk a look of surprise, but quickly turned his kelpie and raced back to the city.

"Sir ... the Mal-mohr are attacking!" Volkk turned towards the familiar whale cry as the massive black shapes moved out of the black mist of the waters with what sounded like a hundred clicks and whistles. The huge mammals swam onto the battlefield, maneuvering themselves, one whale for each machine. Volkk began to worry when he saw one machine after another turn their fire on the rapidly closing Mal-mohrs.

Bolt after bolt slammed into the heads of the whales as everyone heard whistles and chirps that sounded more like anger as each whale flipped its long tail to slam hard into one machine after another. Cheers erupted everywhere as the Mal-mohr tossed one machine up after another like they were toys, only to subside as the mighty creatures began to slam into the sand to rest still.

A scream to his left got Volkk's attention. Turning, he saw that a few of the machines had gotten ahead of the whale assault and were still now approaching the turtle shield wall.

Worse, the machines were now using their bolts to free the others tangled in seaweed, after which they arose and continued their forward march. Volkk forced himself to think. *Machines mean there has to be a way in and out. Where would a man enter the machine?* Volkk stared at the bellies of the turtles when the answer came to him. *Of course, they would climb up to the belly. Like a turtle, the underbelly might be weak ... might!* Volkk cautioned himself against too much optimism as he turned to the hundreds behind him waiting for his order to join the battle.

"MAKE READY!" Volkk cried out as three machines at the center of the line fired red bolts towards the wall. As Volkk had hoped, the turtle shells deflected the bolts, as they bounced off and back towards the machines.

Volkk smiled as the wall held. "Now ... ATTACK!" he cried out. "Aim for their underbellies!"

Within moments, thousands of sea elves and their allies swarmed the machines, covering each other as they sought a way in to stop these armored beasts. Elven warriors swam forward using shells from turtles that had died in the past as shields to deflect the bolts being shot at them.

Still, many elves fell in that first wave of the battle. Volkk grabbed a warrior who was whipped sideways by a bolt that merely grazed him. Pulling him behind a rock to keep him out of the line of fire, he could see that the elf was experiencing a massive amount of pain. Struggling to speak, the elf told Volkk the bolts were almost like the eel bolts, just more powerful and painful.

Nodding, Volkk left the warrior there to recover as he returned to the fray. He and his kelpie maneuvered away from the red bolts as Volkk took stock of the battle. Many of the beasts had been damaged by the whales and the dolphins and struggled to walk. But walk they did, continuing their march towards his city. Worse, those machines that had been turned over like a turtle were still able to emit the red bolts of destruction as they awaited assistance.

"Sir, we are taking heavy loses … Do we continue?" One of the warriors swam over, just missing a bolt that had been shot at him. The warrior's face told Volkk everything: they needed to reassemble and fall back.

"No. Order the retreat. Get those turtles to cover us as we fall back. Tell the zool to do their best to cover the surviving Mal-mohr as they get themselves to safety!" Volkk replied.

He watched bitterly as his forces quickly scattered behind the wall of turtles after being given the order. The dolphins and whales dispersed soon after, leaving the battle in different directions as Volkk stayed behind to take in the scene before him.

The sandy bottom of the ocean was virtually littered with the bodies of elves and their kelpies, dolphins, whales, eels and even a few unlucky crabs. So much loss. His people had cut the number of machines more than in half, but he feared that there were still enough machines to damage Vigaluna beyond repair. His people had never faced a threat such as this, and with their power … his city wouldn't last long

It was clear to Volkk as he turned away to return to the city. He needed more help.

Chapter Sixteen

*D*espite the death of Halashii, the city of Manhattoria was in celebration mode. The populace filled the streets, celebrating something that most had never even believed, let alone thought would come to pass. The legend had been fulfilled. A girl from the north had come to be named empress of the land. The streets buzzed with excitement as the parade moved slowly down the main street so that their new empress could be seen by all.

Shermee waved back at the crowds with a smile that hid her nervousness. She wore heavy blue and green robes adorned with the emblem of each of the provinces of the empire: Kaznori, the flying horse; Vostoki, the roaring bear; Rakhanik, the swimming zool; Kustik, the flaming sword; Petrikbur, the pondering man; Novski, the crossed sword and spear; and Manhattoria, the crown upon a flaming throne.

Shermee had not realized that the empire was so vast, but she was determined to protect and lead them all in the war she knew to be coming.

Her chariot stopped at the temple that represented the empire's main goddess, Messania, one of the oldest goddesses that had ruled over the lands of Marn.

Looking up at the massive statue, Shermee took in the gloved hand of the protector and the ungloved one holding a feather symbolizing compassion. *I hope I can be both!* Shermee thought quickly.

Shermee turned once more to wave at the people of the city, who cheered and screamed out her name, before turning to climb the steps leading up to the open massive doors behind which clerics awaited her arrival.

Standing in the threshold was the city's head cleric, Nergu. An elf at least a hundred cycles old wearing a long white robe, he waited with hands clutched before him.

As she had been instructed earlier, Shermee knelt as she stepped up to him. Nergu lifted his hands to silence the crowd. When everyone had quieted themselves to his satisfaction, Nergu began the ceremony.

"People of the Empire of Pendore'em and Edlaii, you are here to witness an event of profound historical significance, of prophecy fulfilled. This woman, a princess who came to us from the northern reaches to lead in our time of conflict, having passed all the trials put before her as the legend foretold, will now be crowned empress!"

The crowds erupted in cheers yet again. Nergu again raised his hands and waited for them to quiet down before continuing. "The legends confirm the empress. But what say you? Will you confirm the legend? Will you lead the people of the empire?"

Shermee looked up at Nergu with a soft smile. "Yes. I will." Shermee took a deep breath. She wished her parents were here to see what she had become as she blinked a tear away.

Raising his hands above Shermee, Nergu whispered a prayer to the goddess Messania above, hoping that she would help bring peace to the land and bring compassion and understanding to help the new empress. His voice got louder as he recited the words he had been studying since last night, having never done it before.

"... and for each province, there shall be peace and prosperity for the glory of the empire. The empire, in return, will promise to protect you, your family and the people of each clan. Shermee, you must now vow to provide order and law to the people of the empire. Are you ready to promise to uphold the order of the empire?"

Shermee smiled and nodded as Nergu finished.

"I, Shermee, former princess of Brigin'i ..." she began, ignoring the catch in her voice as she once again thought of her former home, "Empress of the Empire of Pendore'em and Edlaii, shall protect our people and uphold the order of the law of empire and fight for them all. I, Shermee, am ready to command!" Shermee recited the response that had been sent to her by Lord Applori with the other instructions of protocol.

Nergu smiled back at Shermee and nodded as the crowd cheered a boy walking out of the temple, carrying a brilliant crown fashioned out of more diamonds and gems than Shermee had ever seen on a single object. Like her robes, Shermee could see that all of the provinces were represented by the crown as well, with the emblem of the empire front and center. As he reached them, Nergu turned and took the crown from the boy, who grinned and bowed to Shermee before leaving.

Holding the item over Shermee's head, Nergu completed the ceremony. "I, Nergu, of the Empire of Pendore'em and Edlaii, high cleric and priest of this empire, pronounce you, Shermee, Empress of Pendore'em and Edlaii from now until time ends!" When he finished, he lowered the crown upon Shermee's head, who luckily, could just bear the weight without toppling over. Slowly rising to her feet, she turned to the thousands cheering her name.

"Shermee … Shermee … Shermee … Shermee!"

Smiling widely, she looked around slowly, taking in the faces of the people she was now ruling over. She looked down at Quinor, who smiled back at her and bowed his head slightly to acknowledge her position.

Raising her arms high, she waited for the cheers to subside before addressing the crowd.

"I am your empress, and from this day forward, I will work to ensure that our empire remains strong and peaceful. But I cannot do this alone. Will you follow me as we all journey forward together?"

The crowd again screamed her name in response. Shermee sincerely hoped that meant yes as she signaled a smiling Quinor that she was ready to depart. He nearly vaulted up the stairs before bowing deeply and offering his arm. Together, they slowly descended the stairs to the awaiting chariot through a path now covered in flowers and cloth, showing the respect to be afforded to the empress. Shermee climbed up on the chariot and once more waved to everyone before taking her seat. The weight of the crown was one she would have to get used to. Thankfully, it was only needed for the most notable events. The tiara she was to wear daily was far less elaborate, and less heavy. As she heard the crowd continue to scream and cheer, she turned to her friend.

"Can you believe this, Quinor?" she yelled at the man who sat across from her. She laughed again as she saw children jumping up and down, yelling her name and waving at her.

"My empress," Quinor yelled back over the noise, "you know if you wish, you can walk amongst the people."

"Of course, I can. These are my people now, Quinor! In fact, I think I will. Take this heavy thing off my head."

Quinor smiled as he took hold of the crown. He wasn't the only one. The crowd seemed charmed by their new empress ditching her crown. With a brilliant smile, Shermee stepped out of the chariot and made her way towards the crowds that were being held back by hundreds of guards and warriors that were trying desperately to keep order and calm. He had never seen her happier as she shook hands, kissed babies and hugged the children who ran up to her, including one excited lad whose mother shrieked when he ran up and hugged Shermee's leg with his muddy hands. Shermee merely laughed and invited the other small kids to add their handprints to her gown. Soon, her robes were covered in muddy handprints, which she showed off to the crowd with pride, sealing in their devotion to her forevermore.

Quinor stood in the chariot, watching the woman he had fallen in love with. He knew that he would never be her husband. He lacked the pedigree. He wondered if she still had feelings for that ranger back in Brigin'i. She had never mentioned him directly to him, but he had heard her crying out to him in her sleep. Knowing what had happened to the city, the man had probably been killed or taken prisoner long ago. Now that she was empress, she had the means to find out. *What will she do now?* Quinor wondered as Jacoob and a man wearing cleric clothing approached.

"Sir, have you had a chance to talk to her about the rumors of a massive army assembling at Blath 'Na City?" Jacoob asked. As Quinor opened his mouth to respond, the man in the cleric clothing piped up.

"Word has it that there are signs of a powerful evil within ... Does she know?" the cleric asked urgently.

"And you are, sir?" Quinor frowned slightly as he took in the elf. From the looks of him, he had been around for many cycles. His face must have seen battle, as there was a long scar going down the right side and down the side of his neck.

"This is Gereel, Quinor," Jacoob interrupted, sensing the tension between the two men. "He is a cleric in this temple. He is the one who worked with me to uncover Halashii's crimes. I would listen to him, Quinor. He has been around and knows things." Jacoob smiled slightly as both men nodded to acknowledge the other.

"Well, to answer your question, Jacoob, no, I have not spoken to her about any rumors from the north, nor about what she plans to do about the missing people. However, the boy, Applori—"

"Lord Applori," Gereel corrected.

Quinor rolled his eyes and sighed. "*Lord* Applori says that she spoke to him of a coming evil."

As Gereel opened his mouth to respond, Quinor held up his hand. "She has called for us to gather tonight. She said that she wants to know everything possible. I imagine that you will get your answers there." Quinor smiled at Shermee hugging an older elven woman, who then kissed her on the cheek.

"She will let me speak to her?" Gereel asked, not believing that the new empress would let a common person of the empire speak to her.

Quinor turned to the cleric with a look of surprise. Then it hit him: *they wouldn't know anything better.* "Of course, she will … and believe me, when you come to know her, you will love her like … as you can see the people here already do."

Jacoob and Gereel looked at each other and then at the lovestruck warrior, whose attention had already returned to the empress, before walking away. Quinor watched Shermee's delight as she let go from a tight hug with a young boy who, both could see, was filthy from head to toe. His clothes looked like they hadn't been cleaned for over a cycle.

"Shermee … empress of the empire … I am yours forever!" Quinor whispered as he continued to watch the young woman make her way down the road, bonding with the people of her city.

***

General Vana sat in the pub house, brooding over a mug of ale as he waited on General Summ to arrive. He had sent word to Summ that his contingent was needed back at the Father Gate. If the reports were true about what was happening inside of Blath 'Na, he had a duty to return now to make sure the gates of the empire were secure and his men were ready.

Vana thought about how leaving this city might make it harder for Summ to defend, but Vana had his own losses to contend with — losses that would now make the empire harder to defend. Vana was so deep in his thought that he didn't notice the man standing before him until he cleared his throat to get his attention.

"General Vana, is it?" Vana looked up to see an older man who had clearly seen a lot in his cycles and wore it with more than a bit of pride, but with a lot of sorrow also.

"Yes, sir, how may I be at your service?" Vana rose slowly to reach out and grasp the man's arm, shaking it slowly. The man moved a stool out and slowly sat down as a girl walked over with two mugs of ale, placing one in front of each man.

"I am King Dia Vaagini of Brigin'i …" Dia paused as Vana bowed his head to the king. "I understand that you are planning to leave soon. I was wondering if I could travel with you and your men as you journey home."

Vana, a little shocked, lifted an eyebrow at the thought of a king traveling with him. "Sir ... I would be honored to have you join us. However, what of the elves? Won't they need your troops to assist with their defense?" As Vana spoke, he looked over the king's shoulder, where a commotion was happening in the street outside the pub house.

"I have no troops here, son. I was only given a small contingent of riders during the battle to lead, and now the battle is over. As for the defense you speak of, I believe these elves can protect their city. They seem far less inclined to help others — especially non-orcs. Which is why I hope to get to the empire to see if your leader will allow me recruit some of your people to join in the fight that I know will happen sooner or later."

"I have no problem with your coming King Dia, but you understand that I cannot speak for the high minister. He might have a problem with what you are proposing, as he is the only one that can raise an army."

A smile moved across Dia's face as he listened to Vana's worries. "Don't worry about Halashii. I am sure that he will be most eager to help. Especially when he hears where I plan to go next."

Vana couldn't help but smile back at the crafty gleam in king's eyes.

"Okay, I'll bite, sire," Vana laughed. "What is your next stop?"

Dia grinned. "Once I gather help, I'll be marching north to, hopefully, join with my sons, neither of whom Halashii wants to anger. I haven't yet heard of any troubles plaguing their lands, so that seems the next best place to go." Dia turned slightly as he caught Vana's eyes moving from the king to a group that had just entered the pub. He nearly dropped his mug as he recognized them.

"Kalion ... the gods are glorious. You live!" Dia smiled widely as he struggled to stand up. Vana smiled as the group gasped in unison, only remembering to bow as each got over their shock.

"Shermee?" he whispered as he stepped forward, grasping Kalion's arm, whose gaze told the old king that their mission was a failure.

"My king, I … we lost her trail early on. Since then, we have picked up a few leads here and there, but none that have led us to her location." Kalion quickly relayed their steps with such a look of devastation that Dia nodded and patted his ranger's shoulder gently. He had always known that their mission didn't stand much of a chance.

While Dia greeted his people, Vana signaled the barkeep to bring a round of drinks for the group. "Please, come and sit. I would like to hear more if you're willing." Vana motioned to the table where the drinks had been placed.

Amlora and Niallee, who had taken some time off from helping the wounded, all but plopped down on the available chairs, as both were exhausted. Kalion and Kikor grabbed a couple of empty chairs from nearby tables and sat down with the king and general.

"How did you survive the assault on the city, sir? From what we were told, it was completely destroyed!" Amlora whispered, leaning close to the king.

"Survive? I wonder sometimes," Dia said softly. "The empress's body is still there, rotting in rubble, killed by a traitor."

Hearing that the queen was dead made the table silent. Amlora blinked and felt her mouth drop open as she remembered the queen's beauty and kindness towards the people of the city and beyond.

The cleric finally found her voice again. "I am so sorry, sir. I am sure the gods are caring for her as we speak."

Dia looked over and smiled sadly at Amlora. "Thank you, my dear."

"Who saved you?" Niallee finally spoke, hoping to turn the

conversation away from death.

Dia took a deep breath to compose himself before turning to the druid.

"Levenori elves who had survived Methnorick's attack on their forest kingdom to our north. That creature that was on the field — that cyclops giant — he was the one that destroyed my beloved city and theirs. Luckily, they were tracking him when they came upon my kidnappers."

Vana, who was listening intently to the story, found himself more intrigued by the story of the team. There was something right on the edge of his mind. They had crossed a great deal of Marn, encountering opposition and destruction at every stop, which made him all the more worried about his own empire.

"General, your gates ... How many warriors do they hold?" Kalion interrupted the general's thoughts, making him blink quickly and look up to see everyone staring at him.

"Each gate was designed to hold a full battalion of warriors, but I've been able to put almost two battalions on each when necessary."

Vana reached into a large bag he had placed on the ground next to his chair and pulled out a rolled parchment that opened up to reveal a map of the empire.

"Here are the gates of the empire, built to stop anything!" he said, pointing to the dots that represented the massive gates that blocked the north from the south.

Kalion leaned over to look at the gates. Then his eyes travelled along the Great Ravine to the forests southwest of the gates and to the hills that lay southeast.

"What would stop an army from landing on the coast here and attacking the gate from behind?" Kalion pointed to the areas he'd just studied. Vana smiled at the ranger.

"Nothing. In fact, it has already happened, my friend. Shortly before I was called here to help, I was on a patrol that encountered a large force of orcs that had either found a way across the ravine or landed along the coast." Vana pointed to the area on the map.

"We followed them for a bit and met them here in battle." Vana looked up at both Kikor and Kalion, who were taking in the map's information.

"Did you lose many warriors fighting them off?" Kikor asked as Vana shook his head.

"No, in fact, we did very well fighting the orcs. I'm sure by now the field rats are as fat as lazy cats with the number of carcasses we left them to feed on." Kalion smiled from the corner of his mouth at the general's comment.

"Still, you know the old saying, 'Anything built to stand still can be brought down.' Do you think the orcs have found a way?" Kalion asked as he drank from his mug of ale.

"I do know the saying, but no, I don't believe the orcs we encountered ever got the chance to report how they breached our defenses. There have been constant patrols sent out to keep watch since their sighting. No one has sent word that the orcs returned, so … here's hoping for the best."

"General, what do you plan to do?" Dia pipped in then, making the three turn slightly to look at the king, who had crossed his arms as he looked back.

"Send word to our capital for supplies and more men, for one. We suffered great losses in the fight here. We cannot afford to be at less than full strength with such a threat headed our way. And if the forces coming join up with the orcs in the Sernga Mountains …" Vana let the sentence hang, sure that he didn't have to spell the situation out further.

"Interesting that they never joined Methnorick, yes?" Amlora's quiet question made the team nod as the same thought had occurred to them.

Vana smiled widely. "Well … that might have something to do to me. Before we linked up with the elves from here, we captured two men who we think were sent from Methnorick to get a message to the orcs for reinforcements." Vana sipped his beer, smiling as the thought drifted into his mind that, in capturing those men, he might have saved the elven people a little more than they knew — as opposed to the two travelers he had captured earlier that week. Suddenly, Vana's eyes widened. *Could it be?*

Vana turned back to the king.

"King Dia, you mentioned your sons, but do you not have a daughter as well?" Vana watched as the entire table seemed to deflate with his question.

"Indeed, General. My daughter, the princess Shermee, was kidnapped by none other than Methnorick himself." Hearing the Dark Lord's name brought Vana's eyebrow up in surprise.

"Ah, Methnorick!" Vana responded as he thought back to the warrior with the girl. Vana couldn't swear to his identity since the man had blatantly lied to him, but he was fairly certain that the lad wasn't Methnorick. He looked up as Kalion took over the story.

"At first, we followed her kidnappers, but lost track of her. I had presumed she—"

"Wait. Did you say kidnappers?" Vana interrupted, lost in thought again. "So, not Methnorick himself ..." Vana trailed off.

By now, the whole table watched Vana carefully. "Describe her, if you will.""She was the most beautiful woman on all of Marn, yet quite naïve and innocent," Kalion started, only to receive frowns from all three women at the table." Niallee actually rolled her eyes at him. Kikor lifted a hand to signal that she would handle the general's question.

"She had hair the color of the morning sun, blond with the signs of the land within it. Her eyes were sky blue, and her smile ..." Kikor trailed off as Vana's eyes widened yet again.

"General?" Niallee also saw the look and spoke up, which brought Dia out of his trance as he looked upon the general's face.

Seeing everyone now looking at him, Vana took a sip of his beer and coughed slightly to clear his throat.

"After we cleared up the plains of those orcs I mentioned earlier, we encountered two travelers who claimed to be making their way from the eastern coast to the capital. One of those travelers was a young woman of obviously good breeding, fitting your description to a tee. As such, I put her and her companion on horses and sent a group of soldiers to accompany them back to the city. They are probably still there." Vana nodded.

For a moment, everyone at the table stared at Vana in shock. Then, suddenly, it was as if floodgates opened. Words flew at Vana as everyone started asking questions at the same time.

"I do not remember if she spoke her name. If she did, I am sorry that I cannot recall it. The man that was with her was indeed a warrior. A bit of a wily type, but no threat to her. As I recall, she was the one in charge. He stood behind her, as a protector, as we discussed their journey … both were a bit tired and dirty from their traveling. No, neither were harmed as far as I could see."

Vana's answers made Dia smile widely. Suddenly, he let out a joyous cry.

"But," Vana said cautiously, "she did not seem very naïve."

"It has to be her. She's alive. By the gods, she's alive and in the empire of all places!" Dia cried out laughing, slapping the table hard as he did.

"She somehow escaped Methnorick. That is indeed a feat I would have never thought her capable of, but the man with her … Someone who helped her maybe?" Kalion said aloud, clearly confused about the woman he thought he had known.

Dia laughed and slapped Kalion on the back. "You're a fine ranger, son, but you've got a lot to learn about women. Shermee has always been as wily as they come," he finished with a decidedly pointed look at Kalion.

"You are all certainly welcome to accompany King Dia to our capital if you want to continue searching for her!" Everyone in the group nodded immediately and then laughed at their own eagerness to see if Shermee really had escaped Methnorick.

"It's agreed then. We shall accompany you, General, but first, a drink in celebration, shall we?!" Dia motioned for the servant to refresh their drinks, standing up to wait for it as Vana also stood up to join in. Quickly, the rest followed along.

"We need to find Whelor and Meradoth to see if they want to join us, Kalion," Kikor reminded the ranger, who smiled and nodded.

"Agreed … and let Summ know as well," Kalion replied as the barkeep delivered another round of ales to the table. Lifting their mugs, they smacked them together, spilling the ale with a laugh as Kalion saluted.

"To King Dia and Princess Shermee … May they forever rule!"

"To the empire!" Vana yelled then, making the others cheer, quite boisterously, "To the empire," which was the sight that greeted Whelor and Meradoth as they walked into the pub and saw their friends cheering and drinking with … King Dia?

"Well, it seems that we got here at just the right time," Meradoth said, smiling at Whelor as they approached the group. "King Dia, it is good to see you alive and well. And certainly a fine reason to celebrate."

"That's true, but that … that's not why we're celebratin'—" Niallee hiccuped. Whelor took the mug out of her waving hand before she spilled it all over.

So, what are we celebrating?" Whelor asked as he moved to set the mug back in front of his friend. Meradoth grabbed a mug of ale off the top of the server's tray as she walked past, thanking her quickly for it.

Kalion cried out the good news, making Meradoth nearly choke on his ale, while Whelor, who had yet to let go of Niallee's mug, lifted it up to his lips and drained the cup dry in a few gulps. Whelor looked at Dia, who nodded back at the big warrior.

"Well, then, to Shermee, to King Dia!" Meradoth's words brought another round of cheers to the table that were drowned out by yells outside the pub.

"Let us see what is happening outside, shall we?" Vana bellowed as he rose from his chair and headed out the door, followed by Whelor, Kikor and Kalion.

Grabbing a monk that was walking right in front of him, Whelor turned the elf around, who looked up a bit surprised at the size of the man grabbing him.

"What is happening?" Whelor's voice came out a bit softer than the elf expected, which made him blink a moment, trying to compare the two.

"The council has decided to prepare God's Haven for war," the monk responded, looking nervously at the crowd of warriors gathering around him.

"Preparing them to hide?" Vana sneered as he looked at a few of his own warriors standing on the far side of the street, pulling their armor back on.

"No, sir. God's Haven is going to war!"

Whelor let go of the monk, who bowed gently and continued on his way, looking back once at the group to see if anyone followed.

"God's Haven heard you, Kikor!" Kalion looked at the elf, smiling wide. When Kikor could only muster up a tight, half smile in response and turned her back on him, he frowned at her, confused.

"I think you two have some talking to do." Meradoth's voice snapped Kalion out of his trance.

Chapter Seventeen

Kaligor sat upon his massive beast, holding the reins tightly as his army boarded the ships that had carried many of them just a few days ago from the far eastern world. High above, Chansor continued his patrol, watching over the city and the army below.

The last of the ships would serve as his flagship. It was smaller than the others, but quick upon the water, with the ability to hide if attacked, according to the masters. He watched as the Blingo'oblin in charge made his way over to Kaligor. Bowing, he informed the cyclops that the ship was ready for him. Kaligor nodded as he watched his guards clear a path to the gangplank, pushing orcs to the side as they did.

"It's going to be a fun journey!" he whispered as he kicked his mount forward and galloped up the gangplank of the ship. Once aboard, he jumped off of the giant beast, handing the reins to the first orc he saw, who looked none too pleased to have to deal with the creature.

"My lord … your fleet is ready!" one of the Blingo'oblins yelled over from the bow of the ship, pointing forward.

"Then let us commence. It is time to give those elves their comeuppance once and for all!" Kaligor yelled to his assembled troops. Stepping up to the rail, Kaligor counted the number of ships now slowly departing from Blath 'Na's port.

Over twenty ships carried hundreds of his warriors, in addition to supplies and war machines that had been constructed in the depths of the city, away from the prying eyes of spies. Looking up, he caught the sight of Chansor flying out over the water, slowly flapping his massive wings as their armada headed south.

"This is it … Masters," Kaligor murmured under his breath. "The point of the sword is moving closer to their neck. The pointy ears are coming to their end!" Kaligor whispered as he pulled his hands behind his back.

Far from the ships, standing on the top of the tallest building left standing in the city, four black-robed figures watched silently as the fleet of ships slowly left the port of the city, making their journey south.

"The cyclops still disobeys. Shall we kill him now?" the first one asked angrily.

"No, not yet," the second responded calmly. "He might yet succeed."

"Is the prisoner ready for his next mission?" the third one asked with a bit of an edge. He was tired of listening to the screams from such torture.

"Almost. Methnorick is resisting … but he will break soon. I shall have him in the land of the ice when all is ready," the fourth one whispered back, adding a slight giggle afterwards.

"I still don't like that cyclops changing the plan," the first one muttered.

"It was ordained. Everything is moving perfectly now," the second one soothed.

"Just make sure Methnorick knows if he fails this time … he will meet his gods!" the first one lowered his hood to look at the fourth, who merely nodded with a sly smile.

The first one was about to ask the fourth one what he found so amusing when a figure covered in black and red clothing appeared on the wall. His high black boots gleamed in the moonlight, but it was the hair that caught the attention of the master.

"Well, Chenush … is everything ready?" the first one rasped.

Bowing slightly, the vampire's silver-white hair whipped in the wind as he nodded his head slightly.

"My masters … let war begin!" Chenush smiled slightly as he

walked up to join his masters. Together, they silently watched the fleet below sail away.

* * *

Volkk entered the council chamber to chaos, as everywhere he looked, people were arguing about what to do about the machines. It hadn't taken long for the news of the army's failure to stop the machines to sweep through the city like a hurricane.

Ignoring everyone who tried to approach him, he sped down one of the halls, looking left and right for the one elf he hoped might be able to help him stop the unstoppable machines. Swimming past a few assistants hurrying to get to their families as the evacuation call went out, he hoped that the elf he was looking for hadn't left earlier.

Volkk finally swam down a small hallway that was hardly used by any of his people. Maneuvering around a seaweed barrier that was blocking a small room, he entered cautiously, looking back and forth. In the center of the room were three globes glowing brightly with tiny lights moving around within them. Each one was a different color, but the colors moved around like they were alive.

Volkk peered into one for a moment as the misty colors moved around. He blinked and shook his head, for he could have sworn he had just seen ... the city itself inside. He was about to take another look when he heard a cough behind him.

"Volkk, my friend ... why are you here? Shouldn't you be out there preparing the city?" Volkk turned around to see an old sea elf sitting on a bench, holding a large jar, which the warrior could see held what looked like a small fish moving around.

"Gulbra ... Your guidance is, I believe, what is needed most now. See? I did not even ask how you know what is happening." Volkk swam closer to the sea elf, who gently smiled back at the warrior.

Gulbra was known to all of Vigaluna. As one of the oldest elves, he was valued for many roles: historian to some, councilor to others. But to Volkk, he was just a good friend.

Gulbra motioned for the warrior to sit. Volkk quickly told Gulbra what happened during their encounter with the machines as the old elf sat back with his eyes closed. Volkk thought Gulbra was listening, but when he finished and the old elf continued sitting silently, he wondered if the old elf had heard any of his tale. Thinking he may have fallen asleep, Volkk leaned in to shake him when he suddenly spoke.

"Interesting is not the word I would use for these machines … Did you see who or what might be controlling them?"

"Not up close, but they looked like men," Volkk replied as he noticed Gulbra's left hand grip the jar he'd been holding a little tighter.

"Gulbra," Volkk pressed, "when I was young, you told me the story of how the city was first born. You and Mother protected us from a storm when the gods fought one another. You told me she came to us as a protector after driving our city under the sea." Volkk looked down at the jar again nodding at it.

Gulbra frowned slightly as he thought back. "Those, my friend, were dark times. Marn was young and in turmoil from the war of the gods. We had no choice." Gulbra leaned back against the wall, seeming to get lost in thought.

"These are dark times now, my friend. I need to protect this city, and those machines seem to be impervious to most of our defenses. We were lucky to stop the ones we did, but," Volkk paused as his voice caught, "we had too many losses to be able to stop the rest. There are just too many of them for the city's defenses to hold back, I fear. If you know something, I need your guidance and help right now."

The old elf leaned forward as he looked at the warrior. "Volkk, I am torn. If you are asking me to wake Mother up … I fear for our people as much as I fear for what is marching towards us."

Gulbra closed his eyes again. Volkk was thinking of what to say next when the globes in the room began to all turn red. "Your globes … are they speaking to you?" Volkk asked.

"They are speaking to me ... but they are not telling me anything different from what you have already told me. Those creatures approaching were fashioned by evil ... from the darkest of the east. They are warning me."

Volkk straightened himself up upon hearing the last part. "Warning you about what, sir?" Volkk looked from his friend to the globes. "Do they say how to defeat them or what they are?"

"Those beasts are not ... are not of this world." Gulbra looked at the floor for a moment and then at his friend. "They were made by gods. They are not meant for Marn. They destroy life."

"Are we doomed then? Can nothing save our city and people?" Volkk's voice could not hide his worry.

Opening his eyes and smiling, Gulbra slapped his thigh with his right hand and jumped up. "Of course not. This city is ours, and we will fight and die if need be. But let's try to stop them without that last part!" Gulbra winked at Volkk.

"But ... how?" Volkk followed Gulbra as he floated over to the globes, leaning closer and almost putting his nose on the glass of each one while moving his lips like he was talking to them.

"Come, lad, time to go." Gulbra looked at the warrior, who was giving him a suspicious look back.

"What is it, son?" Gulbra's smile made Volkk wonder suddenly if the old elf was not in his head for a moment.

"Were you just talking to those things?" Volkk nodded to the globes that were now changing in color again from red to blue and green, swirling around as he spoke.

"Talking? No, no, my friend. I was observing what they were showing me. Now let's go. We have a goddess to awaken," Gulbra said as he left the room, leaving the warrior standing with his jaw dropped open.

* * *

Bennak and Ame-tora peered over the cliff again, careful to avoid the brightness of the moon, which might give away their position.

"Those fires … There are many!" Ame-tora whispered as the frost giant moved his head to get a better look through the bush he was hiding behind.

"Many is a small word, my friend. I would say thousands really!" Bennak moved to lay on his back, looking up at the bright moon.

"I do not think they are orcs, though, my friend. I hear none of their awful singing." Ame-tora continued to look at field before them, hesitating for a moment to move closer.

"They could be orcs under orders not to celebrate!" Bennak looked over and saw the disbelieving look his friend gave him and grinned back. Being half orc himself, Bennak knew that orcs not celebrating was as unlikely as humans not sleeping. They always sang whilst sitting around campfires.

"Man or elf then!" Ame-tora whispered as he squinted his eyes, trying to see any sign of who was camped below in the glen.

"Meanwhile, those mountains you see straight ahead in the distance, my friend. I think — and I could be wrong, of course — but from their height and look, I think they are the Sernga Mountains."

Ame-tora nodded. "I see forests in the east. We could go that way, but it's going to take a while." Bennak moved to see what the giant was talking about.

"Hmm … I see some type of lake too. I know you hate water, so that way is out," Bennak teased.

"I told you that I didn't like water … I can still walk through it without a problem," Ame-tora grumbled, making Bennak almost giggle.

"If we travel down to that camp and it's full of orcs or worse … we will have a battle on our hands." Bennak looked to his right as he whispered and saw what could be a possible trail. "Hey, look over there. We can use the cliff face that runs along the edge of this glen to skirt around the glen and try to make it down to that main road that way."

Ame-tora nodded. "The brightness is coming soon, so we must go!" Ame-tora gestured to the east, where the sun was just starting to peek over the forest treetops.

"Then let us make our way." Bennak pushed himself up and stepped back from the edge, looking around for anything that might be watching them. Seeing nothing, he signaled Ame-tora and waited for the giant to repeat his steps. They slowly pushed their way through the brushes, making their way to the western edge of the glen, when Ame-tora moved one branch of a dense bush, only to cause another part to snap back hard enough to knock Bennak off balance.

Snap.

"OUCH!"

Snap.

"DAMN THE GODS"

Snap.

"OH HELL!"

Chapter Eighteen

Empress Shermee leaned over the massive table, pretending to study a map of the empire. She had chosen to wear a simple blue dress and leave her hair down to meet with the council, as she had no intention of being overly formal in her daily life just because of her title.

For the past few minutes, she had listened surreptitiously to all of the conversations going on around her. Some objected to her simple dress. Some objected to her style of rule. Quinor was nearby, lecturing a few councilors as to why they now had to represent the people of their districts as opposed to the empress. She could fend for herself. Their people couldn't. Her main concern was the welfare of her people and how best to protect them from the coming darkness.

Just as she was about to put an end to the bickering, she noticed a range of mountains near the upper left corner of the map that stretched from the southwest to the northeast, cutting off the ability for any traveler to get through. "The Forbidden Mountains," she murmured aloud.

"Can I help you with something, ma'am?" a voice asked, making her look up to see one of the councilors smiling at her.

"Councilor … Timor, isn't it?" She smiled when he nodded back. "Yes. I was just going over the map here and was taking in the names of many of the places. I noticed that here at the map's edge lies a mountain range. Why are they called Forbidden Mountains? Are they holding something in or something back?"

Timor smiled broadly, as did two other councilors that were listening in on their conversation. "As the tale goes, the gods built the mountains to keep the snow and ice from our lands, for on the other side of the mountains, it is so cold that no man could survive. However, legend has it that many dark creatures live on the other side."

"Legend, eh?" Shermee looked at the councilor as she straightened herself up, ignoring the teasing gleam in his eyes. "The map cuts off here. How big is the area?" She couldn't see any indication of routes around the mountains.

Seeing that she was serious, Timor stepped closer until he was only a foot or so away from her, almost as if he was embarrassed to speak of the place aloud.

"Its size is unknown ma'am, and beyond it … lies darkness, where tales speak of a land that the stars never touch." Timor looked away from her. Shermee could tell that the subject bothered him. Now, that was interesting. She would have to speak to him alone one day. For now, she changed the subject.

"My father once spoke of lands beyond the ocean where, legend says, man and elven kind once lived. Could this be the land he spoke of?" She peered closer to look for any writing that might tell her more about what was to the right of the map's edge.

"Your father spoke the truth. We believe our own people came from there," Timor whispered, looking down at her head and noticing how beautiful she really was.

"Why, then, is it dark—"

"Empress," Timor interrupted, "of the few men or elves known to have travelled that way, most have never returned. The few who did were different … in the darkest of ways." Timor squeezed his lips tightly together.

"Are there any living near the mountains who are friendly?" Shermee asked, looking down at the map again.

"Not that I have heard of, ma'am … The mountains are dark, and many say it gives one an eerie sense of being watched." Timor pulled in a breath, remembering the one time he and his family journeyed near the mountain range for a week. Each night, he was sure that someone was watching.

"Watching," Shermee whispered. "I wonder ..." She let the thought trail off as a new, irritated voice spoke up.

"Where is this empress? Why are you chaps just standing around? Are we here to plan our strategy, or what? It's going to take a bit of time to disperse our armies and thicken our defenses."

All eyes turned towards Shermee, who exerted every ounce of control she had to resist blushing. She had forgotten the time as she spoke of legends and maps. Nodding, she smiled and gestured for the councilors to take their seats as she made her way to the head of the table, with Quinor standing behind her left shoulder.

"Tell me your plans then, councilors. I trust that you know how to comport yourselves." Shermee smiled as she looked around the table.

"Empress. We ... uh ... we have decided on troop placement."

Shermee narrowed her eyes as she recognized the man who spoke up first. He had had accompanied the loud old codger into the hall. Leaning left, she waited for Quinor to fill her in.

"That is the master general of the empire. General Atwolf is in command of the combined armies of the empire," Quinor whispered as Shermee took in the man's injuries. Not only was he missing his right eye, but also part of his cheek. The entire area was covered by a partial mask made of silver. It reminded her of armor.

"... but first, I would be honored, Empress, to introduce you to my most trusted general," the man's voice rasped as he lifted his chin.

"Please," Shermee smiled, "proceed."

"Ma'am," he said somewhat loudly, gesturing to the rude old man, "this is General Hartwig. He is in charge of the forces of the Mother Gate at the western edges of the Sernga Mountains." Shermee turned her head slightly, prepared to narrow her eyes at the old man when she noticed his instead. If he squinted any harder, his eyes would be completely closed.

157

General Hartwig slapped the hand away of an aide who tried to help him rise and bowed deeply at what appeared to be the flag stand in the corner of the room. He smiled widely, showing her that he was missing a few teeth. "Empress," he bellowed across the room, "I beg your forgiveness, ma'am. My vision has been struck with a few problems as of late, and it is a bit difficult for me to see much."

As he spoke, she heard some of the councilors giggle quietly as General Atwolf's face tightened. He had been watching her intently since Hartwig rose. Now she understood why. She also understood that she could show no sympathy to the general.

"Thank you, General," Shermee answered somewhat loudly. She waited for him to turn towards her before continuing. "I appreciate your explanation for the misunderstanding. However, I trust that, in the future, you will be content to rely a bit more on your aides when you enter council rooms, at least until your sight returns. Disrespect will not be tolerated in these chambers," she finished, looking pointedly at the now-silent councilors.

Turning to General Atwolf, she returned to the task. "Your plans, General. Let me hear them!" This time, the leader of the armies rose and bowed deeply to Shermee before turning towards the map table.

Taking the hint, the rest of the councilors followed Shermee and Quinor to the massive table, surrounding it completely as General Atwolf explained their plan for defending the empire.

"Empress, the Great Ravine of the Empire has for many cycles been our best natural defense. Four bridges were built to cross the ravine hundreds of cycles ago," Atwolf explained as he pointed to the four marks Shermee could see indicated bridges.

"I know of them, General. I heard one, at least, has fallen into the ravine," Shermee replied as she leaned over the table to read the names of the bridges: Mother Gate, Gate of the Hand, Gate of the Eye, and the one farthest east, Father Gate.

"Well, yes, ma'am ... In fact, two of the bridges have fallen apart. Both the Gate of the Hand and Gate of the Eye have broken apart in places, making it very hard to cross. However, the other two are still useable."

Shermee turned to Hartwig. "You say you command the armies at the Mother Gate. Who is at the Father Gate?"

"That would be General Vana and Commander Tevanic, Empress. Both very capable leaders that are working to build that gate to full strength," Hartwig answered.

"Both gates are built to stop a war machine. However, if ever necessary, each bridge can be collapsed by a lever that only the commanders of the gates know of." Atwolf smiled.

Shermee lifted her head upon hearing about the lever. "What happens if the necessity comes after the commander's death? Too risky. From now on, the location of the lever must be known by two."

Quinor looked at Atwolf to see his reaction. He had expected the man to show irritation at being advised by a young girl, but to his surprise, he looked as if he was ready to genuflect to her. The man was definitely impressed by her. And trying to impress her, if his puffed out chest was any indication.

"At once, Empress." Atwolf snapped his fingers and signaled two aides, who ran out of the room to execute her commands. "Our main army will be positioned just south of these gates, ready to march at a moment's notice."

Shermee nodded, clearly approving of what she had heard thus far. "What of our sea borders?" she asked.

"The western and eastern coasts are now watched by patrols of cavalry that Hartwig, here, is in command of. If anything approaches, we will be notified."

Shermee nodded again. "It is a sound plan, General. The only hole I see is here, these Forbidden Mountains. Do we have any troops patrolling that area?" Shermee asked.

Atwolf snapped his fingers again, sending two more aides out of the room. "We do now. Nothing shall get past my warriors!" Atwolf boasted. Smiling back at him, Shermee felt a sense of pride that she had won the respect of this group of intelligent and knowledgeable men.

"Councilors, generals, if I may." She gestured to Quinor, who handed her a scroll. Unrolling it, she continued, "I understand that the empress has the prerogative to appoint Guardians of the Empire. After speaking to the high cleric I would like to fill that position once again. This empire is under threat; we need powerful leadership at the front."

The room filled with a few gasps of astonishment as a few councilors looked at each other. Timor stepped forward, motioning for calm as he explained. "Empress. Uh … that position is more ceremonial, not one the military needs—"

"Maybe we should change that too. My guardians will need to be men or women capable of fighting with a blade and knowledgeable about strategy. Doesn't that sound acceptable, councilors? Generals?" Shermee could see that both generals were keeping quiet.

"Empress, though I do agree that the position has always been one of ceremony, in this time of change within our empire and with rumors of a darkness approaching from the north, a symbol of a guardian would be the best thing, I think, to rally our warriors together and put the people at ease." Hartwig's words made Atwolf blink in surprise.

"Thank you, General. But I was also thinking of more than one guardian. One for each part of the empire." Shermee looked slowly at each face, which either returned a nod or smile.

"Did you have someone in mind, ma'am?" Timor quietly asked, wondering who she was thinking of for these positions.

"Uh, might I remind you, Empress, that each of these guardians will need to have an army behind them in order to lead and carry war to the enemy. Having more than two will separate and stretch our forces too much." Atwolf placed both hands on the table as he looked directly at Shermee, hoping she understood what she was doing now.

All of the councilors also stared at Shermee to see how she would handle this problem. She thought for a moment and then returned the general's stare. "In times of war, we will add two additional guardians. We will position one of the War Guardians here in the west and the other in the east to watch both the gates and coasts as well as lead troops at a moment's notice. How does that sound, General? Think that would work?" Shermee watched Atwolf's eyes move across the map as he hid his smile.

"Indeed. Two War Guardians should be quite adequate."

"Empress, there is no need for a guardian to be watching the southwest of the empire. The Forbidden Mountains are there, and nothing lives to the west of that mountain range," Timor stated.

"The Forbidden Mountains is just a mountain range, correct, Jacoob?" Shermee looked over at Jacoob, who had been quiet for the whole conversation. However, Shermee knew that he had grown up in that region of the empire and still knew the area well enough.

"Well yes, it is, Empress. But I don't know of any passes that would allow an army to pass through to that part of the empire, which is why the army has never placed a post there; only scouts keep watch." Jacoob could feel the looks from many of the councilors wondering why he was in the room, but Shermee had asked him to join them, so here he was.

"What is the closest settlement to the mountains?" Shermee looked over at the map, seeing a few names that looked like they lay near the perimeter of the wall.

"That would be Chiconogo, Empress. It is a small castle town, mostly old men and women ... in fact, one of the older settlements of men," Timor piped up, wanting to impress the empress with his knowledge of the area.

"Are there enough able-bodied men and women to keep an eye to the west there?" Shermee looked up from the map to Timor, who shrugged, and then to Jacoob, who shook his head. "It is mostly a town of old and retired warriors of the empire. There are, Queen, no real forces housed there."

Shermee caught the hesitation in Jacoob's answer and stared at him. "What do you mean by real forces, Jacoob? Who is up there?"

Quinor came to Jacoob's rescue. "You may as well tell her. She will hear the tale from someone."

"They will not fight for us, Quinor. They have never had any love for the empire or its people," Jacoob muttered as the rest of the group showed looks of confusion.

"Maybe not, but they might love the fact that the empire has an empress now!" Quinor's words made Jacoob tilt his head, as if considering the idea.

"What or who are you two dolts talking about?" Hartwig bellowed.

Quinor waved a hand to Jacoob for him to explain as everyone looked over at him. Jacoob blushed and looked like he'd rather face a firing squad, but nodded his head and took a deep breath. "There is one thing that keeps an eye on the mountains ... but it is only a tale that I remember being told once," the warrior qualified as he looked at the faces staring back at him.

"Many cycles ago, during the wars between man and elf, there was a group of elven maidens — princesses, according to the legend — who were ... let us say, attacked by a large group of men, who didn't kill them, but ..."

"We get the idea, son," Hartwig yelled. "Move on."

"Like I said, the men did not kill them, but left them for the wilds, believing the wilds would finish their job. But when they sobered up and returned to the area the next day, there was no sign of the women anywhere. Legend says that the wilds rescued them and turned them into ... well, a nightmare for man." Jacoob looked over at Shermee.

"What type of nightmare? Who are they?" Shermee asked, wondering just how many legends she would have to deal with in this place.

Swallowing deeply, Jacoob blinked as he answered her. "They're known as Nightwitches!" She watched in amazement as many in the chamber began to shift uneasily at the mention of the name.

"What makes these Nightwitches nightmares, and what makes you think these nightmares might be able to help us?" Shermee grilled Jacoob.

"Well, ma'am, any man who faces them dies. No man or male elf has ever seen them and lived. Quinor may be right, though. You might be able to convince them." Jacoob shifted on his feet, suddenly realizing that he would have to go with her.

With the exception of General Hartwig, every eye in the room followed her as she began to pace with her hands clasped behind her back. Stopping to look up at a carving of a battle scene from a long-lost battle from history, she turned to see expectant eyes waiting for her response.

"Councilors, send me your candidates for guardians. As for War Guardians, I believe that Quinor and Jacoob are both right for the job. I need to journey to the south to speak to these Nightwitches." Turning to Quinor, she added, "See that preparations start immediately. I want to leave at first light." Turning back, Shermee stood and smiled at the stunned reactions throughout the room, including on the face of General Hartwig.

No one moved. The response was short and sweet. "What!!!?"

Chapter Nineteen

Methnorick knew the footsteps he heard moving closer were those of his jailor, the master. *This is it … My death has finally come … Oh, please let this end now.*

"So …" the familiar voice quietly spoke as Methnorick looked back at the floor. The steps moved from the doorway into the room. "I went over many ideas as to what to do with you, Methnorick."

Methnorick swallowed as best as he could; however, his throat was so dry he was sure it cracked inside his body as he did.

"I have one idea that might work, though … In the end, it will both help and entertain me." Methnorick saw the tips of the boots of the master as it stopped pacing to stand directly in front of him.

Methnorick groaned as a powerful grip lifted his head so that he looked directly into the eyes of the master who had tortured him for his failure to destroy the elven menace.

"So, let's end this now, shall we!" Methnorick waited for death as the master moved so quickly that he never saw the flash of bright red light that emerged from his other hand, nor the pain that he momentarily thought he had felt across his neck. He opened his eyes to see that they were still at the same level as the master, who was now smiling.

"This is mine now!" the master whispered as he turned Methnorick's head around so that he could see his detached body still hanging from the chains. Next, a flash of light erupted in the chamber, blinding Methnorick. All he heard was a long haunting laugh coming from the master and then nothing at all as the laugh slowly drifted away.

* * *

Kaligor stood at the bow of the ship, looking south as he pondered the plan to land his army along the coast of the empire and march towards its massive capital of Manhattoria that lay many days' march from its eastern shores. He had always hated ships. He felt enclosed by them, not being able to do much. Now all he wanted to do was to hear the screams of man and elf at the end of his sword.

More than enough time for the empire to organize any type of counterattack ... From the plains to the many mountains, this will be his hardest campaign ever, he mused.

Clasping his hands across his armor-covered stomach, the cyclops watched a flock of birds fly past, only to scatter as the shadow of Chansor flew close enough for them to sense the dragon.

Looking up, he saw that Chansor was doing well in keeping his eyes open for any threats. For the past three days, the only trouble amongst his fleet of ships was orcs that were experiencing sea sickness.

At least two more days until we land at the first shore ... just east of a tower called The Father Gate. Where do men come up with these names? Kaligor laughed to himself. *Stupid creatures!*

Looking to his right, all he saw along the shoreline was the thick forests. He wished more fog covered the ships. Plus, he couldn't shake the feeling that he was being watched from shore. After all, the trees provided more than enough cover from both Kaligor and Chansor for any elf archer who might be watching the cyclops from the shore

"ALL IS CLEAR AHEAD, MASTER KALIGOR ... A SAFE JOURNEY AWAITS YOU!" The cyclops heard Chansor's voice in his mind as he looked up, noticing the dragon was circling high above but looking down at him.

"Let us have the wind on our back then!" Kaligor whispered as his ears finally returned to the sounds of the ship.

* * *

The winds had calmed, but the sun was still barely visible through the heavy clouds hanging over the snowy land. The only signs of movement and life were two silvery-white bears playing in the snow. Atop a black horse covered in heavy furs sat a man, also covered in furs, scanning the landscape.

Pulling the reins of his mount, the man slowly moved off the cliff and returned to the camp, which was far more crowded now that creatures from within the Forbidden Lands had made their way east to join the god amongst them. Seeing his black horse moving down the hill, they cried out to hurry themselves.

He entered the center of the camp, where he sat quietly, listening, as orcs dismantled the camp and prepared to march.

One of the ice giants who had been in camp a few days slowly approached the man, taking care not to crush any of the orcs as he knelt before him. Looking around at the activity going on, he swallowed as he formed a question in his mind.

"What we do now? We train, we wait, we train and now we march? Where?" the giant asked. No answer came from the man, so he repeated the question again. Still no answer. Exasperated, the giant stood and turned to rejoin his comrades when the man finally spoke.

"He is coming!" The voice came out with foggy breath from under the hood.

"Who?" the giant responded, looking around the camp, not understanding.

"He is coming … now!" The man lifted a fur-covered arm and pointed. The giant followed the finger to gaze to his right slightly to the edge of the camp … and saw nothing.

"I see no—" The giant's words quickly stopped when, in the clearing, a small red ball of light appeared. He, and everyone else, stared as the red light pulsed and then grew larger until it reached the size of a horse.

"He comes!" the rider rasped.

"Who?" the ice giant whispered, in awe of the magical sight before him.

"Why, your leader, of course," he replied.

All eyes watched the ball of light as it hovered in the air. Suddenly, the ball flashed, emitting a light so brilliant that all but the man threw their arms and hands up to shield their eyes. At the same time, a sudden gust blew wind and snow around everyone, and then just as quickly subsided. Before anyone could figure out what was happening, a piercing scream filled the air, so intense that most in the camp fell to their knees, including the ice giants.

Finally, the unbearable noise trailed off. As the camp recovered, they looked up to see a man and a massive black horse now in the place where the ball had been. Like the other rider, he wore black, almost burnt-looking armor, and his clothing was ripped in tatters.

The rider who had observed the entire event without having moved now slid off the saddle and, without a word, stepped forward to stand a few feet in front of the being. Kneeling in the snow, he lowered his head. "My lord, your army awaits you!"

"Where ... where am I?"

"You are in the Forbidden Lands, my lord, to lead us to victory," the rider responded.

"Who are you?"

"I am called Edvar, my lord. I have been ordered to be your servant."

Edvar pulled back his hood to reveal himself fully. He was completely bald, yet his head had been adorned with a large tattoo that looked like a snake running from ear to ear. Or, at least, where his ears would be if he possessed them. Instead, Edvar had holes where his ears should be.

"Ordered? By whom?" The words drifted across the snow.

"By our masters, my lord. I was sent here to prepare this rabble for you." Edvar lowered his voice. "Are you not happy, my lord?

They are under your command!" Edvar's voice sounded worried, especially when the rider said nothing.

"My lord, are you well, sir?" Edvar gently asked, looking up slightly, wondering why his lord seemed to be hesitating.

"Who ... am I?"

Still kneeling, Edvar lifted his head to look at the rider fully, not understanding.

"My lord, you ... you are Lord Methnorick!" Edvar answered urgently, as if willing him to remember.

"Meth ... nor ... ick." The rider tested the name on his tongue and then blinked and moaned as memories flooded back. He looked out over the army before him with such a menacing stare that every creature in the camp dropped to a knee and bowed just like the one calling himself Edvar now bowed.

"I am Methnorick. I am your lord. I am fear. I am death!"

The words drifted across the snow, accompanied by a chill that cut through all of their bodies like ice, including those of the Hel-tors.

Methnorick turned to look out onto the tundra of ice and snow that was blowing. Peering across the landscape, he wondered where on Marn he was and why it seemed ... familiar. He tried to probe the memory, only to stop when a sharp pain shot through his body like a shock, making him moan in pain.

"My lord, are you well?"

"DO I LOOK UNWELL!?" Methnorick snarled at the servant as he dismounted. "And stand up. You can hardly be of any use to me from there. There will be time enough for you to grovel on the ground."

Edvar slowly stood up, grateful that the furs he wore hid his shaking. Fear moved through him as he looked upon the creature standing before him, lowering his eyes until he saw writing on the breastplate.

"Lord of the Forbidden," Edvar whispered.

Edvar never saw Methnorick move, but the next thing he knew, he was being held in the air, with Methnorick's hand clasped around his throat. Gasping and struggling, Edvar wondered what he had done wrong.

"I am Methnorick!" he yelled as he threw Edvar to the right, where he landed hard in front of a group of orcs, who didn't move a muscle as the new lord raged.

"Hear me. I am Methnorick. I am your lord, and death follows me. From this day forward, everything will die under my hand. Follow me and you will be masters of Marn!"

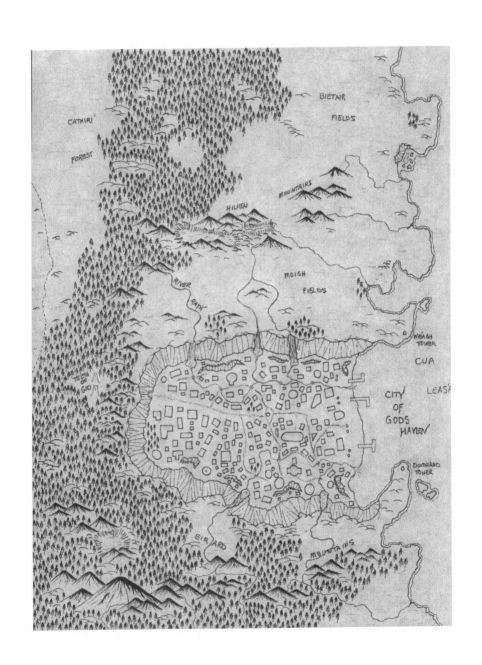

Chapter Twenty

At that same moment in God's Haven, King Dia, Kalion, Meradoth, Amlora, Kikor and Whelor all stood at the edge of the massive square, where residents gathered to hear the news of the north falling to the orcs, who were now marching south.

"Sounds like we need to decide what to do," Meradoth said. Kikor nodded in agreement with the mage.

Kalion also nodded as he uncrossed his arms and began to walk away.

"Where are you going then?" Kikor asked, unable to keep the annoyance out of her voice.

Looking at the elven warrior, Kalion took in her beauty for a moment and smiled.

"We shouldn't be separated now, my friend. You of all people should come south with me to find out if it is true about my daughter, do you not think?" Dia calmly spoke, placing a hand on the ranger's shoulder.

Kalion turned towards his king with a smile. "Of course, sire. I won't be long." Satisfied, Dia patted his shoulder once more and stepped back, leaving Kalion alone with Kikor.

"Who will you speak to then?" Kikor muttered as the rest of the group moved away to collect their packs and weapons.

"General Summ first, to see what he has planned." Kalion nodded towards the elven banner on the far side of the square.

"Before you leave, tell me, Kalion, are your feelings for her the same now as they were before this world began to fall apart?" Kikor wanted to hear the man say it before he left her.

Images of Shermee rushed through Kalion's mind as his chest tightened. He tried to think about her in the way he had before this quest … the times when they met secretly without King Dia's or her mother's knowledge, although now he wondered. But then there was the time he promised her that he would be by her side forever and protect her. Yet, if she was in the empire, he would have to accept that she didn't need his protection. Coming out of the trance quickly, he swallowed, gently clearing his throat as he took a breath, thinking of the right words.

"Kikor, yes, I still have feelings for the princess, but," he added quickly when he saw her eyes narrow, "they have changed." Kalion sighed and continued. "I have been a fool, Kikor, but no," he said, shaking his head, "Shermee is not the woman for me. No, another now owns my heart. A woman of great courage and even greater beauty, and a warrior to be reckoned with, especially when a bow is in her hands. An elf, in fact. You might know of her," he teased with a grin.

"Oh?" Kikor teased back. "Well, let's see. I know of many elves. There's Niallee and—"

Kalion's roar of laughter interrupted her … and surprised her. It was the first time his laugh seemed truly happy. But it was the love she saw in his eyes that filled her heart with joy and caused her to lose her heart to the man now staring at her with an intensity that nearly took her breath away.

"I am committing myself … my sword, my heart … everything to you, Kikor Ru'unn of the Eagle People. Will you take me even with all my failures?" Kalion said gently to the woman he loved.

Kikor let out a laugh as she grabbed the ranger and hugged him hard. They were both so caught up with each other that neither saw the pair of monks walking by, smiling at them as they embraced.

Letting go a moment later, Kalion felt as if a massive weight had been lifted off his chest as he stole a quick kiss from the shocked elven maiden. Winking at her, he turned to leave. "Go to the main road with the others. I will meet you there, soon!"

"Wait," she said dazedly, touching her lips. "We need to get organized and ready to move. Now that we know where the princess may be, I fear that the monks may have been right. God's Haven isn't their target."

Kalion's eyes widened as he caught on to Kikor's meaning, and then narrowed almost menacingly as he nodded to Kikor.

"Did I have 'brilliant' on that list earlier?"

Kikor shook her head.

"Add it," Kalion said grimly as he squeezed her hand. "And keep an eye out. I will be back soon!" Kalion let go of her hand and quickly moved through the crowds of elves in the square. Judging from the amount of activity going on around him, it appeared that nearly every elf with a weapon was planning to join up with them to stop what was coming.

* * *

Volkk had been following his mentor through what seemed a maze of corridors until Gulbra stopped. As he peered around Gulbra and saw nothing but a thatch seaweed covering the path, he was annoyed that he had wasted precious time, and sad that the old elf had lost his senses. Gulbra laughed as each expression crossed Volkk's face, winked at him, and backed into the thatch, disappearing completely from sight.

A moment later, Volkk joined him. Gulbra nodded and then began swimming through the waters faster than Volkk had ever seen the old elf move. Following his mentor, Volkk was fascinated to discover that he also had the ability to swim faster than before. *The old elf has some explaining to do*, Volkk thought as the two made their way along a ledge and then circled around a grouping of rocks that took them to what looked like an entrance of some type.

"Remember, my friend, this is very dangerous. We could easily destroy our city if we do not do this right and with respect to our surroundings." Gulbra looked over at the warrior, who nodded as they swam through tall seaweed and large schools of fish to the small ravine that Volkk never knew existed before.

"What is this place, Gulbra?" Volkk whispered as he slowed down and took in the beauty of the valley before him. Everywhere he looked, coral of incredible colors grew.

Gulbra smiled. "There is no name for this place; this is her realm!" Gulbra answered as he unscrewed the large jar he'd been carrying to release the creature inside.

"Her realm ...? I thought the oceans were her realm," Volkk said incredulously as he watched the tiny creature dash off to slip through a crack in the rocks.

"Marn *is* her realm, my good friend, but this trench valley is her home of homes, where she found peace from her sorrow," Gulbra replied, still staring at the point in the rocks where the tiny creature entered. Just as Volkk again wondered about the old elf's mind, he felt a sudden piercing pain in his head.

Instantly, Volkk realized this had to be what Gulbra was searching for. As he felt the water around them move, he watched the rock wall before them, where sand was shaking off the top of the cliff to fall to the sea floor. He looked down to see the sea floor itself shaking, and as a few rocks fell away from the wall, Volkk felt the pain in his head subside enough to whisper to his friend.

"Is this her, the legend that you whispered about for cycles? Volkk suddenly felt a sense of calmness pass through his mind and body.

"She is Marn, my friend!" Gulbra said with reverence as he began to feel her approach. Volkk watched in fascination as Gulbra slowly raised his arms as he heard what sounded like a roar, but one that seemed to exist inside his chest.

From the gods' hands! Volkk's mind screamed in fear as the sea floor began moving up and down like a wave. Even the very water around him felt heavier than normal and warmer to his skin.

Tampering down his fear, Volkk watched as the seabed began to swell. The hill was getting larger by the moment when, suddenly, an invisible hand grabbed them and slammed the two hard against the rock wall behind them.

Groaning from the pain, Volkk turned to Gulbra to see how he fared, only to see the old elf gazing at something with a serene smile. Following Gulbra's line of sight, Volkk turned his head and looked up at the face of the creature of legend.

"By the gods!" Volkk whispered in shock as the beast slowly burst out of the seafloor to stare back down at them.

Chapter Twenty One

Raising a clenched fist, the cyclops held the rail of the ship with his free hand as it violently rocked back and forth. Screams and yells could be heard from the crew trying hard to hold the ship together. For almost a full day, the ship had been rocked hard by this storm, making the general wonder if something — or someone — wasn't behind it. Meanwhile, he knew that he needed to find the landing area soon.

He peered through the heavy rain, considering his options. Suddenly, a snapping sound caught Kaligor's attention. He looked up to see a familiar black beast burst out of the heavy dark clouds, flapping his wings as he circled the ship. Orcs and goblins alike scattered as the beast dove straight for the deck, only to disappear in a mist where it should have landed. Kaligor crossed his arms over Chansor's dramatic approach but reluctantly conceded that he had certainly mastered the move.

"Yes, General Kaligor?" the clothed man rasped as he stepped up to the cyclops.

"I have a task for you — that is, if you are game." Kaligor leaned down slightly, smiling down at the man, who instantly nodded back, smiling from the corner of his mouth.

* * *

In Manhattoria, half of the newly installed council, chosen by their new empress, watched in horror as the lady now mounted her horse. Jacoob, already seated on his mount next to hers, turned to hide his grin as the twenty warriors he'd ordered to accompany them arrived from the stables to form up behind her. The battle of the sexes had begun, as the three female councilors stood far off to

179

the side, making their opinion clear, while their male counterparts grumbled and shook their heads at the proceedings.

Like the empress herself, the troops now lined up behind her were all dressed in simple clothing, yet another thing that seemed to disturb the council. Shermee had learned quickly that being popular could sometimes be as much a curse as a blessing. It took her nearly an hour to get anywhere in the city when she left the tower. There were always hands to shake and babies to kiss. She had no time for either on this trip. In fact, they needed to get started if they were going to make it to Chicanogo by dusk. With an air of impatience, Shermee turned to the hovering councilors.

"Yes, kind sirs?" She smiled, leaning down in her saddle.

One day, they would all recognize the futility of arguing when she turned that icy, determined, steely smile on them, but for now, the men on her council were still learning the ropes.

Bowing their heads slightly, the middle of the three men cleared his throat before he spoke. "Ma'am, we are very worried about you taking this journey. Not that the empire isn't safe, ma'am—"

"It's the destination we are concerned with, ma'am!" the older man interrupted his fellow councilor.

Shermee leaned back and placed her hands on the pommel part of her saddle, staring down at the three with a raised eyebrow.

The man who had spoken first looked at his other councilors for a moment and then back up at Shermee. "Ma'am, there are many female warriors that could make the journey. Even a few councilors volunteered to go there in your stead," he added, glancing at the female councilors still glaring at them. "We just worry that if something ..." He let his last words drift quietly.

"Do spit it out, sir. I have a long journey ahead," Shermee said without changing her expression.

The councilor glanced at his companions and pulled a lip as it dawned on him that they would not be able to stop her. Resigned, he stepped closer, glancing at the restless warriors out of the corner of his eye before speaking. "Empress, there … there are elements within the empire who may seek to do you harm." He sounded so earnest that Shermee dropped her air of indifference and leaned down closer.

"Explain," she ordered the nervous councilor.

"The high minister had many friends and allies in the empire, ma'am. Most are, frankly, happier that he's gone, since he often used blackmail rather than diplomacy to secure their allegiance. However, since your ascension, a small number have disappeared, most violently, and … well …" He looked around a little nervously before lowering his voice even further. "There is a rumor, Empress, that one of those allies has set an assassin on you!"

Shermee leaned back and quickly processed this possible problem, ignoring the shocked look on Jacoob's face for now. The journey, she had been informed, could take five to six days one way. That meant six days on the road, with only twenty warriors to protect her. However, they were twenty of the very best, nine of which were Manhattoria's best female fighters. Even General Atwolf agreed that they were indeed the best in the heat of battle. Shermee felt confident they would be able to protect her. Smiling gently, Shermee soothed her anxious councilor.

"Well, that's hardly new, is it?" Leaning down, she patted the man's shoulder. "I do believe we will all be well, my friend. I am counting on you and the others to take care of making sure the city is prepared for what will be coming."

Swallowing, the man nodded and then smiled up at his new empress and wished her well on her travels. Standing back, the men watched Shermee and her entourage slowly leave the tower's large courtyard and make their way through the city, where, even in plain clothes, Shermee was swarmed by adoring crowds, who stopped what they were doing to yell and cheer as she rode by.

As they disappeared down the road, the councilors who had kept themselves back walked up to join the man who spoken with their new empress.

"What did she say?" a young man who secretly was falling in love with his new empress asked.

"She ordered us to run the empire until she comes back and prepare the city for war, so that is what we are going to do: take care of the affairs of state and run our great empire as best as we all can."

"And what of the rumor, my friend? Did you tell her about the assassin?" an elven woman spoke, as she was concerned for the empress.

"Of course, I did. To which she informed me that she has the finest warriors in Manhattoria beside her. There is no doubt that she is correct about their capabilities, but send word out to General Atwolf that she has left. I want him to know any information that you hear about this assassin." With that, the group of councilors all bowed to each other and quickly walked their separate ways to manage their specialties.

As the riders left the valley, the weather slowly turned from a sunny morning to a wet drizzle. Trying not to let the nasty weather bother her, Shermee turned her thoughts to another as she pulled her cloak tightly around her face.

She thought of Quinor, the man her heart was telling her to miss as it ached inside her chest. She wondered how everything had gotten so complicated. The man had kidnapped her, by the gods, but … She frowned. That word kept coming up. There was always a *but* in the tale now. He had kidnapped her, *but* he had only been doing a job for hire. She had to admit that he had been fiercely loyal to her since that day on the beach, risking his life more than once to save her. Then there was the prophecy, and his role in it. And how she would not now be empress *but* for the fact that he had kidnapped her. Now her pesky heart was involved, urging her to ignore everything in her head … and failing spectacularly. *Think of something else, Shermee.*

Per General Atwolf's orders, messengers were sent out to each province to prepare a standing formation of two battalions of warriors and cavalry. Commanders were ordered to train the volunteers as fast as possible. All units had to be ready to march by month's end, which was just under four weeks away.

Shermee also thought about what Atwolf had told her as they spoke quietly during the evening meal, after having given him the first honor of sitting beside her at the high table.

"Truth is, ma'am, if you speak to the people up there, most admit that they've never seen them. Not even the kids who wandered up the mountainside on a dare. But there is certainly something strange about what happens to men who visit the place. And so, the legend of the Nightwitches continues," Atwolf finished with a decidedly impertinent grin.

Shermee smiled as she remembered what had happened next. How she sighed and daintily placed her fingers on her wine glass before looking him directly in the eye. "Yes, I suppose we ladies must do what we must to solve all the mysteries in the world men can't," she murmured with such an air of innocence and sweetness that Atwolf felt his good eye begin to water before finally giving up and lifting his napkin to his mouth to hide a snort of laughter. His eye still twinkled as he replied, "Yes, Empress, I suppose you must," with such good cheer that Shermee found herself soon lifting her napkin to hide her own grin. She was really beginning to like the general. He reminded her a lot of her father — gruff, direct, yet fair minded and fiercely loyal — as she recalled her introduction to General Hartwig. She had easily surmised that he would never be afraid to tell her what she needed to hear. But now, she also felt that he trusted her, which is why she trusted him.

She continued to think about what she had been told about the area they were headed for, Chiconogo. Its capital, if it could be called one, lay along the southeastern edge of a massive forest from which it had taken its name, according to legend. The Chicono Forest had been settled by man when they first entered what would one day be called Pendore'em, having traveled from the eastern lands many cycles before.

However, during the wars, when the elves of Edlaii reached the

Chicono Forest, they met resistance from men who had settled on the continent, where for many cycles some of the heaviest fighting took place. Here, both sides had taken heavy losses, but in the end, the battle proved one too many for the men and a fairly easy win for Edlaii as their elven archers were easily in command of the forest, ending any chance of men controlling this area. Many cycles later, after peace had returned, the two peoples became one and named the area Chiconogo out of the respect for the forest and the people who died within.

"Empress? Are you doing well?" The voice brought Shermee out of her thoughts as she looked over and saw Jacoob's smiling face as he pulled down the hood of his cloak.

"Of course," she answered back with a smile of her own as she noticed the sun peeking out. "It's not like I haven't ridden before, you know!"

"I was hoping to speak to you, Empress, about what you plan to say or do once we enter Petrikbur." Jacoob had been wanting to ask her for a while now, but the rain had made it impossible for him to speak to her without yelling.

"I have already told you. The plan has not changed," she answered a bit testily, annoyed that Jacoob would dare to question her yet again. Impertinence was one thing; insubordination was something else entirely. She had no intention of tolerating the latter, not even from a friend.

"You plan on really trying to speak to the Nightwitches?" Jacoob's eyes told her he still really didn't believe her. Shermee decided that it was time to make herself clear.

"Are you calling me a liar, Jacoob?" Shermee looked Jacoob directly in the eyes. "Because this marks the third time you have questioned me. Now, I believe that I have allowed you far more latitude due to your elevated position than you have ever enjoyed before, but there are some protocols that will not change. Do you understand me?"

"Ma'am," Jacoob swallowed, "it's just that … they might not want to listen!" Jacoob looked ahead as the pair rode just ahead of the rest.

"They will listen to me!" Shermee said with far more confidence than she actually felt. Truth was, she needed their help. She needed everybody's help. So, she would at least try. The reward was worth it. If she succeeded, who would say nay to her then?

Jacoob stared off into space as he thought back to his youth and growing up in that cold province. He was one of the few who had actually seen a coven of Nightwitches. He was still haunted by that memory of the witches screaming and destroying everything that lived on the river bank.

Just then the sun came back out fully, signaling the end of the rain for now. One of the warriors near the back with a booming baritone began to sing a cheerful drinking song that soon had everyone in the group singing along. Shermee smiled, glad that these warriors were at least trying to enjoy the journey.

For three days, the group travelled south, meeting groups of farmers and merchants on their way to the capital. As they stopped for lunch while traveling around the massive expanse of Lake Berlini on the fourth day, they met up with a group of dwarven merchants making their way north to the capital. As the warriors broke out the cooking equipment and the dwarves cut down some wood, Shermee took in the beauty of the lake. Jacoob walked up, offering a piece of fruit that was eaten far more quickly than she intended once she realized how hungry she was.

Smiling, the old man knelt down, noticing how she was looking out towards the lake.

"It's beautiful, is it not? This place always gave me peace. It has a long history of battles. Would you like to hear of them?"

Shermee looked at him quizzically. "Do you not think that strange, that thoughts of battle come to you in a place you say gives you peace?"

Jacoob shrugged, as if he had not thought of it before and most likely would not think of it later. His next word confirmed her suspicions.

"So, do you want to hear the stories or not?" he asked, nodding at one of the dwarves striding up to stand nearby.

"The history of our empire you probably know — how it used be two smaller kingdoms, one of man and the other of elven kind. They fought for many cycles over the lands and borders."

"What finally ended the fighting?" Shermee asked, remembering the tales her father had told her and her brothers.

"That is an interesting tale in itself, ma'am!" Jacoob smiled as he nibbled on some cheese and bread he had brought with him. "One legend says that the land stopped it. My favorite tale is that of the elven maiden who fell in love with the warrior who came to kill her and together they both stopped it. Then there is another tale that tells of a tremendous army of orcs who took advantage of the war to march out of the Sernga Mountains." Jacoob lifted his pouch of watered wine, taking in a deep swallow of it.

Remembering one tale from her father, Shermee said, "My father told me once that he never believed that the gods had anything to do with it ending. He always said that it was numbers in the end, as in how both sides had killed so many of the other that neither could place a full army on the field in the final cycle of the war."

Jacoob laughed slightly, as did the dwarf, who nodded a few times, as did a few warriors who were lying in the grass nearby, making Shermee look over and smile at them.

"The elven peoples had thousands, if not hundreds of thousands, of warriors on the north and western shores who never fought or saw the war, according to many written tales of our people!" one of the elven maiden warriors murmured as she smiled at her queen.

"Okay, then. If it wasn't numbers, what do you all believe it was that ended it?" Shermee asked the elf, who, upon seeing every eye turn to her, shrugged and dropped her gaze back to her food.

"The most popular legend is that it was the land that woke up to the horror of what was happening and ended it," Jacoob quietly answered as a few warriors laughed.

"Do not mock something you clearly do not know of, friends!" the old dwarf standing near the water's edge spoke, shifting everyone's attention yet again.

"My people are known by legend to be the oldest race upon Marn. Our tales in the beerhall speak of the truth. We were there. We know what happened!" the dwarf said fervently.

"Please, kind sir, what are these tales? I would like to know!" Shermee moved herself to get more comfortable on the grass as she smiled at the old dwarf. For his part, the dwarf pulled out a pouch and took a long swig before turning to his captive audience.

"There are few still alive who know of this. My people wrote it down to make sure the truth was told. Listen, Empress, so you understand the way of Marn, as she was the one who ended the war!"

Chapter Twenty Two

*G*ulbra struggled to get up from where he had fallen against the rock wall as Volkk stared in stunned silence, for before him, floating in the water, was a massive head swinging slowly back. It slowly moved closer until they could clearly see a pair of emerald green eyes staring down at them, looking none too pleased with either of them. Volkk struggled desperately not to show fear as he could almost feel the creature scanning his mind.

"Gulbra Bolorrma, you dare to disturb me!" The voice slammed into both sea elves so hard that they both instinctively grabbed their heads in reaction to the wave of pain that instantly shot through them. Neither realized at first that they had also been pushed back in the water by the tremendous power of the creature before them.

"Empress … I … I am sorry my … empress … You are in great need!" Gulbra winced through the pain as he spoke. Volkk felt the creature's presence in his mind, and although it — no, she — hadn't spoken to him, the look she had given him when he dared to peek up made him rethink his very existence.

Water around the beast stirred up sand. The sea elf felt another frisson of fear as each massive claw slowly became visible. The creature was larger than several Mal-mohr whales, which, before today, Volkk had always thought was the largest creature in the sea. Each giant appendage was covered in massive scales, larger than the largest turtle's shell he had ever seen. Volkk reckoned that each scale alone could stop even the strongest spear point.

Suddenly, the beast slammed her claw on the seabed, causing sand to cloud the water. This time, the sudden movement of water sent shock waves, pushing Volkk backwards towards the rock cliff again. This time, however, Volkk was ready and braced himself well enough to minimize the impact. Shaking his head, he looked straight ahead to get a better look at the terrifying creature. The first thing he noticed was that the scales were a bright red. Then they almost seemed to change to a deep seafood green.

Rows of sharp teeth that looked as if they could easily cut a whale in half jutted out of her mouth. The claw that was positioned on the ground in front of him looked like it could crush a whale.

"Why do you wake me when I know all is lost to me …?" Again, her voice made the two elves wince as the words screamed loudly in their minds.

Volkk saw that Gulbra was having a difficult time recovering from her latest blast, so Volkk quickly spoke up, hoping that the creature wouldn't kill him on the spot.

"Queen of all creatures," Volkk began, keeping his head bowed, "we need your help!" Volkk resisted the urge to shudder as her blue eyes stared down at him.

"Darkness is spreading. I have known of it for many cycles. Why should I care what it does to your people — people who pushed me away, Volkk, son of Besswaa, protector of my children's mightiest city."

Volkk thought for a moment and then lifted his head to stare back at the being. "Because, Empress, we are still your children. Our city has come under attack from an evil we have no way to stop or understand! I beg you, please bring yourself out of the darkness so your children can see you again!" Volkk's voice sounded desperate, but he knew that they were all running out of time.

Feeling the water swirl around him, he braced for another hit. Instead, the beast lifted her head and looked towards his city and then slowly back, looking down at him.

For a while, no one spoke. Volkk turned to check on Gulbra and saw that the old elf was still struggling. He needed help, and he needed it now, as he looked back up at the creature.

"I beg you … Mother of all Marn. Please, help us!"

* * *

Methnorick sat upon his horse, ignoring the chaos around him, his attention solely focused on a range of mountains that lay far away in the distant glow. So much so that he failed to hear the crunch of snow and ice as one of the orc commanders ran up to speak to him.

"M-m-master," the orc stuttered, "the bridge has collapsed. We lost twenty or more warriors in the ravine, Master, and there are still two battalions trapped on the other side!" The orc pulled his fur cloak closer but still could not stop his shaking as he waited for his lord's response, hoping he wouldn't become the master's latest victim. Since his arrival, Methnorick had killed over thirty orcs and even a few dark elven warriors that he deemed useless. He had seen one of the massive Hel-tor giants lose the fur along one side of his face when Methnorick hit him with a burst of fire in anger.

"Move the army forward, Commander. Let those stuck behind figure out a way across!" Methnorick answered as he kicked the side of his mount and turned towards the mountain range now in his sights and galloped off.

Turning, the orc commander signaled to those nearest him to follow Methnorick as he walked to the edge of the ravine, where he saw that a few orcs had been able to climb back over the edge.

Having seen their leader ride away, some of the orcs were already grumbling when their commander appeared on the other side. Their expressions quickly turned from annoyance to shock and anger as the commander barked out orders for those on the other side of the ravine to get themselves across or be left behind without the food or supplies that were now on his side.

"Commander, they have no way of crossing," a goblin engineer said softly.

"The lord wants to keep moving, so we move forward. Always forward … never back!" The orc looked down at the goblin, who was

191

already shaking from the cold.

"To leave part of the army over there …" the goblin said, shaking his head, "…could be a death sentence for us. Without them, what kind of chance will we have against the elves, sir?" The goblin looked over, pointing to the orcs and other still screaming and swinging their arms and weapons in the air for help.

"Always forward … never back!" the commander whispered to himself for a moment. Then, calling over his guard and leaving the goblin, they turned and began to follow the rest of the army that was just moving over a dune of snow not far away.

"Never back!" the orc repeated again and again, staring at the back of his lord, wondering and hoping that Methnorick had a plan.

* * *

Kalion and the group were securing their packs to the sides of their horses when an elven rider galloped into the barracks area, stopping his horse so quickly that the animal kicked up dust in its wake. Kikor raised an eyebrow as the rider dismounted on one fluid move, impressed with his riding skill, until she saw him frantically looking left and right. Curious as to its cause, Kikor approached the rider.

"What is it?" she asked. "Whom do you seek?"

"I need to find General Summ. I have urgent news for him!" The elf's breathing was labored from his hard ride. Kikor offered him her water pouch as she nodded.

"Drink," Kikor ordered. "He is with the war council. Come with me. Twill take you to him."

The scout followed Kikor as she briskly moved through horses and other riders exiting the barracks. As soon as the elf saw General Summ with the council, he rushed past Kikor, turned back to return her water pouch with a rushed "Thanks," and ran up to the general's side. Kikor hung back but stood close enough to hear the rider.

"Ah, good. You're back," Summ said absently until he glanced up and saw the scout's face, at which point he turned his full attention to the elf.

"Report," Summ ordered.

"Yes, sir. I was contacted by one of our mountain scouts. Sir, it's the Sernga orcs …signs show they are marching out of the city!"

Upon hearing that the Sernga orcs were on the move, Kikor quickly turned and made her way to where the king and the rest of there friends were all saddled up, just waiting for her return. She vaulted on her horse and turned to the others.

"Sernga is on the move!" Her words brought one of Kalion's eyebrows up as he quickly calculated how much time they had to reach the empire in order to beat the orcs.

"Were's Vana now?" Kalion looked over at Amlora, who shrugged her shoulders, not knowing where the commander might be.

"Last I heard he was making his way to join the rest of his men at the tunnel entrance, getting ready to move out south. He was going to wait for us there if he could." Amlora spoke, nodding towards the huge gateway that led to the tunnel.

Looking back down at Kikor, Kalion asked, "You think he knows?" The elf shrugged her shoulders.

"He would have seen the scout ride past him, I would think," Meradoth piped up.

Kalion thought quickly and then saw the big man to his left. "Whelor … find the general and see if he knows. We'll be just behind you, after King Dia and I find out what Summ plans to do."

The big warrior nodded and kicked his horse forward as Dia dismounted and nodded at the ranger. Kalion swung himself off his horse, and both made their way to where the general and his staff were again in deep discussion about the new threat they now faced.

"If we can use the waterfalls here, that will make it hard for anything to launch an attack on us … Flood the road as a mast movement." The elf pointed to a spot on the map that marked Fanniloo Springs and then quieted as other members of the council presented their opinions, including a forced march.

"Those warriors who stayed within the glen to clear the daed, sir, are already marching back. Should we keep them there or have them gather and block the road, sir?" another piped in as Summ considered this.

"Get word to them quickly to continue marching south and secure these springs!" Summ looked at another runner, who nodded and left to carry out the order, when the general caught sight of Dia and Kalion standing behind the council.

"You two best hurry. General Vana has already left for the empire!" Dia raised his eyebrows as the elven general grabbed his helmet from a passing servant without turning his head.

"Will you be marching to the empire, General?" Kalion asked, tilting his head slightly. Summ shook his head, surprising both warriors.

"I am marching out a portion of the army to join the one coming from the battlefield. We will keep the road clear of anything ugly and nasty. If it looks like this city is defended well enough, then I will march south and join you within the empire." Reaching out, Summ shook both Dia's and Kalion's arms in farewell.

Nodding, Dia turned to return to his horse, leaving Kalion for a moment longer with the commander. "Be safe, sir." Kalion bowed his head slightly and followed the king back to where everyone still waited. Swinging into his saddle, he turned his horse towards the tunnel that would take them out of God's Haven, leading his team to join with Vana, who was already exiting the tunnel with his forces towards the empire.

Methnorick dies and an even larger army returns from the north. Dead beings wandering across the lands, attacking the living. Orcs from the Sernga Mountains are finally marching out, and if we do not march quickly, they will cut God's Haven off. The only way to not get caught is to move before that happens. Summ finally lifted his head up from the map and turned to the others.

"Get the word out now. We march in half an hour!"

Chapter Twenty Three

Bennak and Ame-tora finally made it through the forest, having broken so many branches and twigs between there and the main road of the Northern Reaches that a mere child could track their path if inclined to do so. The pair had decided that speed was preferable to stealth, especially if they could get somewhere safely close to the elven army.

Resting behind a large tree, Bennak, having drunk deeply from a nearby spring to fill his belly, could no longer deny the hunger pains he was feeling, not having eaten any real food for a few days.

"The road looks clear, human. We should be careful though; it looks recently used," the frost giant grumbled as Bennak leaned against the tree, his eyes closed as he tried to rest for a few moments.

"Ame-tora, you know my name. Use it. I feel so tiny when you say 'human'!" Bennak answered, smiling without opening his eyes.

Ame-tora looked down at the man whom he had come to befriend. "Tiny human fill empty belly with water … Ame-tora cannot," the giant teased, only to tense up a second later.

"Bennak, we need to move, friend!" Ame-tora whispered.

Hearing the urgency in Ame-tora's voice, Bennak's eyes snapped open. Swallowing a groan as he pulled himself up, the warrior stepped out onto the road, looking north and south for signs of movement, when the sound of galloping reached his ears.

"Hide!" Bennak hissed, quickly jumping back to hide behind part of the tree as the giant did his best to do the same. The warrior peered around the trunk and listened as the hooves got closer until he caught sight of the rider.

"Elf!" he whispered as the rider sped past their position. Bennak took another peek at the elf, whose hair whipped behind his head as he leaned down in his saddle, obviously urgently riding somewhere.

"Maybe we should follow?" Ame-tora "whispered" so loudly that Bennak was surprised the elf didn't hear.

"Shhh," Bennak gestured, somewhat bemused by the giant's inability to whisper in noisy situations. "Remember, as long as you are right beside me, I can hear you even if there are other noises. Now, let us be careful!"

Both stepped onto the road and looked north, seeing nothing but dark clouds in the far distance that looked to be getting even darker. Turning south, the two warriors made their way down the well-traveled road.

It didn't take them long to hear the unmistakable sound of a marching army headed south. Both jumped back into the woods, hoping for cover enough to hide from whatever was moving closer.

Bennak remembered the elf who had raced by earlier as he hid behind a tree. Whatever that elf was riding from had to be what was coming south along the road. Were they orcs...or worse? Carefully, Bennak moved a branch of the bush he and Ame-tora were hiding behind and almost let go when he caught what sounded like a voice.

He blinked twice and then began to grin. Marching south were rank after rank of elven warriors. Hundreds of spears glinted as they reflected the morning sun. Their armor bore the various emblems of the elven peoples as banners fluttered above their heads.

"Elves ... can you believe it?" Bennak whispered, looking back at the giant, who had found a depression which hid most of his massive body.

"We should be safe with them, do you not think?" Ame-tora whispered back at a volume that sounded closer to a roar to Bennak's ears.

"Stay here ... Let me find out who they are!" Bennak sighed.

"Or, the two of you could save time and come out together now," came a voice from the other side of the bush. Bennak sighed again and nodded. It had been too much to hope that the elves hadn't heard them this time. He turned to Ame-tora. "Slowly, my friend," he warned as he pushed himself through the bush. He knew seeing a massive giant like his friend might cause a sudden movement of arms.

"Hello there!" Bennak said cheerfully, raising both hands to show he wasn't holding a weapon. Ame-tora listened, gripping his axe tightly, getting ready to jump out if his friend called for him, but all he heard were muffled shouts and boots moving closer to where he was hiding.

"Ame-tora! You can come out now. It is safe … They are allies!" Bennak's familiar voice yelled out. The giant swallowed and sheathed his weapon as he slowly stood up and stepped through the brush to find himself looking down at the faces of several surprised elven warriors, who were clearly not harming his friend, as Bennak was already enjoying a piece of food that someone had handed him.

"Those campfires we saw from the ridge … They were coming from them!" Bennak laughed as Ame-tora tilted his head.

"We defeated Methnorick and his armies back at the glen. You must have seen the fires of victory!" the elven team leader said as he stared up at the frost giant.

"Where are you marching to now, friend?" Bennak asked, nodding to the elves still marching in formation.

"We were ordered to march back south to link up with our forces. Word is that the Sernga orcs are leaving their mountain. Just what we need with whatever new evil is coming from the north." Bennak listened, munching on the bread he was just given.

"We encountered some creatures a few days back. We thought they may have been part of Methnorick's forces. But now you say that Methnorick is dead. So, perhaps they were part of another army?" Bennak asked.

The elf turned quickly and shouted out orders before pulling Bennak to the side.

"What did you see up north, friend?"

"I have no idea what they were or where they came from," Bennak admitted. "I just know that they are very dangerous foes. Even Ame-tora here had difficulties fighting them." Bennak nodded to his friend, who just stared at the two warriors.

"Explain," the elf said, pulling his hands behind him.

"They rode large wolf-like beasts, larger than any wolf I have ever seen. They wore black clothing and ..." Bennak paused and swallowed, "smelled of death." Bennak shook his head at the memory. "The wolf creatures were easily taken down by our weapons, but their riders did not seem to be affected."

"How did you get away?" the elf asked, raising an eyebrow.

"Sunlight," Bennak answered simply.

"Sunlight? What about the sunlight?" the elf asked.

"When the creature was exposed to the sun, it ... burst into flames and disappeared!" Bennak looked at the frown on the elf, who slowly shook his head as if not believing the tale the big warrior just shared.

"I am not telling tall tales, sir. That is what happened. You should also know that we saw many more of the deadly creatures, whatever they are!" Bennak could not tell if the commander believed him or not, but he had given him the info.

"Where are they marching to?" Ame-tora interrupted their conversation as he noticed that not all the elves marching past looked the same. Those passing by now were wearing brown and grey robes and carrying staves instead of sharp weapons. They did not look like warriors at all.

The elf smiled as he looked up to answer the giant. "Ah. They are returning to God's Haven to rendezvous with the rest of the army." The elf hid a grin as Ame-tora glared at the large group of elven monks smiling up at the frost giant.

Bennak furrowed his brow in confusion. "What's God's Haven?"

Smiling, he turned to the big man. "Why don't you come see for yourselves?" The elf turned to rejoin the battalion but then noticed their hesitation. "You do want to come with us, do you not?"

Bennak and Ame-tora looked at each other and then turned back to the elf and nodded, quickly moving in behind the column of monks, where they were soon regaled with tales of the recent battle and the victory against Methnorick.

Bennak found himself deep in conversation with a young monk. "Wait … You are saying that a man turned into a creature that looks like a wolf beast and that he killed Methnorick?" The young monk nodded vigorously and began to describe the man responsible for the death of the Dark Lord. As he did, Bennak's face changed from the indulgent smile he had started with to an unmistakable look of worry. Seeing how quiet the big man suddenly turned, the monk placed a hand on the warrior's shoulder. "What is wrong, my brother?" the monk asked gently.

The half-orc tried to smile but quickly gave up when the monk continued to wait on his answer, sighing instead. "The man you described … sounds a lot like a comrade I once had," Bennak answered sadly as he thought about his big friend and the others in the team that he had abandoned. No, he amended, betrayed. He wondered what had happened to them. Were any of them even still alive?

"Ah, sad memories then. Well, I assure you, the wolf-man who killed the Dark One is very much alive, and we are all grateful for his … affliction," the monk said kindly as he returned to describing what happened when the beast met the Dark One on the field.

"It's a shame we weren't able to retrieve his body after he was killed," the monk said a bit testily.

"Why is that?" Ame-tora asked, still wondering what kind of creature could kill Methnorick.

"Methnorick has some dragon creatures fighting in his army, and one took his body before we could grab it!" Bennak looked up at his friend, who clearly was as surprised as he on hearing about the flying creatures of legend.

"Can you repeat that? Did you say 'dragon'?" Bennak almost stopped in his tracks, but the movement behind him kept him walking beside the monk, who returned a smile as he nodded.

"Oh, yes. Thus far, we've seen two of them. One is dark red, and the other, the larger one that grabbed the corpse, is black. However, our allies are strong and smart, so, naturally, they successfully kept them back from attacking our forces!"

Bennak listened to the excited monk explain more about the battle and how God's Haven's cavalry of Pegasi had flown in quickly to keep the two massive creatures at bay.

"Incredible. I have never seen a dragon. Have you Ame-tora?" Both Bennak and the young monk looked back to see the giant shaking his head as he lumbered behind the column.

"How you win?" Ama-tora asked the monk.

"When the Dark One was killed, his army fell apart and ran away, giving up the field!" another monk chipped in then. "Unfortunately, we weren't able to capture or kill any of his generals, as they used the retreat to escape. Still, many of Methnorick's army were slaughtered by our warriors giving chase, with the help of those warriors from the empire."

Bennak let out a quiet whistle. "The empire joined in the battle?" Bennak was still thinking about that development when he caught the sight of the elven commander moving down the side of the ranks.

Indicating that he needed to speak to them both, Bennak thanked the monks and stepped out of the formation as the elf moved to the side again.

"I sent word of you both to my commander ... If you two want to join and fight with us, you are both welcome to. He thinks it will be quite something to have a half-orc and an ice giant in our midst. However, he also wanted me to let you know that there is a small contingent of warriors on their way to the empire if it is your goal to travel farther south."

As that was Bennak's goal — he had no desire to chance running into Whelor, if, indeed, that was who the young monk had described — he immediately grasped the elf's arm and thanked him for the food, information and company.

"Then we will depart at the crossroad. I had hoped you would both join us. We need every able-bodied being to fight whatever is marching from the north. I had thought that Methnorick was a danger to my people, but now … the news that I just received tells me that I was wrong, that what is marching is darker, more evil!" the commander stated, trying put on a bright face, but Bennak could tell that he was nervous about this new threat.

"Your battle is at your God's Haven. I believe the bigger battle will be to the south. That is where they will need us more," Bennak said, releasing the elf's arm as Ame-tora grumbled his thanks.

No one spoke as they followed the formation up the road until they came to the crossroad. "You won't have long to wait. I believe I can already hear their horses. Be well, friends, and good luck!" the elf said as he turned and rejoined his troops.

Nodding gently, Bennak and Ame-tora stepped to the side and stood next to the trees to wait. Sure enough, just moments later, Bennak saw the dust of several horses galloping their way. Letting the branch go back slowly, he leaned over to smile at his friend.

"I guess this is the place!" Bennak giggled as the horses made the ground shake as they galloped by, each carrying an armored warrior holding a long spear that shined in the sunlight.

Ame-tora frowned as he looked in the direction the riders were headed and saw hundreds more spear tips marching up ahead.

"I might be wrong … but there is a large group already moving south, just up ahead." Ame-tora pointed to the warriors.

Bennak whipped his head around and blew out a breath, wondering if those were the warriors they were supposed to rendezvous with.

"Has to be … I see not many!" Ame-tora grumbled as he pulled the tree back, wondering how he would keep up with horses. He had long legs, but his people were not known to run fast for long periods of time.

As the pair stared at the formation, neither heard the next set of riders trotting down the road until they were almost upon them. Bennak turned, thinking how lucky they were to be able to get a message to the forces ahead, only to feel his stomach fall to the floor. "Oh, gods!" he whispered.

"Well, well, well. Bennak. Praise the gods you live ... You are alive, right?" The man's voice sounded angry to Ame-tora as he gripped the handle of his axe tighter, wondering if these two were friends or enemies.

"Hello, Kalion!" Bennak answered, smiling tightly at the ranger as the warrior moved his horse so he could look at the two standing under the tree. "Never thought to see you, my friend!"

"Friend? Are you sure that's the word you wish to use, Bennak? You left us!" another one of the riders cried out. Ame-tora relaxed his grip as the second rider pulled back her hood to reveal the most beautiful elf maiden he had ever seen.

"Kikor, I never meant to harm any of you ... Please understand that!" Bennak pleaded. Suddenly, there was a loud laugh from a robed rider, who quickly jumped off his horse and ran over to grasp Bennak tightly.

"Well, I, for one, am glad you have returned and survived the wilds, my friend!"

"Meradoth, it is good to see you too!" Bennak gasped at the unbelievable strength of the mage holding him now. "You can let me go now, friend!" Meradoth laughed again and lightly slapped Bennak's shoulder as he did.

"Well, now, you must tell us how you came to be here ... and who your big friend here is!" Meradoth smiled up at the massive frost giant.

"This is Ame-tora. He ... he saved me from Jebba's clutches, and we've been making our way, trying to catch up with you all. Ame-tora, these are the travelers I told you about!"

"Well, I was told that there were two that were to join us marching south. So, are you ready?" Kalion asked, his voice still sounding disappointed and angry.

"No, we are not," Ame-tora said, looking pointedly at Bennak. "Not until my friend here apologizes … to all of us."

Bennak frowned up at his friend and turned around to hiss at him, "What are you talking about? Apologize for what?"

Ame-tora didn't even try to whisper as he crossed his arms. "For telling falsehoods. I did not save you from Jebba. You were not searching for these people. And you did not tell me that you abandoned ladies to help your mad friend."

Bennak closed his eyes for a moment and then sighed. Turning around, he saw everyone in the crowd sit with their arms crossed, mimicking Ame-tora, save for Meradoth, who kept grinning like a loon.

"Fine!" Bennak barked, glaring at his friend. "I honestly tried to help Jebba. He …" Bennak looked up at Kalion with a pained expression, "he was truly mad near the end. I thought if I accompanied him that I could convince him to return, but …" Bennak said as he looked away, as if racked by guilt, "we got separated during a skirmish with some orcs one day during a blizzard. By the time I had defeated my foe, he was nowhere to be found. I dug through the snow for days, looking for his body. I was almost dead myself … until Ame-tora saved me. He has been a faithful companion and friend ever since, and I … less so."

Bennak glanced at his friend and then his former team. "I'm sorry. I know that doesn't begin to— Oof!" His words were cut off by yet another bear hug from Meradoth. This time, the faces that looked back at him were no longer filled with anger, including Ame-tora. As for Bennak, he felt as if a weight had been lifted from his shoulders.

"Do you have a horse for me?" Bennak asked just as a horse came into view, being pulled by another man. "No. It can't be. Is that …?" Bennak pointed, getting the rest to look back.

"King Dia? Yes. Alive and well and journeying with us to the empire. Allegedly, his daughter, the princess, is also alive and well," Kalion added.

"King Dia, I am glad to see you!" Bennak smiled up at the man before bowing deeply.

"By the gods' hands, Bennak! Well, son, you are a sight I never thought I would see again. It is good to see you! And Ame-tora," Dia added with a nod towards the giant.

Turning to look up at his friend, it occurred to the warrior that they may not be able to accept their help in any case, as there was no way his friend could keep up with the horses. "My friend here will not be able to keep up with the pace, so—"

Ame-tora had been thinking the same thing since the moment he saw the horses. It was time to say goodbye. "I believe that our time has—" Ame-tora cut Bennak off, only to have his words cut off by Meradoth.

"I can help with that, Bennak. Take my horse. Your friend and I will travel together." Meradoth grinned as he pulled a rolled-up rug out of his saddlebags.

Stepping up to the giant, Meradoth unrolled the rug on the ground, sat down and then gestured for Ame-tora to sit as well. Bennak laughed as Ame-tora looked around in confusion.

"Do not worry, my friend … You are only about to fly!"

* * *

"Wait, you're saying that your people are two separate beings …? I am lost, friend!" Shermee had been listening to the tale from the old merchant dwarf while the rest of the group finished up their meal. The old merchant dwarf nodded back at her.

"In the beginning, no. We were one of the two beings that lived upon Marn. At that time, we were of one mind, capable of building the greatest things out of the ground that Marn would give us … until the gods came. They destroyed Marn. The legend says that, in doing so, our people were ripped apart. Split into those with a mind to continue building Marn and those bent on destroying it."

Shermee said nothing. Ordinarily, she would have dismissed such a tale as unbelievable, but for some reason, it also made sense as well.

"Our people have a legend that is quite similar to that one," one of Shermee's elven warriors piped up, getting everyone's attention.

"That, I believe, will be a good tale to tell tonight, don't you agree, ma'am?" Jacoob had been enjoying the conversation, but knew that time was short on this journey as well.

Shermee nodded and stood up with a smile. Looking at Jacoob, she gestured her head towards the dwarves as she returned to her horse. Nodding, Jacoob walked over to the dwarves, where he pulled out a few coins and thanked the merchants for their help in providing food and drink before mounting his horse to catch up to the party.

As the dwarves watched the riders disappear in the distance, an old dwarf, who had remained quiet the entire time, finally spoke up.

"So, that was her, eh? The new empress. She's a pretty human, do you not think?" The old dwarf laughed at the expressions on his companions' faces as they finished packing up.

"Very pretty, indeed!" he whispered to himself as he snapped the reins to leave the area, hoping that before he left Marn he would meet her again.

* * *

"Empress, please, my people do not have the means to stop the machines. Please, save my people!" Volkk pleaded again.

What happened next made him blink, for he thought his eyes were playing tricks on him. The creature before him changed into different ocean creatures. Volkk could do nothing but watch in awe of the power of the being before him.

Volkk felt Gulbra begin to shake, much like one trapped in a cold river, something he had only felt a few times in his life. Those deep-sea rivers were terrible if caught in them and were known to be strong enough to move an elf miles from where one started.

"Your people!?" The haunting voice brought the elf suddenly back to the scene before him as he squeezed his eyes tightly at the sound of her voice.

He looked up as her form changed again, this time into a massive whale, one he had met once cycles ago with a long horn sticking out of its forehead like a spear. As she floated easily in the water, his mind eased from the pain so he could think.

"Gulbra told me the tales of who you are, Empress, but he never told me that you were a living being … that you were real. I had been brought up believing you were a legend!"

"LEGEND?!" her voice screamed so loudly that Volkk grabbed his head to stop the pain as he fell to his knees in the sand.

"Your council knew of my presence, but did nothing. Your cousins upon the land fight other beings for nothing but greed whilst my world is destroyed around them all. Tell me, child, why should I come to your aid? You have all forsaken me. None of you have ever even made the smallest sacrifice—"

"I will sacrifice my life here and now if it will save the lives of my people and friends within our oceans."

Volkk felt more sure of his words than he had ever felt about anything. And not just because he could already see the red bolts in the distance, where he knew the city to be. It felt … right. He felt at peace with his decision. Nodding, Volkk looked back to the creature to see her changing once again. This time as the sand cloud settled, the most beautiful elf he had ever seen floated before him. Emerald green eyes looked directly at him, cutting into his mind sharply. Her green gown looked like it had been fashioned with the tightest spin of seaweed cloth, perfectly complementing her gorgeous mane of blue-green hair. He could see a smile form on her face.

"You speak and believe in the truth for your people and the creatures of the oceans. If I do what you desire, this world will be cleansed of those that seek to dishonor and destroy my world. Are you certain that you want this?" Her eyes stared directly at Volkk, almost like they were beams of fire into his very soul.

"Yes, Empress," Volkk whispered.

Smiling fully now, the queen placed her hand on his head as she closed her eyes and began to speak in a language he had never heard before. Suddenly, a rush of images flashed within his mind, most of a past he had never known existed. He saw the entire story of Marn in a matter of seconds.

Lifting her hand off Volkk's head, he swallowed deeply and opened his eyes to look up seeing her smiling as she looked at him.

"You and I are one now, Volkk of Marn. Now go to your city and get as many out as you can. Leave Gulbra here to recover." Volkk noticed that her voice no longer caused him discomfort. Nodding, he looked down at his friend and then back at her.

"What are you planning?" he asked when he saw her smile.

"Just get our people to safety," she answered as she closed her eyes and began to speak in that unfamiliar language he couldn't recognize. Something began to emanate from her body as she lifted her arms slowly and opened her hands.

Volkk turned and quickly grabbed his sword that now lay upon the sand. Sheathing it, he swam up to the ridge and headed for his city, where explosions were now erupting.

Chapter Twenty Four

The castle didn't resemble any structure bearing that name that Shermee had ever seen before. It was more of a large fortified house with wooden walls made of large cut trees. She could make out a few men staring down at them from the top ramparts as she and her entourage approached what appeared to be the front gate. According to Jacoob, this was the largest settlement in the province of Petrikbur, making Shermee keenly curious about the other settlements in the region as she and the rest of her group galloped through the gateway that opened up for them.

Their horses caused dust to rise up in the large courtyard that was used between the wall and the large building, where she could see a smiling man wearing a simple brown robe with the emblem of the province on his chest waving at her as she pulled her reins to stop her horse.

Walking down the few steps, the man grabbed the bit of her horse as if he didn't quite trust her riding skill.

"Welcome, welcome. I trust you didn't run into anything nasty out there before your arrival," the man said, looking at her as her horse whined a bit from his grip on the bridle.

Smiling tightly, Shermee lifted a leg and swung herself off the horse before the man could offer his assistance. At least he had let go of her horse's bit in his haste to reach out to help her, only to pull his hands back to his sides as she used her hands to brush the dust from her simple jacket.

"No, my warriors are quite bored by now, not having had even a rogue bush to defeat. I am glad to be off the saddle, of course!" She giggled as the man smiled widely back at her.

"I am glad to hear this, my lady. I am Lord Nikuass, Keeper of Chiconogo and this province, and my home is, of course, at your disposal." Nikuass bowed slightly as he finished and gestured to the house behind him.

"Thank you for having us, Lord Nikuass. We have much to discuss. I will be most eager to converse with you after my team and I have a chance to freshen up. Shall we say … an hour's time?"

"Yes, yes, of course, Empress!" Nikuass smiled as he turned and motioned to a servant, who began to shout out orders to other servants waiting nearby. Shermee followed the shy housemaid who came to lead her and her female warriors inside while the men followed another group of servants to the large building where they were told they could freshen up.

Nikuass pulled his hands behind his back. As he watched the young empress walk up the steps and into his house, another man joined him.

"So, that is our new empress. So young. I would have thought her to be older from the rumors," the man said quietly as they watched her disappear inside the building.

"You will show her respect, Sir Erek. The woman may be young, but I feel that she knows exactly what she is doing," Nikuass responded. "But what is she doing here when the whole of the north is exploding into war? Maybe to recruit us?"

"We are too few. She should know that," Erek retorted, looking at his lord as he did.

"Go and order everyone to gather in the hall. If she is looking for recruits, there is one direction I could send her," Nikuass said, nodding towards the mountains that lay almost a hundred miles away yet could still be seen from the castle.

Erek's eyes got bigger as he caught on to his lord's meaning. "Gods! Not them. Seriously? Of all the things …" Erek shook his head as he looked at the main house.

"It is one way to make her reign short!" Nikuass spoke, causing both to laugh loudly as they stepped forward to walk into the lord's house.

"What a waste!" Nikuass and Erek laughed quietly as they walked up the stairs towards the house's large entrance.

"Yes, a waste!" the lord repeated as they both stopped laughing. "Send a message to the camp. I want them to be ready to move at a moment's notice!" Nikuass whispered before walking down a hallway towards the room where they would wait for the empress and her warriors.

* * *

The dungeon of Blath 'Na City hadn't been used in many cycles before the masters came. There never seemed to be a need to house any criminals within it; the city had been more or less safe for those living and traveling through it. Now it echoed with screams, cries and more as prisoners and slaves were brought down to be tortured.

The room where Methnorick had been kept was now a burnt-out chamber. A single hinge was all that held the broken door up. As the black-robed master walked by, silently looking over it, a smile formed on his face.

Walking down the hallway, the master came to a room that once served as the guards' quarters, but now as the master stepped closer, he could hear the noises of construction.

Pushing the heavy door open, bright light flew into his face as he looked towards the area where the hammers were clanging away. Looking around, he saw scores of dead prisoners hanging from the ceiling, some from their arms, many from their feet.

Most were naked, a few still had rags on their bodies, but many more had no skin at all, removed by one of the workers who ran over to kneel before the master.

"My master, I am sorry I did not—" the man began, only to fall silent when the master interrupted.

"I was curious to see your work." The master looked down at the head of the man kneeling before him. "You may stand. Explain your progress!"

The man rose up and swallowed as he pulled in a breath to speak.

"We have a small number of new creatures ready for you, Master, over here!" The man waved a hand to direct his master to a large secured room where the experiments were being kept.

As they got closer, the master could hear sounds almost like those of a wounded man or elf. It also sounded like things were being dragged across the stone floor.

Peering in, he smiled widely as he took in the first round of the newest soldiers, meant to counter anything the elves or men might put against them in future battles.

"When will you have them ready?" He leaned back, looking at the groveling man, who was clearly shaking.

"The ... the number we are working on, my master ... We should have a full battery ready for you by week's end, sir."

"Hmmm, week's end. I want two batteries upon the field in ten days ... understand?" The master pulled his arms back as the frightened man nodded.

"Then my time here is done ... Continue with your work, slave!" the master ordered as he turned and slowly walked out of the room.

* * *

Elesha flew high above clouds now thick with rain and thunder as she made her way south to explore. Heavy forests stretched everywhere, with the occasional river winding through the green trees. Here and there she could make out a few small lakes, but nothing stood out to her until she caught the sight of a new lake that had been formed within the Ribbwa'nor Glen, where Methnorick had met the elven armies.

It sparkled just enough for her to recognize that it was now a permeant feature upon the land as she flew slowly over it. Elesha wondered for a moment where the elves were. Suddenly, a flicker in the far south caught her attention.

"The road!" she whispered to herself as she turned to follow it. Soon, Elesha caught the sight of movement within the rolling hills. Elesha flapped her wings excitedly as she caught sight of her target. The elven army was marching … the wrong way.

What are they doing? she wondered. *Why are they headed south?* She lifted herself up into the clouds, knowing that those creatures could see her.

Using the winds to carry her over the long line of elven warriors marching and riding along the road, Elesha tried to figure out where they could be headed when she caught another flicker of something out of the corner of her eye.

"Orcs, moving out of the mountains!" Elesha whispered as orcs numbering in the thousands streamed down the ravines and small roads intertwined throughout the Sernga Mountains.

Elven warriors marching to meet the orcs! Elesha was happy to see that the orcs were finally leaving their city to go to war. *Elf kind are marching quickly* … She would give the elves something else to think about while they engaged the orcs. Turning to join them, she began to climb. Just before she reached the clouds, another sight, far more brilliant than thousands of orcs, lay below … an entire city.

"It cannot be!" she gasped as she hovered in midair, staring at the large port that lay wide open along the shoreline. Before her stood high buildings of stone. Many were temples of gods, she could see from the emblems. Everywhere she looked, she saw the wealth and comfort of a people who had never seen war. Suddenly, she remembered that she had stopped short of the clouds. By now, she knew she had been seen by …

"ELVES!" she yelled angrily. "*My brother, I have found an elven city. A hidden city!*" Elesha thought to Chansor, who at that very moment was flying cover for the fleet of ships.

"*Elves? City? Where, sister? What do you plan to do?*" Chansor responded back.

"*Have fun, of course. You will see it soon enough … and tell the general!*" she roared loudly and pulled her wings in closer to her body to direct her flight over the city.

Those in the city cried out in horror as Elesha flew herself over the city, quickly releasing three massive balls of fire. Debris flew everywhere, killing many nearby elves.

Stupid elves! she thought to herself as she flew up into the clouds to prepare for another run. *Hiding within the land. You cannot hide from me!*

Turning herself around, she pulled her wings in close and opened them again just as quickly, as scores of armored Pegasi burst through the clouds, holding

heavily armed elven warriors, whose arrows all seemed to be aimed right at her as they surrounded her.

"NONE OF YOU CAN STOP ME!" Elesha roared loudly as she pulled in enough air to release a bolt of flaming fire at the first group of elves, who quickly scattered as the fire flew through their formation.

Laughing, Elesha didn't hear Chansor pleading with her to flee as she flew through the horses, feeling arrows hitting her sides. She was trying to ignore the fact that she had felt their impact as a spear flew so close to her face that it made her pull back hard.

"STUPID ELVES. YOU THINK YOU CAN STOP MEEE!!!" she roared loudly, looking for the leader. Finding him, she pulled in a breath to release another bolt of fire when she felt something unfamiliar, something she had never felt before. She felt pain.

Elesha screamed as the feeling of massive hot fire shot through her. One of the elven spears had embedded itself deep in her right wing.

"*Elesha, get out of there. Those are elvish monks. They can harm you!*" Chansor's voice finally burst into her mind.

It was already too late. Suddenly finding herself surrounded, she didn't have time to move as three elves threw their spears at her head. Only one connected, but that one embedded under the scales that lined her forehead, causing her to roar in pain. Next, her sight began to wane from the blood leaking into her eyes. Soon, she saw nothing but bright stars.

Using her claws, she desperately tried to pull out the spear, only to break its shaft, leaving the spearhead still inside. Roaring again, Elesha let out two more bolts of fire to clear a path as she blindly, but quickly, retreated, flapping her wings as hard as she could.

Despite the pain and blindness, Elesha was able to outrun the slower Pegasi pursuing her after a few minutes. Seeing that she had made good on her escape without slamming into a mountainside, Elesha landed in a quiet wood to recover. But first, she needed to tell Chansor and Kaligor about the orcs coming out of mountains, and the hidden elven city.

Chapter Twenty Five

Volkk returned to the city to find most of the residents already gone. The only elves still around were rescue teams searching for survivors in the rubble of collapsed buildings throughout what was left of the city.

He gripped his sword handle tightly as he watched one machine after another moving through his city, attacking and destroying building after building. Even worse, the ground was littered with the corpses of the hundreds of warriors who had tried to stop them, only to be hit by those deadly red bolts.

"Marn'azzi, where are you?" Volkk whispered, using the queen's — no, mother's — name for the first time. Just as he started to despair, he heard a familiar sound floating through the water from behind.

Squinting his eyes, he looked through the debris for the source of the sounds now getting louder by the moment when he finally spied the dark shapes of not one or two but hundreds of whales. And they weren't alone.

Swimming in between their massive bodies were hundreds, maybe even thousands, of dolphins, and moving just below were just as many massive sea turtles.

Volkk began to smile as even more creatures came into range. There were scores of electric eels as well as manta rays moving themselves to land on the turtles. But it was the sight of what followed the animal army that made his smile widen.

The seas were filled with hundreds of thousands of sea elves from different underwater communities. Some rode kelpies. Others preferred the backs of the turtles and dolphins. But each one of them carried long, sharp tridents as well as shields.

"Our people!" Volkk whispered to himself as he caught sight of another massive creature, one that made even the largest of the whales seem small in comparison.

"Marn'azzi?" he whispered to himself, blinking a few times as he watched the enormous creature flap her large wings. This was truly the goddess of Gulbra's tales. Volkk raised a hand to feel her power moving through his mind and body as he acknowledged that Gulbra had been right all along ... His people had been lost.

"Marn'azzi!" he repeated proudly.

"WE HAVE COME TO TAKE BACK THAT WHICH IS OURS!" Volkk heard her roar loudly as the ocean filled with battle cries. Lifting his sword high over his head, he let out his own battle cry and swam to join the other elves as they together lifted their own spears and charged forward.

* * *

The group sat around the large wooden table, laughing and eating loudly as food and drink flowed throughout the hours. Shermee sat in her chair, laughing with one of the leaders as they joked about what life was like in Brigin'i and the northern areas. Others, including her own guard, were laughing with warriors from the castle about life within the province. Off to the side, Lord Nikuass glared at his new empress as she enjoyed herself, slowly sipping at the wine he had in front of him. His people were making it hard for him to hear, but he was sure the girl was retelling a story about some far-off barbaric city she once was princess of.

"Oh, you cannot believe my brothers ... always fighting about whose castle was stronger and such!" Nikuass hear her say and shook his head slightly, wondering how this girl thought she might be able to bridge the hate that the Nightwitches felt towards all men.

"How many do they have?" the man she was laughing with asked as he pulled on the chicken leg with his teeth.

"Well, altogether, my family had five castles throughout the north. Not all of them are still standing now," she said, taking another sip of the drink in her hand. "I must compliment you, Lord Nikuass. This is delicious wine you have here in Petrikbur." She nodded with a smile, wondering what bothered him.

"Thank you, Empress. Grapes from the sky, goes the legend. Grown on the cold vines in southeastern parts of the province!" he replied as he took a sip of it himself.

"Well, please give my compliments to the vintner," Shermee said, turning her attention back to her plate.

Realizing that he may not get another chance, Nikuass leaned forward and cleared his throat. "May I speak to you privately, Empress?" he whispered to her, making her turn slightly, smiling up at him.

Excusing herself to the men around her, Shermee got up, taking her glass of wine with her, and let Nikuass usher her over to a corner where the two could speak without being interrupted.

"Your quest to recruit more troops for this war coming to our borders is commendable, but I am concerned that you might be risking yourself—" Nikuass stopped when Shermee lifted a hand.

"My lord, a few of your men have already tried to convince me not to go, so believe me when I say that I am well aware of the risks. Our empire is desperate to get as many men, women, elves and anything else willing to fight under our banner. However, know that they are not the only beings that I plan to reach out to!"

Nikuass was taken aback by the thought that the new empress was recruiting beyond his province. He had thought his province special because of the Nightwitches. "Where else do you plan to go, Empress?" Nikuass asked.

"I cannot travel all of the empire, Lord Nikuass, but I have riders reaching out to each province. They will relay the news of what is coming."

"Every province?" Nikuass asked skeptically.

"Yes, Lord Nikuass, every province. From Sokol to the province of Vostoki. I hope they will join me as well!"

Nikuass looked shocked. "The white warriors are barbarians! They cover themselves in white to hide themselves in the snow until you pass them, and then they attack. But do you know what else they are known for?" Nikuass raised a brow as he spoke, hoping his queen knew what she was doing.

"Eating their prisoners and enemies. They are known for their fierce fighting abilities, sir, and that is what we need!" Shermee said as she finished her wine. Nikuass shook his head in disbelief.

"I will not allow any of my men to go with you, Empress. I cannot risk their lives on such folly." Nikuass quickly smiled as he leaned back.

Shermee merely nodded. He would soon discover that she was fully aware of the extent of her power, meaning that she knew full well that she didn't need his permission to recruit whomever she chose. For now, however, she turned to rejoin the others, nodding politely to the castle commander as he strode by.

"So?" Erek asked once he got close enough to speak without being overheard.

"She knows what she is getting into, that is for sure ... and she knows that I can help her too, but ..." Nikuass paused as he watched her laugh along with a few of his warriors.

"I can escort her to the Blue Tree, if that is your wish," Erek stated. The Blue Tree had been living for more cycles than anyone knew — just like how no one knew why its leaves reflected a blueish tint.

"Yes, the Blue Tree but no farther. That is the boundary of their lands, and I will not lose you to those witches."

As Erek nodded and left, Nikuass suddenly felt exhausted and left the party, walking towards his own chamber that lay at the far end of the large wooden building they were all occupying at the moment.

Entering his plush chamber, Nikuass simply pulled his robes off as a servant came over to assist him. Nikuass looked down at the boy for a moment as a question came to him.

"What do you think of our new empress, my boy?"

"She seems to know much, sir … much more than I!" the boy whispered as he helped his lord out of the trousers and folded them before moving to undo the shirt.

"No, I mean what do you think of her? Isn't she beautiful? Speak freely. I won't punish you." Nikuass could see the boy hesitate. "Unless you don't answer me," he added menacingly.

"She is very pretty, sir … beautiful. More beautiful than I thought an empress could be, sir!" the boy said quickly, still maintaining his smile.

Looking away as the boy pulled his shirt off, he held his arms out so the boy could pull his sleeping robe on. Nikuass whispered to no one in particular for a moment.

"She is beautiful, all right. It will be a loss if she dies tomorrow. I am in need of a wife, and the empire deserves an emperor!"

Shermee saw their host leave the chamber without saying goodnight. Strange man, but in this case, she was grateful to be able to end the party on her own. Turning to her escorts, she simply announced that she needed to be at her best for the next part of the journey. Quickly, the rest of the warriors took that as the end of the party as they slowly got up and made their ways to their rooms. Shermee entered her room, disrobed and fell asleep even before the last man had cleared the hall. Those on guard duty stood watch over their companions as the room quickly filled with snoring.

* * *

The courtyard of the Father Gate was crowded with men and elven warriors as Quinor and the men accompanying him rode in and dismounted their horses, all groaning from the long and hard trip.

A boy ran over to take his horse's reins as Quinor took in the sights. He was still settling into his new position as guardian of the empire. Riding next to him was General Atwolf, who had come to decide where to deploy the armies and to explain the events that had occurred in the capital over the past few days.

"Tell me, lad," he asked as he handed the reins over, "who is the man in charge of this place?" Quinor smiled as he stretched his back again.

"That would be General Vana, sir!" the boy said proudly. Quinor smiled at his enthusiasm.

"Point him out to me, son. I've come from the capital and need to speak with him immediately!" Quinor watched as the boy's eyes widened.

"Oh, the general is not here, sir. He's in the north, battling with elves!"

"Then who is in charge now?"

"Commander Tevanic, sir, right over there!" the boy answered, pointing to a group of men that Quinor saw talking together near a large well.

Thanking the boy, Quinor adjusted his sword belt as he strode towards the well. As he closed in, he saw one of the warriors nod to a man whose back was to Quinor, when he suddenly turned around.

"Can I help you?"

"I am Quinor, guardian of the empire. I have come from the capital with General Atwolf and these warriors here to get an update on the situation here, sir." Quinor waved his hand slightly as more men slowly streamed into the large courtyard.

"Well, I thank you for the men, sir. We are certainly going to need them. I am Tevanic, Commander of the Father Gate." Walking past his men Tevanic gently grabbed Quinor's arm to pull him along with him as he led Quinor to a place where they could talk without interruption.

"Now tell me, sir, what exactly is a 'guardian of the empire'? We heard rumors that something significant happened within the capital! Indeed, until you mentioned Atwolf, I was ready to have you locked up."

"Well, then," Quinor said dryly, "It's a good thing he came along," he added before giving Tevanic a quick rundown of everything that happened in the south.

Tevanic's eyebrows lifted in surprise as they entered his chamber at the far end of the courtyard, shaking his head slightly as he listened to the news.

"So … we have an empress now," Tevanic said when Quinor was finished. "One who speaks of impending war." Quinor nodded. Tevanic sighed as he sat down. "All right, then. Have a seat, Quinor. I need to know everything about this threat that you can tell me!" Tevanic spoke calmly, but Quinor could see the worry across his face.

Chapter Twenty Six

The three elves to Volkk's right nodded at him to take the lead, moving their spears to point at the belly of the beast.

Gripping his spear tightly, Volkk and the other three elves slammed their spear points hard into the armor of the battle beast, just as an explosion occurred to his right.

The shock that went down his arm was like nothing he had felt before as he looked wide-eyed at the effect of the spear points. They had managed to make a large rip in the beast, which stopped its movement but also damaged their spears.

Knowing they wouldn't be able to use their spears much longer, Volkk and his team fell back to allow another group to charge. Then he noticed something else. As the head moved, it exposed its unarmored neck. Though small in size compared to the overall beast, it was more than large enough to aim at. Calling out to the closest elves, Volkk directed them to move in and attack the neck area, which was instantly was covered with spears. Volkk was sure he could hear the beast cry out as black liquid began to leak out of the damaged neck.

"Move in!" he screamed at another group of elves, who were waiting for their turn, when he felt the water around him rumble as the machine before him shuddered, releasing a large amount of the black stuff into the water. Directing his kelpie over the machine that had stopped moving, he saw bodies floating in the water, and not those of his people. *Those have to have come from within these beasts. They have to be the enemy,* he thought.

Volkk swam to one of the bodies. He needed to see the face of his enemy. As he turned the body over, he saw the charred flesh, as it had been through some type of fire. However, what made Volkk's jaw tighten was the part of the face that hadn't been melted by the fire. He had suspected it when he saw those the first two swim away during the battle, but now he knew for sure.

MAN! Volkk hissed in his mind. "There are men within these beasts!" Volkk hissed loudly as he let go of the body. Volkk shook his head as he looked around.

Three of the beasts he could see were down, their necks cut open by his warriors' spears. A few of his warriors were floating along with two dolphins that had been caught by the red light.

Volkk turned his kelpie towards the area where Mal-mohrs and crabs were working together, having Mal-mohr's knock over the battle beasts while giant crabs cut open their necks to release the black blood.

"Sir, we have been able to trap a large number of these beasts in the middle of the city near the main square!" Volkk turned to look at the warrior who was moving up behind him.

"How many?" he snapped back as he turned to look at the young warrior. Sure enough, he could see a large number of the beasts gathering near the statue of the god that protected the city of the sea elves.

"At least three score," answered the elf, who, Volkk could see, was young and foolish enough to still be excited by the idea of battle. Volkk wondered how the lad would react once he had a true taste of it. Or, worse, once he lost someone close to him.

Looking back where the beasts were gathered, Volkk noticed that not only were they making a stand, but they were also maneuvering themselves to face outwards.

"Your orders, sir?"

In fact, Volkk was at a loss as to how to proceed as he looked around at the massive numbers of the dead, but he answered, "Have every warrior left form a perimeter around the city, but they are not to move in until the order is given. Do you understand me?"

The young warrior nodded eagerly and raced off to spread Volkk's order. Volkk, meanwhile, sighed as he felt Marn'azzi's presence in his mind. *"Perhaps a little warning next time, before snatching my body for your own use,"* Volkk thought back.

"Prepare yourselves!" Her words floated into his mind as a shadow appeared over him, causing him to look up to see the massive beast slide over him towards the city center. Again, Volkk could only wonder what she was planning as he turned his kelpie and raced to the perimeter.

In the far northern edge of the city, three elves who had gotten separated from the main assault force were maneuvering around rubble along the edge of the street. Each had lost their mounts earlier when the red fire hit, so now they silently approached a trio of battle beasts that seemed to have gone off on their own, when the call for them to move out of the city hit their minds.

"What do we do?" the youngest sea elf whispered over to his sergeant, an elf named Soryn, who, even with the loss of his left hand to a shark, remained a formidable warrior. Soryn ignored the young elf for a moment as he leaned on the edge of the rock wall, looking at the three beasts that were for some reason not moving anymore but just standing there.

"Sir?" asked another elf, who was kneeling not far behind, holding tightly to his spear as he and the young elf looked at each other. "Do we leave?"

Leaning back, the sergeant shook his head as he looked at the two elves who were the only ones to survive from the group of thirty he had started with: Tibool, an elf of about two hundred cycles, who was no longer much of a warrior, and Keenzo, an elf that should have still been with his mother at home. But when the call had gone out for all able-bodied elves, Keenzo had not hesitated to protect his people.

"No," Soryn replied. "Whatever the call is for, we are far from the main part of the city. I want to know why these three are just sitting there." He moved back to let the elf behind him look around the corner as he looked at the youngest member of his group.

"Soryn … what do you think they are doing?" Tibool whispered as he moved back.

"Only the gods know. Do you not find this strange, though, finding three of these things in this area of the city just sitting there?" Both Tibool and Keenzo nodded, when they heard a loud roar that made the rocks around them shake.

Soryn motioned for the others to stay where they were as he moved up to the top of the rock wall to look down to the city proper and gasped at what he saw.

Marn'azzi's dark shape was moving slowly as she floated over the city. Soryn watched in horror as the beasts lifted their heads towards her.

They hope to kill her in one massive strike! Soryn thought as red beams flew through the water to slam hard into her body.

"*You dare to attack my children!*" Every being heard Marn'azzi's haunting words calmly float into their minds as she circled around the city a few more times while being constantly attacked by the machines' red bolts.

Suddenly, Marn'azzi stopped circling. As she hovered over the machines, she opened her mouth, causing the very water to shake around her. Her roar erupted as a white glow with such tremendous force that every elf grabbed their head. The white glow then exploded out of her mouth, quickly encompassing the machines that still tried to harm her.

"The gods are mighty!" Volkk whispered to himself as he watched the machines melt away to become part of the bedrock.

She is truly a god! Soryn thought to himself as Marn'azzi moved away from the city center and swam into the dark mist of the ocean. Yet, before he had time to properly register what he had just seen, Keenzo's worried voice reached his ears.

"Sir … sir … they are moving!" Soryn peered around and saw that two of the four machines were moving, leaving the others hidden in place.

"Go find an officer," Soryn said, pointing to where he saw many of their fellow warriors gathering. "Let them know we still have more of those things in the city. And Keenzo," Soryn added with a stern look, "hurry!"

Keenzo nodded and took off, staying low and in between the buildings, out of sight. Soryn and Tibool continued to watch as one of the machines began to open.

"They have creatures within them!" Tibool whispered as they watched about a dozen beings swim out from the small opening in their bellies. "What is that covering their faces?" Tibool squinted.

"Something to help them breathe, maybe?" Soryn watched as half of the beings swam into one of the buildings, leaving the other six to stand guard.

"They come from above … What should we do?" Tibool whispered.

Soryn shook his head. He couldn't take on six of them by himself and had no intention of risking Tibool's life for a lost cause. Suddenly, he felt thoughts trying to enter his mind. Thinking it might be Marn'azzi, he closed his eyes to concentrate.

"*Soryn. Sergeant Soryn, do you hear me?*" Soryn nodded as the words became clear in his mind.

"*Volkk? Is that you, my friend? Where are you?*" Soryn thoughts drifted loud and true, bringing a smile to Soryn's face.

"*Here with young Keenzo, who tells me that you still have three machines in your midst.*"

"*Aye. Here in the Sokol district. But I must tell you, these machine beasts seem different. The two that moved positioned themselves near a building, after which several beings exited the machines and entered the building, leaving the other half to stand guard. I have no idea what they seek to do, so make haste, my friend.*"

"*I will attend quickly. However, be advised that there are reports of small groups of the beasts throughout the city, so do nothing until help arrives!*"

* * *

Chansor had relayed Elesha's information about the hidden elvish city she had attacked to Kaligor, who seemed less than impressed after being told that she had come under attack by a group of Pegasi.

Standing behind the group of dark elf commanders and Kaligor as they poured over the map, trying to figure out where this city could be, he folded his arms across his chest, not understanding why they were arguing.

"You all realize that this news could change everything. This has to be the city that reinforced the elves in the battle with Lord Methnorick. If it is destroyed, that leaves the north completely open!" Chansor said.

"Your sister did not share where this city was located. And she was stupid enough to take on a group of Pegasi rather than return with the information. What do you expect us to do without a location, just sail up and down the coast, looking for a city that has been able to hide itself for hundreds of cycles?!"

"Doro Amnach magic!" one of the dark elves grumbled.

Chansor just looked at Kaligor as the big cyclops studied the map for a moment more before throwing his hands up in frustration.

"Fine! Where do you think it is?" the general asked as he gestured towards the map.

Stepping up the table, Chansor looked down at the map and pointed to an area that looked like nothing more than a large forest not far south from where the disastrous battle had occurred.

"Here ... I believe she was near here!"

The rest leaned over to see where he was pointing at, but before anyone could argue, Kaligor lifted a hand for silence as he placed both hands on the table to look closer at Chansor.

"Why there?" Kaligor asked.

"This forest is old ... very old, and thick. Seems like a perfect place to hide!" Chansor looked at the elf, whose eyes tightened as

Chansor answered his question.

"Do you still trust her? She is, after all, the masters' favorite!" The elf's word stung Chansor, who, pulling in a large breath, pushed his chest out slightly. He knew he could kill everyone in the entire fleet within moments. Unfortunately, he would then have to face the wrath of the masters for killing their forces.

"Yes, I trust her. This is where their city is!" Chansor spoke clearly and a little more slowly than normal, wanting the cyclops to understand that he meant what he said.

Kaligor stared at Chansor for what seemed like minutes before he nodded slightly and looked back at the map, placing his finger on the area that Chansor had pointed out. He thought about what could happen if he attacked this city. The masters were clearly allowing him to launch an attack behind the gates, as the orcs from the Serngas came from the north … but if this city could be destroyed… an elvish city hidden for the ages, it could be his path to the glory. *Yes,* Kaligor thought to himself, *I want this. If I take this city and am still able to circle that tower to its south, the masters will praise and give me anything!*

No one had spoken as Kaligor pondered the map. Chansor didn't care what the cyclops decided. One way or another, he was going to find his sister and then destroy that city for causing them harm.

Kaligor finally lifted his head as his eye fell on the man standing quietly in the corner. "Captain, I want all sails pulled tight. We need the best possible speed to this area." Nodding, the man ran out of the room and began barking orders as Kaligor continued.

"Chansor, I want you keeping watch over the fleet for now. If these elves have a hidden city, they might also have hidden traps. The rest of you will return to your ships and pass along the word. Today we will hit the elves at their heart!"

The dark elves looked at Chansor for a moment and then nodded and departed, leaving Chansor and Kaligor alone.

"If the elves do have a city there, it has been quiet and kept secret for ages. I know you want revenge for your sister, and you shall have it. I want nothing but destruction and death there, my friend … Understand? My orcs need a victory!"

"I'll leave the port for you to deal with. The rest is MINE!" Chansor hissed, staring directly at the general.

Kaligor nodded, watching the man leave the cabin and transform into a dragon, rocking the ship slightly as he launched himself off the deck.

As the sound of flapping wings receded in the distance, Kaligor looked down at the map again and reached for his mug. Lifting it, he smiled. "I'm going to crush you all, once and for all!" he hissed as he drank.

Chansor only half-listened to the sounds below as he peered ahead at what looked like another storm forming until he began to hear something … something that made his skin crawl as he slowed himself down. Suddenly, the word reached his ears, making the massive dragon shake in the air.

"CHANSORRRR."

"Marn'azzi," he gasped. "Mother … she's awake!" he moaned, suddenly racked with fear, wondering what he should do now.

* * *

The orc general rode his beast quietly at the forefront of his army, pushing his chest out as he proudly listened to the horns and singing that came out the mouths of his orcs marching just behind him. He was a large orc compared to the others, almost two feet taller than the rest, with shoulders that made him very powerful, but like all orcs, he still wore his black cloak, tightly covering his face and body.

He never understood much about the lore that they were singing about; he never cared for it, but he knew enough that they were singing about glory in battle, something he wanted them to feel at this moment as they spread themselves across the open areas.

Word came from a few riders who had ridden farther south to check for any elven movement. He didn't want to take any chances that word might get to the elven camp about his army's approach. *Especially with these creations in tow*, he thought as he looked at the hundreds of dead beings slowly trampling through the grass. He was glad the masters designed them to not attack orcs. Else, the whole march would have been a nonstop fight.

As the riders rode up and circled him, he quickly ordered twenty of them to make their way across the plain and rendezvous with the orcs in the Sernga Mountains; he wanted them to know he was coming.

Yelling out, the orc riders quickly disappeared into the mist, leaving the army to continue its singing and marching.

"This will be the final destruction of those ugly things!" The words rasped through the orc's mouth as he envisioned the battle plan forming in his head. Mainly, attack fast and cause disarray in the elvish ranks.

A smile born of dreams of impending glory disappeared a moment later when he caught sight of an object flying in the air, coming towards him.

"Hmmm, come to me now!" the orc whispered as he watched the dragon moving closer by the moment. Moving was the only word he could think of to describe it. Something was definitely wrong with her. She seemed … wounded.

"How could anything …?" he rasped again, watching Elesha approach and fly directly over them to land hard on the ground about half a mile ahead of the marching army and roll onto the ground hard.

Kicking his beast forward, the general rode up and ran over just as Elesha burst into mist. A loud and echoing groan made the warrior stop in his tracks until finally the mist finally cleared, leaving the dark-clothed form of a dark-haired elven woman kneeling on the ground, holding an arm tightly against her chest.

Quickly approaching her, the orc knelt down, lifting her head slowly with a hand as he peered into her eyes. He almost felt the massive pain she was feeling.

"What happened?" the general whispered, looking at her and then to the south, wondering what could harm this creature.

"Elves have weapons that sting and hurt me!" Elesha's voice sounded of pain as she breathed roughly. The orc looked down at her arm. Blood was slowly leaking out of a large gash that looked like one made by a sword or something else sharp.

"How many do they have?" he asked as his military mind forgot about caring for the creature.

"I met a dozen of those flying horse things. I killed a few, but they were able to hurt me!" she rasped as a spasm of pain moved through her arm.

"They sound like the same beasts that fought your brother before. Don't recall him saying anything about them being able to harm him … They must have come up with something!" The general looked at nothing as he wondered where and how the elves had put something together when Elesha's quiet laugh made him look at her again.

"They have a city where they could have put it all together!" The word made the orc's mind race.

"City? What city? The elves do not have a city this far south." He reached into his side pack for a rolled parchment map that showed the northern lands of Marn. He quickly rolled it out to examine it, trying to find the city she had spoken about.

"I see no city, Elesha!" The orc held it out so she could see as he shook his head.

"It is there. I know because I attacked it, destroying and killing many of those damned creatures within. It is there!" Elesha closed her eyes as she felt yet another sharp pain move up from her arm.

"Point to it!" he whispered as he stepped closer to look at Elesha with the map. As Elesha looked up at the orc general, she clenched her teeth tightly, anger moving through her body at the embarrassment she was feeling at that moment. Letting go of her arm, she looked at the map for a moment and then touched the parchment, leaving a bloody fingerprint to mark the city's location.

"It is surrounded by heavy trees and high cliffs, hidden from the world, very large too!" Elesha looked into the general's eyes as she spoke quietly. "The elves built it to make sure those passing by would never discover it, but I did!" Tired of talking, Elesha closed her eyes once again, but this time, she pulled in a deep breath, forgetting about the world around her as she concentrated on her wounded arm.

Standing up, the general pondered the news of this hidden elven city between him and the Sernga Mountains. As he considered his options, he turned and signaled a healer to tend to Elesha, not realizing that she was already tending to her arm.

Her abilities gave her the means to repair herself, so long as she removed objects lethal to her human form first. It had taken her hours to remove that spear tip that pierced her head, and hours more to heal the hole in her head in dragon form before changing back to human form to heal her sight. By then, she knew it was time to move. She just hadn't anticipated how the blood loss from her arm would affect her.

"Attackkkk this cityyy!" The voice brought Elesha out of her trance as she looked up and saw the black-robed figure of their master standing quietly behind the orc general.

The general jumped at the sound of the voice, turning quickly to face the creature, feeling a bit taken aback that he could approach without his knowing.

"Away with you. The creature has no need for you," the master said to the approaching healers, whom he flung back twenty feet with the flick of his hand.

"A thousand pardons, Master. You … startled me. What did you say again?" the orc said tightly, trying to tamp down the humiliation he felt. He heard Elesha stand up behind him and felt the heat coming from her body, a sign that she was angry as well.

"I wantttt youuu to attackkk!" The eyes of the master glowed from under the hood as he turned his cloaked head towards Elesha.

"If I attack a city such as the one described, it will take resources, warriors and most of all, time, something I thought you didn't want wasted!" the orc angrily spoke through his teeth.

"Attackkkk!" the master repeated again, making the orc nod his head.

Turning to look at his army that had stopped to watch him and the dragon, he yelled clearly, "DID I SAY STOP?!! FORWARD … FOR TONIGHT, WE EAT FLESH OF ELF!!" A roar returned from his orcs as they began to march.

Turning, the general looked at Elesha's tired face. "Are you all right? Does General Kaligor know?" he asked, glancing back at the spot where the master had been standing to find him gone.

Elesha nodded. "I was able to send out the word, so …" The news brought a wide smile to the general's face.

"Ah, so that is why." The general looked south and nodded. "This is good. Our masters' plans are almost complete! It is almost over." Elesha did not know what to say. She had never thought past an end to the fighting.

They stood quietly, watching the army march by when Elesha smacked her forehead and looked up at the general.

"I almost forgot. The elves are no longer in the glen either; they have retreated south!" The orc's smile disappeared for a moment as his mind raced through the scenarios that suddenly looked possible

"Back to that city you speak of?" Elesha nodded.

"They are marching — more like running — to the south along this very road in fact!" Elesha grinned at the orc leader.

"Interesting." He smiled slightly from the corner of his mouth. If the elves were already retreating, it might be easier than he imagined to attack that city. The orc laughed slightly at the thought of how pompous elves always seemed, never believing they could be outwitted. Though, in fairness, no one ever had. Until Methnorick.

"After my army clears that glen where Lord Methnorick met

his death, we will move to finish that city. I do not want anything behind me when I move into the empire," The general said cheerfully as he turned back to Elesha, who was staring at the sky in terror.

"What is it? Where is it?" the orc grumbled as he squinted into the sky, seeing nothing unusual. Elesha, on the other hand, was beginning to sweat from her forehead. Her body shook slightly as she stood, staring towards the south.

Cocking his head slightly, the general wondered what could be frightening this creature that he had seen destroy whole buildings and kill off hundreds of men and elves in a single attack.

"What is it?" he asked again. He could see her lips moving like she was speaking, not to him but to anyone that might be able to hear.

"She has awoken. She has awoken …" Confused, the orc leaned in, hearing her repeat the words over and over again under her breath as she stared off into the sky, until the general, afraid for her sanity, turned to face her, grabbed her by the shoulders tightly, and pulled her closer so she could hear him.

"What are you saying, woman?" The orc's voice brought Elesha back to the situation as she blinked at the ugly face staring at her from under the hood.

"What?" she gasped as she brought herself back to where she was.

"Who has woken up? Woken up from what? What are you talking about?!"

Elesha's jaw shook slightly as she formed the words she had never thought to say. "Marn'azzi. My mother … She has awoken!"

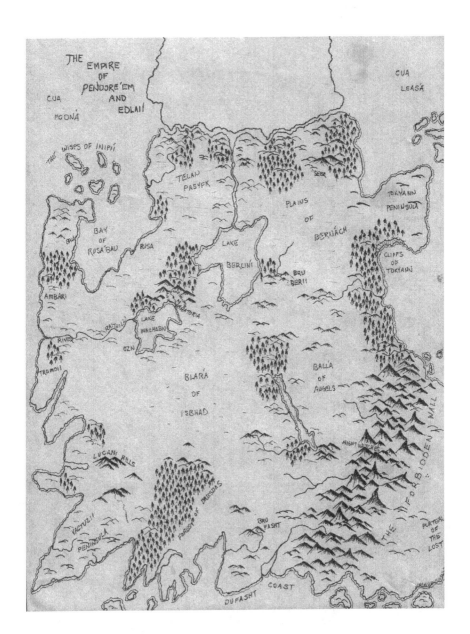

THE
EMPIRE
OF
PENDORE'EM
AND
EDLAII

CUA
FOONA

CUA
LEASA

THE WISPS OF INIPII

TELAI
PASYFK

SEBR

PLAINS
OF
BERNACH

TOKYANN
PENINSULA

BAY
OF
RUSA'BAU

RUSA

LAKE
BERLINI

CLIFFS
OF
TOKYANN

AMBARI

PATHILII

RIVER

TROMDII

OZN

LAKE
WACHABN

TORIA

BRU
BERII

BLARA
OF
ISBHAD

BALLA
OF
AUGELS

LUCANI HILLS

NIGHTWATCHES

THE FORBIDDEN WALL

VICTUZII
PENINSULA

FOREST OF PRISONS

BRU
FASHT

PLATEAU
OF
THE
LOST

COAST

DUFASHT

Chapter Twenty Seven

Soryn swam hard into the metal being, thrusting his blade deep into its chest so hard that his combined force of body and sword slammed the creature hard against the rock wall just behind him.

The two sea elves had decided that whatever these beings were doing inside their city secretly while others of their beast machines continued to destroy and kill his people, there had to be something to what they were doing.

Their attack had been hard and fast so that the metal beast that the beings were climbing into and out of didn't even have time to maneuver itself to return fire. Tibool sliced through one of the creatures coming and going from the metal beasts, causing reddish blood to pool out into the water around him as the body floated silently.

Tibool's anger rose as his blade cut through one of the weird tubes that came out of a pack on the back of one being's helmet, causing it to instantly shudder and scramble, fighting to repair it as bubbles rushed out of the tube.

Within moments of their attack, four of the beings hung in the water, dead from the quick strikes before the first burst of blueish fire exploded out of the metal beast to slam only inches from Soryn's head, causing the rock just behind him to turn blueish white and crack.

"Can you get into that beast, Tibool?" Soryn called over as he ducked around another being that was using one his own people's trident spears again him. He easily moved himself down and around the creature, and for a few moments, the two were taking hard slams on one another until Soryn's blade, being shorter, was able to cut the creature's helmet open as his blade cut through the metal.

"I think I can!" Tibool swam towards the opening that both had seen at the rear of the beast. Moving himself around the massive leg that was lifted up, he smiled, for the opening was wide open.

Snapping his feet, the sea elf shot up into the opening, watching for anything that could be inside waiting for him as he peered inside.

"There's nothing … It is empty?" Tibool's words sounded like a question more than a statement.

Soryn was about to take on one of the two last creatures that were outside the metal beast when he noticed behind him that the head was lowering to level the tube that released the blue fire right at him. He noticed it must be about to fire, as he could see within it a blueish glow appearing.

Reacting quickly, he ducked himself down onto the sand bottom of the seafloor, just as a blueish fire burst out of the tube, and luckily, he was quick enough as it streaked across the distance. Instead of hitting him, it slammed into the being trying to get at him with its spear. Instantly, the creature became enclosed in a state of death as its whole being turned blue and quickly became still.

"*Close!*" he spoke quietly as he moved himself over to the last creature. It seemed to realize it was alone as he watched it step back a few times as he moved to stand just below the head of the beast.

"Who are you?!" Soryn screamed, hoping the creature could understand him, but all he got was silence as it lifted its arms up to aim the spear directly at his chest as he moved closer by the second.

"Men … from the land up above!" The voice could be heard through the water by both Soryn and Tibool, who was still inside the beast.

Soryn recognizing the voice. Snapping the spear aside, he moved to plunge his sword into his chest as they danced around for a moment, trying to get at each other.

From the corner of his eye, he could make out a score of his brothers moving towards them. The beast also must have seen them, for seeing that there were more threats, it turned its massive head quickly, shooting off a few bolts of the blue fire, striking one elf instantly.

Soryn didn't have a chance to watch more as his blade was pushed away by this man creature, but that didn't stop him, as he could see that whatever was giving the creature the ability to breathe was also making it a bit hard for it to fight him off, making it slow.

"Don't kill it, Soryn ... We need him!" The words came as a surprise to the elf as he was lowering his blade, just about to make the kill.

He wondered what the captain was about, trying quickly to deflect a butt strike from the creature.

"We need to find out who they are and where they come from." Volkk's words drifted in as the elf sent three detachments of his warriors to fight and destroy the small numbers of the battle beasts that had escaped Marn'azzi's attack.

Soryn's anger was getting the best of him as he stabbed at the creature. "They killed our people without mercy ... They must ..."

"JUST DO IT!" Volkk's scream cut Soryn off quickly enough that the only thing he could do to make sure the creature was kept alive was to knock the spear away and knock him out with blow that sent him tumbling back.

Above Soryn another burst from the beast shot through the water, trying to get the reinforcements, as Volkk directed three of his warriors to make their way to the building that Soryn and Tibool had seen a bunch of the creatures move into.

Moving his mount and himself around as the fire flew past him, the captain swam over the beast's head and body so he could direct his attack at the neck area, which, from what he had seen a few times, was almost undefended by armor.

Keenzo, the young sea elf that Soryn had sent away to get Volkk, was swimming hard to catch up to the captain, who saw the young elf moving up.

"Hit that area there as hard as you can!" He pointed to the neck as Keenzo, nodding quickly and moving down, struck the area hard a few times with his blade. Volkk, now unable to see Soryn, hoped the sergeant was keeping the prisoner alive. The beast below him suddenly began to shudder as Volkk heard cheers as the blue fire quickly stopped. Volkk looked at the surprised Keenzo, who lifted his sword up, checking his blade like it had done something.

"What did you do, Keenzo?" Volkk, confused, swam over, seeing Keenzo shrug his shoulders.

"I kept hitting this area ... Maybe I ..."

"You can thank me later!" a voice interrupted the young elf as they both looked to the rear of the beast, seeing Tibool slowly drifting up, holding a huge smile on his face. "Oh, hi, Captain ... When did you get here?" The elf's smile made the captain's confusion disappear as he smiled as well and moved next to the happy elf.

"Ahhhh, what did you do, Tibool?" Volkk asked, seeing that Tibool was striding like he had won a game or something.

"I shut the beast off!" Tibool smiled from end to end as he crossed his arms. "I went inside and found what makes these things do what they do ... so I switched it off!" Tibool laughed proudly as the sea elves gathered closer to see the beast now standing still.

"Interesting!" was the only word that came to Volkk's mind as he smiled slightly at the elf, seeing how happy he was for doing what he did.

"Soryn ... Soryn, you still alive down there?" Volkk asked loudly as he remembered the sergeant.

"Alive and well, sir ... Come and speak to this creature before I kill it for looking at me!" Volkk, Keenzo and two others swam around and under the beast to find the sergeant standing, pointing his blade at the kneeling creature, who lifted its helmet towards the approaching sea elves.

"Captain Volkk … there are a few of those creatures still within this building … What do we do?" asked one of the warriors standing at the opening of the building he was sent to guard. The voice made the captain look over at the warriors waiting for his signal to burst in and attack them next.

"Keep them back if they decide to come out!" Volkk answered back after a moment's thinking of what to do with the creature looking at him.

Kneeling down, he looked into the creature's face. Volkk quickly put his sword in the seaweed-sewn scabbard, raising both hands up, hoping the man understood what he was doing, showing that he meant not to harm it.

"Who are you?" Volkk's gills opened and closed slowly on the sides of his neck as he stared at the creature. He could just make out what had to be eyes inside the helmet darting back and forth when the eyes suddenly looked directly at him, squinting slightly as well.

"Do you understand me?" Volkk asked again, hoping it could, but he was getting the impression he would have to take it to the upland chamber, where upland creatures met to talk … if it still was standing.

Seeing no response from the creature, Volkk stood himself up, and lifting an eyebrow slightly, he stared down at it and then at Soryn, who returned a look of confidence.

"*Now what, my friend?*" Soryn calmly asked.

"*If it is still there, take it to the upland chamber … Maybe there we can speak to it … Take four warriors with you. I do not want it to get away from you!*" Volkk placed a hand on the sergeant's shoulder, griping it slightly.

"*Sir!*" Soryn grabbed the creature by its arm and lifted it up, finding it a bit heavier than he thought, but when he did, the creature struggled in his grip as Volkk could sense it was looking directly at him.

Just then, the voice of the creature inside the metal helmet could be heard.

"Why fight us?" the voice echoed in the water.

"We fight because we must … You attacked my people … the oceans … You harmed us!" Volkk responded quickly, understanding that it could hear him through its mind, but from the helmet it was wearing, it must not have been able to return the thoughts.

"You will all perish!" the creature quickly answered. Everyone could hear the anger in the voice.

"Like yours did earlier when they were melted?" Tibool snapped back, smiling at the joke as a few in the group nodded, agreeing with his words.

"My master will make sure your people pay!" The creature seemed to be laughing when it answered this time. Volkk was wondering what these masters were.

"Master … Who is your master?" Soryn asked before the captain could respond.

The creature stiffened slightly and was quiet.

"Talkative thing to suddenly quiet up … These masters must be so scary!" Soryn reached out and gripped the being's shoulder.

"Take it away!" Volkk moved a hand across his face as he turned and looked at the door being guarded. Soryn acknowledged him and started to take his prisoner away, who struggled in the elf's grip for a moment, turning to look directly at Volkk.

"My masters are coming … You won't be able to stop them … They are coming!" The creature was quickly grabbed by the three elves accompanying Soryn, who quickly dragged it off as Volkk concentrated on the doorway, crossing his arms as he did.

"Now what, sir?" Keenzo asked, moving himself up to stand next to the captain.

"Care for our wounded and dead; repair the destruction of our city!" He looked at the young elf, who realized he had asked a stupid question.

"Mmm, yes, sir."

"We wait for those creatures that are inside … If they do not come out … we will have to go in!"

Volkk looked up and watched the prisoner being swum away by his warriors. As he thought about the creature's warning about these masters, a slight shudder moved up his back, and he wondered, *What are these masters, and where are they? … I'll have to speak to Mother about this news.*

"Tibool, my friend … Tell me about this beast, would you?" Volkk quietly asked, not looking at the warrior as he did. He looked at the dark doorway for a moment and then followed his warrior to the rear of the massive machine as he listened to the elf's explanation of what he did to shut it down.

* * *

The empress and her entourage rode off into the dim morning. Erek's wife stood at the top of the ramparts, looking on, when she heard a shuffle of movement coming up behind her. Without looking she crossed her arms across her chest as she watched the dust rise slowly into the sky and she lost sight of her new queen.

"Are they gone?" Nikuass quietly asked as he moved, placing his hands on the wooden wall, looking around as the sun's rays broke the clouds high above, turning them red and orange.

"Just left … She was in a rush to get moving, it seems, and didn't want to wait." she whispered, forgetting that it was just the two of them standing there now, as the troops that normally stood here were walking and keeping a patrol on another wall.

"Any news on what the cause was of all the animals going crazed over night?" Nikuass yawned as he leaned backwards to stretch out the night's cramps.

"None … It was interesting that every animal within and many outside the town just went … crazy for a bit." She let the last few words in her mouth disappear, as she was confident that she was alone, when she looked around, only to find Nikuass staring at her with curiosity.

"What?" Nikuass tilted his head when he noticed her uneasiness.

"Do you think she knows?" she whispered, pulling her heavy cloak around her neck as a cool wind moved by.

A small giggle left the lord of Chiconogo's mouth as he looked over to where the last of the dust caused by the hooves disappeared and then looked back at the woman's face, now hiding under fur, shaking his head slightly.

"No, Washa, my dear … I am sending a detachment to the camp just in case though!" Nikuass turned and strode over to the stairway that led down to the ground level.

She looked over the rail towards the courtyard, seeing the servants preparing horses, armor and weapons for a ride out. She looked back at the lord of the province as he walked away silently.

"Are you sure they are coming back? … The last time a man went that way …" She stopped speaking as Nikuass just waved her off as he made his way back to the main building. He had some parchments to sign before sending his queen the needed warriors she requested, which wasn't much, but he wanted her to think he was behind her on this war idea.

She turned to look back at the distant area where Erek had taken her new queen as she silently said a prayer to the gods for him to return safely, knowing that he was entering the most dangerous area of their province.

* * *

Ame-tora was confused, wondering why the flying creature hadn't attacked him but had quickly disappeared as he observed the large numbers of orcs dead lining the road. He only stopped for a moment to catch his breath and take a sip of water. Then he picked up his feet and continued to try to catch up with his friend Bennak when he ran around a rock, looking at a scene of a small skirmish that had happened, including a large number of orcs frozen like in ice, almost like what his people did to their enemies.

As he trudged farther down the road, the numbers of orc dead began to lessen, but the giant kept his grip on his axe tight, not knowing what could be around the corner. *Orcs are tricky!* he thought as he almost ran over a dead horse. As he moved past, he noticed that it was one from his group. He looked around for any sign of the rider, but seeing no body and no blood, he sucked in a breath and ran as fast as his big legs could carry him

Got to find Bennak ... Wish they would slow down, he thought as his breath quickened. He ran down the road, coming over the next hill to find that the road continued to make its way into the hill range, cutting through large rocks as it weaved around, but seeing no sign of his group. Not having the best hearing or smell, the frost giants relied on their sight more than anything, so as he continued moving through the gully, he noticed movement to the west of the road.

"Orcs!" he whispered as he watched them moving along cracks and small gullies, trying to get down to the road, when he caught movement of something else along the road.

"Frost Giants!" he gasped under his breath at the sight of his people. They appeared to be fighting off groups of orcs.

He moved forward towards the frost giants as fast as he could just as two orcs flew out from behind a large boulder, not to attack him but in trying to make their way behind his people.

"Hello, there!" He lifted his axe up as they turned to see who was speaking to them.

All Ame-tora saw was their wide eyes looking up at him as he swept his axe down, cutting their heads completely off in one quick snap, leaving the giant to watch their decapitated bodies collapse to the ground. He looked up to see where they both had come from and to determine if there were more coming. Seeing nothing, Ame-tora turned to run down the road towards his fellow giants as he heard grunts and yells from the battle on the road.

Coming over the last small hill in the road, Ame-tora saw his chance to maybe turn the tide when a large group of orcs burst out of some bushes directly in front of him. Thinking quickly of the word needed to release his icy ability, he stomped across the dirt road, getting closer by the second, watching them charge at his people.

He saw one of the giants take a direct hit by a spear to the side of his body as a tremendously painful yell erupted. He lifted his hand up, pointing the palm at the center of the orcs charging ahead of him.

Releasing the spell in his mind, he felt the energy move quickly down his arm. His hand felt suddenly cold and jolted him backwards as the bright white/blue ice burst out of his hand to streak across the distance between him and the orcs.

Still believing they had the element of surprise on their side, the orcs lifted their swords as they roared battle cries when, suddenly, the yells stopped

Those still battling the giants suddenly stopped to find their comrades encased in a block of ice, and before any could react and defend themselves, one orc was cut down from behind by one of the frost giants. One by one, the giants quickly cut the last of the orcs down within seconds.

"Brother!" Ame-tora cried out, nodding his head at the others, who nodded back and grabbed the last orc by the head, who screamed a high-pitched scream of terror as the giant quickly ripped the body in half. The wounded giant then fell to his knees. Another stepped over to care for him as Ame-tora made his way towards his brothers.

"Brother Gunbaater ... I am glad to see your axe covered in orc blood!" Ame-tora smiled at the warrior, who turned to see who was speaking. Gunbaater's reaction was one of good tidings, for a frost giant anyway.

"Ame-tora ... brother ... We thought you died within that man city." Gunbaater put his hands on Ame-tora's shoulders, squeezing them as Ame-tora quickly told him what happened back at Brigin'i.

"Interesting ... Now is not the time to speak of tales of battle, my brother ... We need to make our way south now!" The captain of the frost giants released his friend and turned to ensure that their brother that had been wounded during the skirmish was at least able to stand with the help of another.

"You live, brother?" Gunbaater walked over to look at the giant, who just grunted.

"He will live, brother … but we need a healer before the sun goes to the west!" the giant holding his wounded brother spoke for him.

"Brother Rabitan … how far?" Gunbaater turned to look at the group's tracker, who at that moment was cutting off the head of a dead orc, placing it on the point of a broken spear he found, holding it up like a trophy.

Being small gave Rabitan the ability to run and move quicker than the rest. While most of his kind chose to wear armor along their legs and torso, Rabitan chose just to wear shoulder metal, always saying that it was the gods he would have to protect himself from, not the little creatures that roamed Marn.

Smiling at what he had just done, Rabitan turned to see his captain staring at him, waiting for an answer.

"Sorry, brother … We need to cross through the Valley of the Ever Night, but we should be there by sun's end," Rabitan spoke knowingly, as he was one of the few of his kind to venture beyond the borders of his people back within the Pilo'ach Mountains.

Gunbaater clutched his jaw tighter, knowing that this valley was not a deep nor a long valley, but it held no light and was famous for ambushes.

"It shouldn't be a bother for us, brother … We are the masters of the mountains, are we not?" Gunbaater boasted loudly and lifted his arms up slightly. As he did so, many of the giants slowly nodded as he continued, "Do we not cause fear for those in the dark?" He looked at each giant in front of him before saying, "Let us move then … We need to be at the gate of the men creatures!" Gunbaater joined in as everyone cheered, all raising their weapons high into the air.

Quickly, their wounded brother began his journey with help of two others as the rest began to make their way down the road, leaving Gunbaater and Ame-tora alone for the moment to look west up at the mountain passes they both knew were filled with orcs.

"What is at the men's gate, brother?" Ame-tora asked quickly, as he was sure he could see movement within the rocks.

"Men are assembling there behind a gate the man creatures built … General Summ of the forest elves asked us to go ahead to clear the road." Gunbaater looked at his brother, who raised an eyebrow at the comment.

Ame-tora then looked around the ground, seeing dead orcs, many frozen in ice.

"Good job!" Both laughed at the joke as they turned to catch up to their frost giant brothers. Gunbaater moaned that at any moment more orcs could attack again, so they kept their eyes open to the west for any movement.

***

Ribbwa'nor Glen had been quiet for a day since the elves left to gather at God's Haven. Now, thousands of creatures burst out of the forest in the eastern part of the glen, all running out onto the glen that opened up to the grasslands of the wide-open glen itself. Their war cries made the ground shake as the thousands of voices echoed within Ribbwa'nor.

Moments before these thousands of orcs came out of the trees, hundreds of the already dead had been moving through the glen, spreading out onto the grass fields, traveling south.

Every creature erupted in loud roars of pleasure, believing they had scared away the elves. The northern entrance to the glen grew crowded as large bodies of giants slowly moved through to join in the cheering as a few left the machines they were pulling to stand still for a while.

High above, watching the activity below while sitting upon his horse quietly, the orc general looked proudly at his army below. He didn't realize that he was standing on the very space where just a few days prior both Bennak and Ame-tora stood, watching the elven camp and thinking it was an orc camp instead.

"Your orders, sir?" A dark elf standing at the edge already knew the answer even before he asked the question, but he wanted to make sure.

The general gave him a look as he turned to look down at the army below them cheering and waving their banners around.

"Let them celebrate a while longer. Then assemble them to march … We have many elves to kill!" The orc held the reins of his mount tightly as the dark elf relayed the orders when they were covered by the shadow of Elesha slowly making her flight over the rise to fly down over the orcs, who upon seeing the dragon, cheered even more.

The general watched the beast fly down and then drift up into the sky as she circled around slowly in the air. Not understanding Elesha's warning about her mother, he couldn't tell if she was still shaken or worried, but he didn't care. The master would be able to take care of this mother like they had with all other creatures.

"Give the order!" he snapped angrily, realizing that he was wasting time thinking of some mythical creature.

The dark elf, feeling the anger, ran back quickly to jump up on his own horse as he reined it around and rode down the trail. He yelled for the army to gather itself and prepare to march, quickly leaving the orc general to steam for a moment longer as he thought to himself.

You gave me the ability to bring my sword to the elven scum … He stared directly at the sky like it was going to answer him back.

For a moment, nothing came out of the sky except wind and small drops of rain, making the orc wonder if his masters were listening or dismissing his anger when a voice almost made him cry out in pain as a voice erupted in his head.

"You aree in chargeee of alll before youuu!" The words from the masters sent a chill down the orc's back, but he kept the fear hidden as best he could as he continued to listen.

"Attackkk elvennn cityyy … Destroy ittt and continueee to the empireeee!" It almost sounded like a there were a few talking as the voice echoed into his head, bringing him to lift his chin up slightly as his anger rose up again.

"Where is Kaligor, then … Does he know of this city?" The general had been wondering where the cyclops and his fleet were.

"Heeee knowssss … He will be withhh you soonn, General … Attack and heeee will be thereeeee!" The words struck, bringing a smile to the corner of his mouth.

Tilting his head slightly, the general quietly growled to his masters for the information and good news as he turned himself back to look down at the field below, seeing the columns of orcs slowly being assembled together into their familiar formations that would soon be marching.

"So … you have left the field where you beat Methnorick to retreat south … What is your plan, elf?" he whispered to himself as he waited a moment longer as horns echoed across the glen.

"Upon the darkness, I ride to you!" the orc cried out as he kicked the hind of his horse hard, causing it to bolt down the trail that would lead to the glen and the field below.

Chapter Twenty Eight

The landscape was colder and drearier than Shermee thought a land could be. Drifts of snow flew constantly, and she saw some type of animal moving along the ridges of some of the hills, watching and tracking her group.

No one had spoken since passing the huge tree that Erek had left them at. Their parting was a bit tense, as Shermee tried to convince him to continue with them. However, for the first time since entering Chiconogo, she could see that these men were deathly afraid of going farther.

A few hours later, her male warriors were hardly any better, as the road they travelled began to show a marked increase of weeds and branches, as if it hadn't been used in a long time.

Now Shermee could hear whispers from a few of her warriors as they kept looking left and right. Others even began to fidget in their saddles, holding onto the handles of their swords, as if expecting to be attacked.

Shermee noticed that she and the other females weren't feeling the same uneasiness. *Maybe it is true that these Nightwitches only bewitch men*, Shermee thought, looking at Jacoob, who clearly was nervous as well.

Her thoughts were interrupted by a loud howl, almost a scream, from their right, which made everyone unsheathe their blades.

"We are being tracked!" one of men whispered as Shermee looked to where the howling was still echoing from. She could see just over the rise dark shapes moving along with them but staying just out of sight.

"Keep calm everyone. Whatever they are, if they wanted to attack us, they would have done so already. After all, they have been following us since we left the Blue Tree!" Shermee said a bit louder than normal. She had hoped the figures would have shown themselves by now so she could show the men that there was nothing to worry about. Instead, the figures had kept to the bushes.

"So, you knew all along?" one of the women warriors to her right asked quietly with a shy smile. Shermee smiled as she looked at Aamee. A fierce warrior, she was the only woman in the group who didn't wear a helmet. The sides of her head were shaven, revealing an intricate tattoo along one side of her skull that reflected the history of her family and house within the empire. Shermee could only imagine the pain involved, as the tattoo reached past her collarbone before disappearing under her tunic. The story was that Aamee became a warrior for one reason only: to bring an end to the practice of tattooing women of her family, which she did by killing her father and uncle in combat in order to take over the family.

"Of course, I knew. I grew up with four older brothers. I learned how to spot shadows in corners early on," Shermee answered with more confidence than she felt. However, they needed to continue, and truth be told, she was getting a bit tired of the dreariness herself. Which is why it was now urgent to find these Nightwitches, wherever they were hiding.

"Since you, too, have a good eye, Aamee, why don't you and Jacoob ride ahead and see what's over that ridge!" Aamee nodded as she looked over at Jacoob, who, showing the same fear as the other men, nodded quickly, kicking his horse forward to catch up with Aamee.

As the two rode off, Junack took Aamee's place beside Shermee and leaned over so she could speak to her mistress somewhat privately. "Empress, the men are clearly frightened. It would be funny anywhere else, but … with the creatures we are meeting …" the woman whispered.

"Spit it out, Junack," Shermee pressed.

"Well, ma'am, I am worried about them being liabilities. If they cannot conquer the fear gripping them …"

Shermee nodded as she looked at the warrior. Junack was almost as large as some of the men. Shermee had seen her fight back in Brigin'i during her father's games and now could see the one item that made her different than them: her chest armor, which clearly told others that she was a woman.

"What is your counsel, then?" Shermee whispered back as she saw Aamee and Jacoob disappear over the ridge far ahead along the road.

"Let the men camp here while the rest of us continue on!" Junack smiled, knowing the arguments she would hear.

The empress turned slightly in her saddle to look at the men who still carried their swords out, ready for anything, as their heads darted back and forth, looking for anything hiding in the trees and bushes that lay around them. The howling continued to echo.

Thinking of her next move, she took in the height and massive presence of the Forbidden Mountains slowly emerging ahead. She wondered if she and the group would have to go into them to find these Nightwitches. Worse, how much longer could the men be in such a state? She was thinking of sending them all back to Petrikbur when she spied a rider on the road coming at them. A moment later, she recognized Aamee, riding hard.

One look at Aamee's troubled face was all the warning Shermee needed, and she braced herself for the bad news.

"Empress," Aamee nodded, "the way is clear, but you are not going to like what you see."

"What do you mean?" Shermee was getting fed up with half answers.

"Please, Empress. All she would say is that you must see to understand."

"She?" Shermee asked, raising an eyebrow. Shermee kicked her horse and galloped towards the ridge, pulling her reins as everybody else caught up with her and gasped at the sight before them.

"Gods be with us!" one of the men whispered as Shermee's mouth dropped open.

"In all the lands!" Trofen whispered and then looked at his empress. "Empress, clearly that lord spoke the truth. These Nightwitches are not to be played with!" His voice sounded shaky to Shermee as she looked around.

Shermee thought about Junack's advice and made her decision. "Trofen, you and the men will stay here and camp. Keep watch. I will continue on with the women."

"Empress!" Trofen, taken aback, tried to argue his new orders. "We came with you to protect you. Not just sit and watch!"

Shermee smiled at the young warrior. "I understand why you came here. But don't you see? This place is clearly affecting you against your will, making you uneasy to the point of madness. No, I will not have it when it is not necessary. I came here to broker a compromise, a task that will be far more difficult if your uneasiness leads to fighting the first instance that we meet them. So, please stay here and be ready for anything." Shermee swept a hand to the ground to indicate where they should stay.

"Empress, please. How can you expect us to leave you traveling through this?" Trofen pointed.

Shermee had already seen the reason for his stubbornness. Covering the ground everywhere were hundreds, if not thousands, of corpses tied and stacked to the ground. Some burned slightly. The wood was blackened by the fires giving off smoke that hung along the ground like fog. Everywhere she looked, a burnt figure almost seemed to be moving, sending a shiver down her back.

She continued to look, not listening to the argument that Junack was having with the men as she looked around for Jacoob and Aamee.

"Empress! Empress!" the words were repeated until she looked at the man speaking to her.

"Yes, Sir Reo?" she asked as he removed his helmet so he could speak openly to her.

"Empress, these dead must be a sign to keep people away. Shouldn't that be enough for you to understand that we need to return?" Reo's voice was sounding more and more hysterical.

"I understand your feelings about going ahead, which is why I have already decided that you and the other men will stay here. Junack and the other women will accompany me from here. If anything does come at us, they will be able to protect me!" Junack smiled back as Shermee nodded her way.

Shermee raised her hand to silence them. "No more discussion. Make camp here. If we are not back by the new sun's morning fall, then you can decide: ride ahead or return to town. But do not move from this spot until the sun is over everything, understand?"

The men looked at each other and nodded. Shermee and Junack swung around and rode ahead, followed by six other women.

Trefor watched for a moment and then looked at Reo, seeing the man shake his head as he watched their empress ride ahead.

"Are you going to stay, Reo, or return?" Trefor swallowed, still trying to keep the weird fear under his skin.

"I do not understand our new empress. It is like she wants to die or something. We should have brought more troops with us as well!" Reo said, looking around as if spooked.

"I don't think she wants to die. She seems to have something in mind with these Nightwitches. Meanwhile, we have our orders, so let us break out that jug I know you brought of old Jess' spirits, yes?" Trefor wanted the older warrior to relax a bit and knew he had succeeded when Reo laughed out loud, having been caught.

* * *

Standing on top of the wall of Blath 'Na City, the four beings that Kaligor called the masters looked to the south, quietly whispering to each other about the changing situations as the city behind them echoed loudly like a machine readying for war.

"Sheee iss aliveeee."

"Howww? … We killeddd ittt many cyclesss aggooo … Howww?"

"Nooo maattterrr … Weee diddd it onceee …"

"Weee cannn doo ittt againnn, yesss!"

Silence among the four came for a few moments while the sounds of Blath 'Na behind moved past them as creatures they had brought in the holds of the ships worked hard to build the city to what the masters wanted. Sounds of hammering of metal could be heard when, finally, one of the black-robed beings turned to look into the city itself.

"Weee haveee herrr childrennn withhh ussss … Theyyy fighttt forrr ussssss …!"

The others turned slowly to observe the city as they continued the conversation.

"Eleshaaa speaksssr of a hiddennn elvennn cityyy … General Kaligorrrr willll attackkk itt with Chanssssorrr … who will joinnn?"

Their hoods moved slightly as each one thought about the idea. The first that looked at the city turned to look at its companions as its hands slowly moved out of the sleeves to clasp in front of its robes.

"Joinnnn Kaligorrr, I willl!" The words drifted out as the other masters nodded under their hoods, mumbling that they agreed to the idea.

"What of our ourrrr battle beastsss? … Have they dessstroyedd the elvennn sea kingdomm?"

"Theyy attackkk frommm the east and are fighting as we speakkkk!"

"Findddd the crysstalsss they mussst!"

"It will be found!"

With no words passing for a few minutes, slowly the beings moved themselves in a circle to lift their arms up, clasping the others' hands as sparks of blue and white light streaked and jumped around them until, finally, a bright ball of light covered the masters.

To the creatures working hard within Blath 'Na, all they saw was a bright ball of light that flashed brightly and then disappeared. None having a clue about who or what it was, they continued their tasks of getting the city ready.

* * *

Quinor pored over the news that the northern elves had won the field against this fake emperor that was trying to conquer the lands beyond the ravine, but now another report came in. He read about another army of orcs, larger than the first, that was seen marching south.

Commander Tevanic walked around the fortress, trying to ensure all defenses were strong and in place as Quinor reviewed reports to determine the best course of action.

Even though it was half a mile or so from the bridge that cleared the ravine to the north, it was enough space for an assaulting army to assemble, so Quinor ordered archers to hide on the stone walls that lined the road leading to the Father Gate. These walls were hidden within the heavy foliage of trees and acted like a funnel, with the Father Gate at the southern end of the funnel, where, if attacked by a large force, the archers would be moved out so they could strike the edge of any attacking group.

History, he was told, spoke of many times in the past when the orcs tried to attack the gate. None had ever broken the gate, but Tevanic had informed him that morning that orcs might have found another way into the empire, as General Vana had to send out a cavalry unit to counter their movement far to the south, and this had been the first time they were seen in the empire in many cycles.

The gate stood open as Quinor strode through, taking in the thickness of the wall themselves. *At least two men in length,* he thought as he placed his hand on the cold stone as he walked by.

Looking up, he could see some warriors looking down at him. Each man held a bow, but he had seen spears lining the ramparts when he was inside, enough arms to slow down anything.

Turning to move himself north, Quinor walked to admire the construction and planning that had gone into making this site battle ready. Built many cycles ago by elves and dwarven engineers, each bridge crossed the massive ravine but was in itself a work of art.

It clearly is amazing work of those little creatures, Quinor thought smiling to himself as he looked back at the tower and the bridge beyond. "Someday, Shermee ... you need to see this place!" he whispered.

As Quinor looked up at the tower, lost in thought, the sounds of metal escaped him.

He leaned back to stretch his back slightly, looking up at the mountains to see what else might be moving around, when his eyes squinted slightly upon seeing what had to be smoke of some kind rising up from within the mountains.

His arms lowered slowly as he squinted, looking at the smoke, when his ears caught the echo of familiar sounds of battle armor drifting towards him.

"ORCS!" Quinor whispered, looking down at the road, wondering how far away they were. Who could tell? Sounds could travel for miles before being seen in a place like this.

Turning himself quickly around, Quinor ran back to get through the gate, as he could see a few troops were leaning against the interior section of the wall, lazily keeping watch.

Seeing Quinor running towards them, they grabbed their spears up as the guardian approached, screaming something that they couldn't hear. They looked at each other, wondering what he was yelling about, until they caught the first word clearly: "ORC!"

"Orcs ... orcs are approaching!" he yelled as he got close.

"To arms!" the sergeant of the four men on guard, a tall, older man with long gray hair, yelled back into the courtyard, which responded with loud yells as Quinor stopped to bend over, breathing hard from his hard run in front of the guards.

"Sir ... sir, how many did you see?" one of the guards asked, placing his hand on Quinor's shoulder and bending slightly over to, hopefully, hear the answer.

Quinor pulled in two more breaths before looking up at the man as his chest heaved slightly. "I didn't … but I heard sounds of battle armor within the mountains, and it sounded like it was moving this way." Quinor leaned himself back slowly as a pouch of water was handed to him. Thanking the man, Quinor sucked in a few long gulps of the cool water as he turned to look back up the road and the mountains beyond.

"Whatever is coming from within those mountains … it sounds like it's going to lead to a huge battle!" Quinor stared at the road that disappeared beyond his sight as the other guards moved to close the gate. They moved the wooden devices that were used to hold the massive doors closed and just waited near them for the word to come down from the commander. Quinor hoped he hadn't caused an early alarm as he continued to stare north.

* * *

Volkk's warriors blocked the doorway to the building as they tried to understand what this newfound enemy was searching for within the building. As he was pondering, he received word that all of the beasts had been destroyed within the city.

"Sir … we received a message from those beings inside," one of his warriors said, floating over to get Volkk's attention as he stood looking at the war beast for a moment longer, as if trying to see if it could work.

Leaning down, he grabbed his spear and followed the sea elf over to where a group of his elves had positioned themselves behind a large wall that had been part of another building before the attack.

"What message have they sent?" Volkk asked as he moved up to look over the edge towards the doorway now covered by rocks to make it hard for those inside to escape.

"It was a rock that was tossed out … Here!" One of the warriors leaned over, grabbing the small rock and handing it over to the captain. Volkk could see the rock had writing on it, which made him groan as he turned it over, taking in the writing.

"This was all they sent out?" The warrior nodded yes back to Volkk as his gills flapped.

"Send a message to the clerics ... We need Gulbra here quickly ... I think he is the only one that can read this." The elf next to Volkk nodded and quickly swam off to relay the message himself as Volkk stared over the wall at the building that hid this new enemy.

"I need a volunteer!" Volkk asked as he turned to look at the few warriors.

At first, none spoke until, finally, a young warrior rose his hand up, smiling gently back at Volkk. Volkk smiled back and nodded his approval. The warrior floated himself closer Volkk. When he got close enough, Volkk took his spear and sword belt off him.

"Hopefully, not having these will show that we mean to talk and not attack!" Volkk smiled at the elf, who, he saw, was a bit nervous.

"What should I do, sir?" The words, even in his mind, sounded a bit shaky as Volkk placed his hands on the elf's shoulders.

"When you get close enough that they can see you, raise your hands up to show you have no weapons ... See what they do. We need to know how many are in there as well, but if they speak to you, find out what they want." The elf smiled and nodded. Floating up, he swam over the wall and slowly made his way closer to the door, leaving the rest of the elves to peer over the wall, watching their comrade.

"You know he's going to die, sir?" The whisper caught Volkk nodding gently.

"I know. I'm trying not to think of that, but I need to know what they want if possible." Volkk looked at the elf, who returned the stare, when Volkk caught the sight of a group of his comrades swimming towards them.

"Reinforcements ... Good. I need the help here!" Volkk took a quick look at the young elf's progress and then moved to meet the approaching group of sea elves.

"Captain Volkk, sir," one of the elves whispered as he knelt down.

"Sir Gest, you're alive." Volkk saluted the warrior. He was one of the elder warriors that once guarded the central council.

"What can my warriors do here to help? I was told they were needed here!" The warrior clasped Volkk's arm as they whispered.

"We are waiting for my friend Gulbra to translate this." Volkk lifted up the rock. The old warrior took it and looked at it for a moment longer.

Gest, one of the few that wore his hair in braids instead of letting it flow, was one of the leaders of the council guardian detachment. Volkk could see that the old warrior had taken a beating in the battle defending the city, for the right side of his face was covered in a seaweed wrap, which held a wound tightly. The elf's armor just below his chest was burned as well.

"This writing … I have seen it once, but I cannot remember where!" Gest looked up as Volkk nodded that he understood.

"Try to remember where, sir." Volkk took the rock as Gest gestured to his warriors, who were waiting close by for orders.

Turning back, Gest nodded as one of his warriors handed him one of the sea elves' prized spears. "I believe it was in the Grand Atheneum that I last saw it, and if it were still standing …" The old elf's eyes told the captain the rest of the news.

Volkk's eyes grew larger when he saw his face. "The Grand Atheneum … gone?"

Gest nodded gently as Volkk's face tightened. He cursed this enemy for destroying the grandest of grand buildings of knowledge known upon Marn. "They will pay for that and more!" Volkk clenched his fist tightly when one of his warriors interrupted their discussion.

"Sir … he's at the door!" a warrior whispered, interrupting the two. Volkk and Gest moved themselves to look over the wall to see that, indeed, that elf was now just standing in front of the slightly blocked doorway.

"What's he doing there?" Gest whispered as he also saw the massive battle beast standing still on the far side of the open area before him.

"We caught a few of those beings leaving that machine there and cornered them within that building ... So far, they haven't tried to escape, but one of those creatures we caught told me they are looking for something, and I think they will try to fight their way out," Volkk answered back without moving his sight from the young elf, who, he had been told a few moments earlier, was named Domach.

Volkk and Gest didn't see another group of elven warriors move behind them as they were concentrating on the warrior ahead of them, so they didn't notice that, finally, Gulbra had been brought to the area — alive but in pain. As he was gently placed on the sea floor not far away, another elf handed him the rock. The old elf moaned upon seeing the writings on it.

"How are you, old friend? ... How does our city fare?" Volkk said over his shoulder. As he watched, Domach just stood with his hands high above his body, still noticing that nothing was happening.

"Bad, Captain ... very bad, but luckily a good portion of our people were able to get out of the city before the attack ... Many of the council are still active, but many of our people were killed." Gest's words sounded sorrowful as Volkk closed his eyes for a moment to send out a prayer for those that had died.

"Get that boy back, NOW!" Gulbra screamed suddenly as Volkk turned to see his friend kneeling on the rocky ground, holding the small rock that had the writings on it.

"What?" Volkk smiled, confused.

"Get that warrior back here!" Gulbra repeated, gesturing for Volkk to do something quickly.

Volkk, still confused, trusted what his friend was saying, so he turned himself around and jumped up onto the wall so Domach could clearly hear and see him.

"DOMACH ... DOMACH, GET BACK HERE NOW!!!!" Volkk yelled, catching the elf's attention. The young sea elf, hearing his captain's voice, turned, showing his confusion at seeing Volkk gesturing quickly with his arm, waving to return.

Domach looked back at the door and saw nothing moving within it, so taking his captain's order to come back, he took one last look at the doorway, and then, lowering his hands, he moved to return to the safety of the wall when a brightness covered his eyes.

As Volkk, Gest and a few others who were watching jumped forward in reaction, they watched Domach suddenly freeze as bright red light, all-too familiar now to them, erupted out of the doorway and enveloped Domach.

"DOMACHHHHHH!!!!" Volkk screamed loudly, his gills flapping hard as he breathed in quickly through his scream as the young elf was instantly killed. Gest turned and gestured for those warriors moving up quickly to ready themselves.

Volkk, feeling terrible that he sent the young elf to his death, turned to see the elves around him waiting for orders to do something when his laid eyes on his friend. "Gulbra ... what just happened?" Volkk moved quickly over to the old elf, who, he saw, was still trying to recover from their earlier meeting with Marn'azzi.

"Volkk ... so many things to tell you, but ..." Volkk saw he was at a loss for words now as he stared at his friend.

"Volkk ... we need to move quickly ... This rock has a message on it!" Gulbra whispered.

"What ...?" Gest floated up to join the conversation as Gulbra nodded yes gently.

"It's just one word ... one in a language never spoken within the ocean darkness." Volkk looked at Gest.

"This is not the time, my friend, to go over history. What does it say, my friend?" Volkk's words were gentle, but he was getting impatient as Gulbra lifted his hand up, turning the rock around so the two could see the scribble on it.

Gulbra lifted the rock to look at the scribbles and then at his friend. "It says one word: 'Die!'"

Chapter Twenty Nine

*K*aligor moved himself to the middle of the formations of his troops, ordering them to stay quiet. He didn't want anything in the area to hear what was coming.

The orcs shifted in their boots on the decks of the ships, all tense and ready to pour off the ships and attack this hidden city they had only just learned about. Grumbles slowly drifted across the ship as each creature stared through the fog that Chansor had been able to create as the sun slowly rose to their left.

"You think they can see us?" a dark elf asked, leaning over and looking at the general.

"If they did, we would know it. They would be ringing bells or something to that effect," Kaligor mumbled back as he heard the flapping wings of Chansor high above them. He wanted the dragon to come out of the fog just as his ships landed. The elves, if they had any defense along the shoreline, would be showing themselves, which was a perfect time to roast them, he thought, smiling to himself.

The water slapped hard against the hulls of the ships as they quietly cut through the dark water. Above each ship, the sails were slowly pulled down as the sailors whispered to each other for quiet, worried that any sound might carry across the water. The men knew that elves could hear for miles, so any unknown sound coming from the ocean might give them away.

"The army should be close … very close to the towers that Chansor's sister spoke about. If not, when we hit the beaches, we might for a short time be getting the full brunt of the elvish counter defenses," Kaligor whispered back to the dark elf and then looked over, seeing the blue eyes looking back at him. "You know what to do when we land?"

"As your forces hit the wall, my people will get behind them, sir. We are good at that. Just keep that fog up covering us, and we will win the day, sir!" the elf said. Kaligor nodded and looked back at the ocean.

The water slapped a few times as the cyclops listened to the birds flying gently overhead, gulls that he knew only traveled within a few miles of the land. *We are so close,* he thought, swallowing.

* * *

"Look at that beast there ... It is massive!" Bataoli watched the dragon move far ahead of the marching army below as the Pegasus and the elven captain kept themselves in the clouds, trying to understand where the creature was going.

"God's Haven has been on alert since the first flying beast appeared, but now we need to get what we know back to them without getting caught ourselves," Lugtrix mumbled as he maneuvered himself around and quickly flapped his thick wings as the two slowly rose into the air with ease.

"No, we must find out where that dragon is going. That will tell us more than this army approaching ever could," Bataoli countered. "So, just a bit longer?"

"All right, just a bit longer," Lugtrix answered, for their relationship was one of cooperation and friendship. They flew on, watching the dragon from a distance as it flew towards the sea.

Soon, they saw the dragon they tracked fly out over the sea, where it joined another black dragon that circled high above. Looking down through the fog below, Lugtrix could just make the form of ships. "There are ships below!" he almost screamed.

"What? Which direction are they headed in?" Bataoli asked.

"Straight towards God's Haven," Lugtrix answered.

"We must get back to God's Haven and warn—" Bataoli just had time to grab the mane of his friend before Lugtrix took off toward the elven city, flying as fast as he could.

As he held on, Bataoli looked left and right for any signs that either dragon followed them and sighed with relief that he didn't have that threat to complicate matters.

* * *

The large detachment sent from Manhattoria to scout and station themselves along the ravine that divided the lands came slowly out of the pass that lay south of the Gate of the Eye, one of four towers that the empire had built hundreds of cycles ago. The Eye Tower was built to keep an eye not on those elves or men that lived in the north but on the orcs that lived in the Sernga Mountains that lay just north of the tower just beyond the ravine.

Their city, one that the orcs called home, was situated deep within the mountain range, but the tower smoke from their fires could be easily seen, so the empire had kept a watchful eye. When the smoke rose heavily, it told the warriors that the orcs were on a war path.

As the cavalry rode closer to the tower, the commander rose a hand to stop his men. He squeezed his eyes, straining as he tried to observe what he saw before him. He looked at the elf that pulled up next to him, giving him a look of surprise.

"Am I seeing this right?" the man asked, looking forward and then noticing the elf nodding that he was seeing the same thing. The man waved over two of his scout runners as he continued to look ahead until the men moved up next to him.

"You …" He pointed at the one to his right. "Go find the general and inform him … the Gate of the Eye has fallen to the orcs. You …" He pointed to the other. "Go check the Gate of the Hand, search it out and come back. We will be waiting in the pass behind us here." He pointed behind them. "I want to know if that tower is still ours or not."

Quickly, both men kicked their horses, riding quickly off. The commander hoped they weren't seen as he waved for his men to turn themselves around and quickly rode back up into the pass.

"No wonder we never heard from those men stationed there. They must have all been massacred," the elf spoke as he turned his horse around and looked back at the two massive towers. Usually dark from the cold wet stones, now bright fires were flaming at the base of each tower along with what looked like hundreds of orc warriors moving around the perimeter of the place. He could see that just above the gate hung the familiar banner of those orcs that lived within the Sernga Mountains: black cloth with an arm of a man cut off and bleeding.

* * *

Volkk ordered everyone to leave the area. They had killed one of his warriors without a thought, and he suspected that they were going to try again.

Volkk was joined by Olen, who informed him that all battle beasts had been destroyed but no prisoners were taken alive.

Nodding, the captain grabbed his spear and lifted himself up and over the wall, slowly approaching the opening of the building. He formed a plan quickly as he moved in front of the door. *I will tell them what they are dealing with and that they have no way of escaping and to surrender. See if that makes them do something.*

He was growing impatient waiting around, but as he got within a spear's length of the opening, he observed inside a flash of light, making him duck down quickly, almost losing his grip on his spear as he fell to the rocky ground just in time as another red flash of light erupted out of the doorway, slamming into the wall behind him.

"Right … No more talking then!" Volkk said as he strained to get himself back up.

Volkk pulled his right arm backwards, quickly launching his spear directly through the opening, and without waiting to see where it landed, he turned and snapped his feet hard to swim as fast as he could away from the area.

Olen, who watched Volkk's maneuvers, quickly moved himself

to grab his friend, pulling him back over the wall, both feeling the water around them shake as streaks of red light erupted yet again.

"The gods!" Olen gasped as Volkk thought the same thing. Explosions ignited everywhere as the streaks of light flashed through the water around them, which, oddly, made it feel like hundreds of crabs were crawling over their skin.

What in all the oceans do they want? Volkk couldn't believe that those beings would have such power without their battle beasts. Suddenly, another flash of blue light slammed into the wall above their heads.

The two elves yelled out as rocks flew overhead, just missing them. Volkk got himself together quickly and was able to peer around to look at the building but looked back when Olen gasped, poking him in the shoulder to get his attention.

"Marn'azzi!" Olen gasped as he saw the most beautiful sea elf casually walking up the street towards them. The elf watched as her robes flowed silently in the waters, and her hair, bright blond and silver, floated in the water around her head. Her face looked like she was smiling, of all things.

Volkk turned and caught her walking up like nothing was wrong with the situation.

"Volkk ... what is she doing?!" Olen whispered quietly as they both watched her slowly walk past, smiling down at them as she did.

"She's protecting the city!" Volkk whispered.

Olen whispered something in return, but Volkk wasn't listening as he moved himself around to peer over the now-collapsed wall to watch her walk up to stand in front of the doorway.

His fear for her quickly stopped as three red streaks of light struck her, and like a rock hitting another, they bounced off like nothing happened.

"These are my children ... You will harm them no more!" The elves' heads ached instantly, hearing her words as they both watched her raise her arms up as bright golden-colored light glowed from her hands.

271

Amazed, the elves gripped the stone tightly as they watched more blue light slam into her, causing no harm. Looking at each other, both elves smiled, knowing she was here to end this, but those smiles disappeared when they began to feel the rock under their feet begin to shake, causing them to stand up and lift themselves into the water to look down.

Just as they did, a whole section of the rock floor cracked and collapsed, twisting itself in a circle with Marn'azzi in the middle. The building instantly fell apart and joined this movement of rocks as the elves watched her hand glow brighter by the moment. One by one, the massive battle beasts that lay abandoned fell into the hole that slowly opened under her feet.

The water around the elves quickly rushed past them, almost pulling them with it, so they had to swim hard against the current as the twisted rock opened up into a massive hole. To Volkk, it looked like an endless pit below.

"Gods protect us!" Olen screamed loudly as he watched the rock that moments before had been part of the city fall into the red lava below. Each battle beast exploded as it sank in, causing bits of the lava to leap up and land around the city.

Suddenly, it ended. The fast current trying to drag them down stopped. The sound of rushing water being pulled in stopped. They both saw the lava slowly get covered by newly formed rock as Marn'azzi slowly lowered herself down to the ground to look up at the shocked elves.

"*Come to me!*" The words were loud as they erupted in Volkk's mind. Olen also heard them, making him gasp as he looked around.

"*Come with me!*" Volkk snapped his feet and flew down to watch Marn'azzi pull her wings back, exposing the destroyed area of the city. As Volkk and Olen approached Marn'azzi, she was twisting her massive body around to watch the two elves swim closer. As the two warriors closed in, Volkk watched as she was she quickly shrank down back to the form that Volkk remembered seeing just before the attack.

Volkk and Olen landed softly on the sea bottom, instantly falling to their knees as Marn'azzi, now in elven form, walked slowly across to stand before the two, who were looking at the ground, waiting for her to speak.

"This is just one form of power their masters have to destroy the world, Volkk." Marn'azzi's words made the captain nod that he understood as he felt the anger coming from her as his gills flapped.

Marn'azzi walked past the two elves, who didn't dare move, only to stop at the edge of what was once a few council buildings, now destroyed from the attack, as she peered out into the deep darkness of the ocean.

"They intend to destroy and enslave all beings on this world. I, alone, cannot protect them all or take on these masters without help!" Her words crept into the minds of the elves as they looked at each other.

"Empress?" Volkk thought, not really knowing what to call her except Marn'azzi, and that wasn't how he should address something as powerful as she was.

"Join with me, and together we will save Marn!"

* * *

Shermee swallowed hard, trying her best to remind herself and those few with her to have courage. They were doing something good for the empire.

Aamee looked back to where the men were setting up camp at the edge of the burning field. She was worried that if help was needed, none of them would be able to make it to them in time, but for some reason, she was feeling oddly safe, even though she noticed several wolves keeping pace with their horses.

"Empress … we are being followed!" Aamee whispered as Shermee nodded that she heard her.

"They might just be curious. It looks like there's nothing here except the dead or dying," Junack whispered when she saw a few bodies not far off the road still moving, like they were trying to beg for help.

"We cannot help them, I'm afraid … We must continue!"
Jacoob whispered then. His chances of surviving this journey were
becoming slim, so he wanted to keep moving.

The horses trotted around trees that had fallen down over the
road, leaving them no choice but to go off the road. As they did,
the howls coming from the ridges grew louder, making the horses
whinny, which, in turn, caused even the two lead women warriors to
quickly place their hands on their sword pommels.

Moving down the road that wound itself down into a small gully,
they were amazed at how many corpses littered the fields around
them.

"It is like a massive battle took place here!" Junack whispered,
seeing arrows and swords stinking in bodies.

"Do you recognize any of the shields?" Shermee whispered,
knowing the others would know more about this area than she
would.

Leaning in their saddles, they couldn't recognize anything, for
dust, blood and ripped clothing covered many of the emblems. They
shook their heads in response to their empress.

"Jacoob … JACOOB?" she whispered loudly at the man, who was
staring straight ahead when he heard his name repeated another
time. He looked over as she asked the question. "Do you recognize
anything here?" Her words made the man take a deep gulp of air as
he looked at her smiling at him.

He looked quickly around at the shields and burnt flags and
banners lying on the ground and flapping in the slight breeze. "I, uh
… I do see one shield that I think I know, Empress," he whispered
just as another scream or howl echoed past them like the wind was
moving through, causing him to literally shake. It took everything
he had not to soil himself, and the women could tell how he was
getting very scared now.

His jaw began to shake enough that she was sure was she could
hear his teeth rattle. "Jacoob, please … Calm yourself and think.

It's all just in your mind!" Shermee's words almost disappeared as a wind shot past, causing even the horses to shake under their saddles.

Jacoob pointed to a shield he thought he recognized, which was lying on the ground with what used to be an arm holding on to it. Shermee looked quickly, but she couldn't see if it was man, elf or something else since it was burnt and deformed.

"Yes, that shield there." Jacoob almost whimpered as he spoke, but he pulled in a breath to gather his strength so he could finish. "I think it was a family that ruled along the eastern shores!" His words made the women look at each other and then at Jacoob, whose words came out very shaky.

"Jacoob … calm yourself, man!" Shermee raised her voice a little as she moved her horse over and placed a hand on his shoulder, feeling him shaking. "You will be fine, my friend!" The man looked at his empress. She could almost see tears rolling down his face.

"It's not the fear, Empress!" Jacoob whispered through his shaking voice as another chilly wind blew by, making the warriors grab their cloaks and pull them closer around their bodies.

"Then what it is?" Shermee was wondering if the man was so afraid now that he wasn't making any sense.

She stared at him for a few moments longer as their horses slowly trotted down the dirt road. She left her hand on his shoulder, trying to use it as a way to show her friend that she was there for him, as he swallowed a few times, trying to get his voice strong enough to answer her.

"That family … died over three hundred cycles ago in a battle against orcs rampaging across the west." Jacoob's words made Shermee let go of his shoulder as she turned slightly to look back at the shield. Thoughts ripped through her mind. She questioned what was going on as the others pulled their swords out, gasping slightly to get her attention.

Looking at her warriors and then over at what they were staring at, she could see forms moving in the mist. "Ghosts?" she whispered to herself as she gripped her reins tightly, fear moving through her body for the first time.

The entire group looked around as the howls that had been echoing in their ears suddenly stopped. The screams that seemed to be coming out of the mist also went silent, which caused Shermee to look around nervously to see if she saw anything.

She let out a breath of air slowly when she didn't see anyone, but a gasp from Aamee made her whip her eyes forward, where she saw three forms also sitting on top of horses looking back down at them from the hilltop ahead.

"Well, it seems we found your Nightwitches, Empress!" Junack's words made everyone swallow, wondering what to do now.

Pulling her reins back hard, Shermee felt hesitant for the first time since she had started this quest. Her friend was suffering mightily, but she had come too far to stop now.

"Empress?" Jacoob whispered as he alone felt the massive fear of what was before them. He looked down at his hands, which were turning white as he gripped the reins of his horse, who was having a problem staying in one place.

"Jacoob, they will take you back now. I fear you are too close. The three of us shall continue on." Shermee nodded to the rest of her guard, who nodded back at her.

Jacoob looked at his empress as he opened his mouth to say something, but no words came.

"Jacoob ... we will return!" she whispered quietly so only he could hear her. Jacoob nodded, quickly trying to speak, but his throat was too dry as he watched the three kick their horses forward and slowly trot up the road.

With Shermee in the middle, Junack taking the right and Aamee on the left, the three urged their nervous horses up the road silently. None spoke of the fear they each felt.

Shermee didn't move her eyes from the three beings at the top of the hill as they approached. With the exception of the horses whipping their tails back and forth, there was no movement at all as the riders calmly watched them. She squirmed a bit in her saddle, but she could see that each being was covered in some type of cloak.

Junack was the first to notice what was occurring around them. Making a chirp to get the others' attention, she motioned to her right. Both Shermee and Aamee looked to the right and then to the left of the road at the faces staring back at them from within the mists.

As the three slowed their pace, the faces were joined by skeleton bodies. Shermee licked her lips, wondering if she had made a terrible mistake as she looked directly in the eyes of one of the heads.

"They are …" she whispered loud enough that the others looked at their empress.

"Yes, they are, Empress," Aamee whispered, holding on to her pommel tightly.

"I think you were right, Junack. It seems that we have, indeed, found the Nightwitches!" Shermee said as they stared at the trio before them. The ghost-like figures were female … and elven.

After minutes passed with the ghosts still standing in the same spot, staring, Shermee, her nerves already rattled, lost her temper. "WELL!?!? Are we going to just stand here all night?!" Shermee yelled at the creatures.

When another minute went by without a response, Shermee pulled on her reins to turn around when a cold wind shot through them, causing their horses to whine. Shermee, however, was in no mood for games as she stood her ground and narrowed her eyes at the ghosts. Aamee and Junack moved their horses closer to Shermee, unsure of what they could do if dealing with magic.

"YOUUUUUUU HAVEEEEE COMMMMMEEEE TOOOO ASSSSSKKKKK USSSSSS FORRRRR HELLLLPPPP!" The words pierced through the air around the three, causing the horses to whine again as they moved around in circles.

"Yes. I am here to ask for your help. I am—" Shermee started.

"WEEE KNOWWW WHOOO YOUUU AREEEE, SHERRMEEEE!" the voice echoed back as Shermee peered at the blank faces looking at her from the mists.

Shermee didn't know who to speak to, for none of the riders moved as the voice echoed around them. So be it. She would say what she came to say and be done.

"Then you know that I mean no harm to you. I am here to request your help in the war that is coming. The empire needs your help. I need your help!" Shermee snapped her lips closed. She could only hope her words were convincing the beings as she again waited minutes for a response, making her warriors very nervous.

"Think they're planning to kill us?" Junack whispered to Aamee, who nodded vigorously. Shermee rolled her eyes.

"If they were, we'd be dead already. Both of you, calm yourselves!" Shermee motioned with her hand for them to lower their swords. Reluctantly, they slowly lowered them, whispering back that they couldn't protect her for long if something happened.

"I understand!" Shermee whispered back, never taking her eyes off the three beings, who were now moving slowly towards her.

"This is it … We're dead!" Junack whispered. Shermee shushed her as the three riders stopped directly in front of Shermee's group.

Shermee, Aamee and Junack stared at the three riders for a few moments when their bodies, along with the horses, burst into dust, causing Junack and Aamee to lift their swords and point them where the riders and horses had been.

Shermee watched in awe as the dust flew away. Another cold wind moved through, leaving nothing until the dust cleared. Now standing in front of the three women were three elven maidens where the ghosts were moments ago.

"Are you the Nightwitches?" Shermee spoke gently after getting her horse to stop moving around. Each nodded back.

"We have a lot to talk about, Empress Shermee of the Empire, daughter of King Dia Vaagini and Queen Shermeena!" Shermee noticed none of them were moving their lips, but the middle elf pulled back her hood enough to let them see her face. Another maiden raised a hand with her palm facing Shermee and her warriors as a flash of light covered them.

Jacoob was still sitting on top of his mount, shaking like it was the coldest night he had ever experienced in his life, as he watched his empress and her escort encounter the three riders.

"Hurry, Empress!" he whispered through his rattling teeth as he watched. He really wanted to leave here as the skeletons slowly walked past him, looking up at him through their eye sockets. *If they had eyes,* he quickly thought, so he closed his eyes and kept them shut, wishing they would leave him. Suddenly, a cry opened his eyes to see Aamee and Junack, along with his empress, disappear in a bright ball of green light, leaving the old man by himself.

"SHERMEEEEEE!" he screamed as he realized he was by himself … in the middle of nowhere … with only the dead looking back at him.

Chapter Thirty

"TO YOUR RIGHT!" Kalion yelled directly at Kikor, who quickly turned, only to fall backwards as a blade flew just short of cutting her head off. One of the three orcs charging her miscalculated his run and ended up tripping over Kikor as she fell on her back, making the orc fall forward onto her sword. As he gasped in pain, he looked down to find her smiling up him.

Whipping her legs around quickly, she left the sword temporarily sticking in the orc as she used the shorter sword to deflect the downward swings from the axes of the second and third orcs, both grunting loudly, trying to use their brute force to overpower the elf.

Whelor, not far away, ripped apart an orc who had tried to stab at his stomach. In one motion, he pulled the body apart, spreading blood all over himself and the ground, as another group of orcs, seeing their comrade's terrible death, turned and ran back into the hills in panic. That didn't stop Whelor as he reached forward to grab one of the fleeing orcs by the back of his armor to lift the screaming creature off its feet and over Whelor's head to hurl the orc into a boulder, killing it instantly.

Roaring loudly as he stretched his arms out to his sides, the beast looked left and right for his next victim when he caught sight of Meradoth doing a weird motion with his hands and feet, almost as if he was dancing, that ended with a blast of purple light that flew across to make four orcs instantly disappear as they were charging towards the mage.

Meradoth smiled under his breath at what he was doing when he noticed Kalion not far away exchanging blows with three orcs that had been able to corner the ranger against a large rock. His sword sparked as he kept the orcs just out of the range of his swings, knocking their swords back when they tried for him.

Kalion knew that he had to do something as he felt the rocky surface behind him. Knowing he couldn't move back any farther, he did the only thing that he could. He screamed loudly and, in one quick movement, jumped forward, moving his sword upwards as he rushed past the middle creature. He caught the orc by surprise as the blade cut up from stomach to face as the ranger flew past.

The other orcs saw their comrade fall forward as they turned to face Kalion, finding that their victim was now the predator. Kalion had turned himself around, and in one quick swipe, cut through the defenses of the orc on his left as it tried to bring its broken sword up to stop him.

Even as the orc groaned and fell to its knees, Kalion was turning himself to the third orc, who was swinging its axe at Kalion's chest, but the ranger was again too quick and ducked under the blade to stab forward, catching the orc in the stomach.

Pulling his sword out, the creature's innards fell out as the creature cried out in pain and fell back. Kalion turned just in time to watch Amlora snap her staff on the head of an orc so hard that even from where he was, about ten feet away, he could hear and feel the bone cracking.

The ranger didn't have a moment to think as Amlora slammed her staff on the ground, speaking a word as she did, causing the ground to turn to mud. Five orcs moving towards her instantly sank up to their chests into the mud, which quickly turned back to hard ground.

Hearing more screams, she whirled around, dropping to one knee as she did. Placing a hand on the ground, she whispered something quickly, looking at the large group of orcs bursting out of the brush, charging at her.

As the orcs moved around a small hill to get at the small girl, the side of the hill burst apart as roots from the trees shot across, cutting through the orcs, killing many instantly.

Amlora stood back up, noticing a few still lived. *But not for long,* she thought, smiling, as spiders and small critters crawled out of the ground to run across the roots and begin feeding themselves on the defenseless orcs. Their screams echoed as the druid turned to find Bennak, who cut through two orcs and crushed another with a fist.

Bennak used the moment to reach for a branch of a fallen tree, swinging it around and pushing another group of orcs back. When he got far enough back, he threw it at their faces, hoping it would do what he wanted. He almost laughed as they stopped to grab it, dropping their swords and giving him the opportunity to stab, cut and slash as quickly as he could, dropping and killing over ten orcs within moments.

"Come on, you ugly buggers … Come and get me!" he yelled out. Seeing that no more orcs were coming for him, he ran towards four of the ugly creatures moving in on the ranger, who at that moment was pulling his blade out of the head of an orc that he also had cut through, exposing its guts with a slash across the stomach.

Turning, he jumped back just as the huge form of Bennak slammed into an orc that was lifting its axe to chop at him. Bennak ran over the orc like it wasn't even there, crushing its head as the man stepped over him to swing his sword, cutting another orc's head in half. Before he joined in on the fun the big man was having, he jumped slightly as another explosion erupted on the far side. He looked to find Meradoth, who yelled out with laughter in his voice, smiling at his friend and telling him that he was experimenting on some new things he found back at God's Haven, making the ranger shake his head as he could tell that the mage was having fun.

Looking around for something to kill, Kalion watched as Whelor launched himself up into the air to fall hard onto an orc. This orc was almost as large as a man in height and frame, but unlike his fellow orcs, this one wasn't wearing its robe to cover its mutated and deformed face. Hearing the scream coming from behind, Kalion turned to watch Whelor fall into the orc as both tumbled on the ground.

Knowing he would be fine, Kalion turned to take two orcs that were running away. Whelor quickly leaned his body back, and with a few quick swings of his arms, his claws ripped the orc so completely apart that four orcs that were following their large comrade turned and cried out, retreating back into the mountains.

The few orcs left alive, seeing that their surprise attack had failed, turned and left the area as quickly as they could. Running through the brush, three orcs came into another clearing and were about to run through it when Kikor jumped in front of them from out of nowhere, confronting them with clenched teeth and looking at them, almost snarling.

Not giving them a moment, Kikor moved herself forward, swinging her sword back and forth at the chest and stomach of the closest orc on her right, killing it instantly.

The orc to her left dropped its sword and lifted it hands up, trying to surrender as Kikor turned herself to look back at him. She ran up to the kneeling orc, grabbing its armor behind his head, and with one quick motion, swung herself around the orc. Stepping only a few feet, it found Kikor's sword mysteriously sticking out of its stomach.

The orc looked down at the blade, noticing the blood also dripping from it as it groaned. Feeling a hand on its shoulder, it looked back seeing the face of an elf maiden breathing hard. Grunting, he saw her pull something back when, suddenly, he felt a sharp pain in his chest.

Standing two feet back, Kikor watched the orc collapse forward as she turned around to confront the last orc. She wasn't going to give it a chance to live, raising her sword up, wanting to cut its head into two halves.

"Kikor, wait!" Kalion ran up, grabbing her arm just before it came down. She looked at her friend, breathing as hard as he was.

"We don't have time for a prisoner, Kalion!" she gasped, looking down at the orc who was kneeling, whimpering loudly as it begged for its life.

"Hold on!" Kalion let go of her arm to slap at the kneeling orc.

"Stop your whimpering, orc!" Kalion looked back at the elf, and then, pulling out a knife, he knelt down to look at the ugly face of the creature who was trying to say something, but Kalion hit its face again to quiet it down.

"Where are you from? ... Tell me!" Kalion raised the knife, directing its point at the orc's throat, which, he saw, was heaving as the creature breathed. "How many of your kind are there?" Kalion pushed the point in just a bit as the orc quickly whimpered words.

"STOP ... Tell me slowly, orc." Kalion looked at Kikor, who was still breathing hard from the skirmish.

"We ... we come from mountain city ... We are many!" the orc mumbled as Kalion saw its eyes darting back and forth, looking at him and Kikor.

"How many is many?" Kikor asked, letting the orc see her grip her sword handle.

"Many, many, many!" The orc quickly stumbled through the words as Kalion thought for a moment and then stood back up.

"What do you think?" he asked Kikor looking down at the quivering creature at his feet.

"Well ... who knows how many 'many' means ... but I'm sure it is a lot." Kikor looked at Kalion when she finished. "What do you want to do with this now?"

Mountain city ... Many in number, he thought when he got a question. He knelt back down, looking at the creature. "Where were you going?".

"Amnach city to the east!" it whimpered again.

"Only city to the east is God's Haven," Kikor mumbled as Kalion stood back up, nodding that he had come to the same answer.

"I'll get the others ... You decide what to do now." Kalion smiled quickly as he turned to walk back down through the brush to where the others were finishing up. As he moved through the branches and leaves, he caught the orcs pleading in a high scream, and then there was silence as he knew Kikor had ended its life.

Meanwhile, back at the road, Bennak stabbed a few bodies of orcs when he saw Whelor looking at him. "Just making sure they're dead!" He smiled at the beast, who grunted and turned away, walking to hide behind a bush, leaving the half-orc to finish.

Shrugging his shoulders, he continued his play as Kalion emerged from the brush, looking around. Walking over to where Bennak was standing, Kalion nodded his head as Bennak gave him a "What?" look.

"These orcs were coming out of the Sernga Mountains in force because they got the call."

"The call?" Amlora looked disturbed by what Kalion was saying.

"I get the impression that this call is the opposite of what we want, my friend ... to survive while they want to kill us all!" Meradoth spoke as he rubbed his hands together like he was warming them up.

"I believe the border is just on the other side of the hill ... We need to get to it now!" Bennak spoke, standing up after using one of the orcs' robes to wipe the blood off his sword.

"Where is Ame-tora?" Meradoth asked Bennak

"I am sure he will catch up when we get to Father Gate," Bennak stated.

"Then let us not stop, shall we!" Meradoth smiled. The group walked over to where their horses had gotten themselves to, seeing King Dia move out of where he had hidden during the skirmish. Nodding to the king, each checked their saddle, quickly swinging themselves up and beginning to ride out of the area. Whelor ran out of the forest and quickly joined the group, now back in his normal appearance. Only Bennak smiled, seeing the man move up quietly.

"You and I, Whelor, yes?" Whelor sensed that Bennak was trying to be his friend again, so he nodded back, smiling as Kikor ran up and swung herself onto her saddle nearby and rode off to catch up.

"Friends, yes!" The two men quickly moved up to be the rear guard of the group as they travelled on the last part of the road, moving over the hill, only to stop when they saw, peeking through between two cliffs of rock, massive trees standing tall before them.

"Is that it?" Amlora gasped, sensing the aura coming from the trees.

"Just beyond that, yes ... but we need to cross the bridge that expands over the ravine that cuts across the land." Kalion smiled knowing that their short but hard journey from God's Haven was almost done.

"Let us finish our ride, shall we, my friends? ... I'm hungry, the night is almost upon us ... and my mount here is in need of major fun time!" Meradoth's comment made the rest laugh, shaking their heads as they made their way down the incline, seeing that the road, indeed, stopped at a massive pair of columns that represented the northern end of the bridge.

"I hope they have warm fires and broth ... I'm starving!" Bennak piped in as they trotted up in pairs to the bridge, only to see more orcs moving towards them to block their way.

"Problem!" Kikor yelled out loud as she pulled her sword in a snap. Pulling her reins to turn herself around, she caught sight of large numbers of orcs and what looked like hill giants running down the road towards them.

"How many?" Kalion asked as he held his reins, getting ready to ride hard.

"Too many ... Moveeeee!" She yelled back, kicking her horse to turn around as the others, in one movement, kicked their horses and rode hard across the bridge.

Meradoth leaned down in his saddle as he rode over the bridge, catching sight of a single man running south towards the tower gate the mage was beginning to see.

Turning his head, he saw Amlora seeing the same thing and giving him the look that maybe he was friendly ... *Hoping,* Meradoth thought as he kicked his horse to get it to move faster.

The horse's hooves echoed loudly as they crossed the wide

expanse of the bridge, but the sound was quickly covered as the roar from the orcs overwhelmed them, bringing a bit of anxiety to them to get to the towers quick.

Kikor, being the last to get on the bridge, turned herself slightly in her saddle to look back as she crossed the halfway mark upon the bridge. As she did, she saw the road and edge of the bridge that she had just been on moments before now being crowded with orc upon orc screaming as they began to run onto the bridge. She almost thought the bridge began to shake from the tremendous amount of movement upon it.

Looking back south, the rest of the group was riding hard to get to the gate towers she could see in the distance. She caught sight of men along the ramparts moving quickly to get ready for the attacking orcs.

The two large gate doors were open, but she saw one being pushed closed as two men waved at them to hurry.

Calling and kicking her horse, Kikor could almost feel the eyes of the orcs behind her as she heard their feet tromping on the bridge, trying to catch her. She didn't have a choice but to ride hard to get to that gate, and ride hard she did, seeing her friends enter the one open gate and quickly riding inside.

The screams seemed to be everywhere to her as she got to the south side of the ravine. Both she and her horse lurched forward and rode harder as the screams and roars behind her continued on.

"HURRRYYY!" her ears caught through the orcs' yells, seeing men waving at her. Leaning down lower in her saddle, she could see archers pulling their arrows back and releasing arrows over her head.

Not looking back, she rode through the gate, seeing nothing but blurs of the guards that were to her left and quickly hearing the loud metal sounds as the gate was shut tight, ending with a loud bang as the bolt was pushed closed.

Pulling on her reins, she caught up to the rest of the group, who were all smiling back at her, breathing hard from the excitement of the chase.

You there … Who are you!" A group of armed warriors moved quickly, looking at the group of laughing warriors.

"Who are you? … Speak!" one of the warriors spoke. Kalion could hear the confidence in his voice.

"We have come from God's Haven, sir … This is King Dia from Brigin'i. We've brought him to the empire!" Kalion spoke out so that all could hear his voice as he took in the numbers before him.

He could see there were at least one hundred warriors running around the courtyard of the towers, but he could see archers doing their part, still letting arrows go at the orcs, whom they could hear screaming just beyond the gates.

Looking at a few of his comrades and then back at Kalion, the warrior said, "God's Haven, huh?" At that moment, the group saw a man walk out of the far tower towards them, walking and acting like he was in charge of this place.

"You're with whom, sir?" the man calmly asked as Kalion smiled, seeing who it was finally.

"General Vana, sir … We fought together with General Summ against Methnorick … I bring King Dia with us, sir." Kalion motioned to Dia, who pulled back his hood, revealing himself to the general and the warriors in the courtyard.

"Well, well!" the warrior loudly spoke as he stepped forward to shake the arm of the king. "Welcome to the Empire of Pendore'em and Edlaii!" The man smiled as he looked at the king, who thanked him, smiling down at him.

"I think we should reserve introductions until we figure out what to do with those orcs you decided to bring with you, do you not think?" Vana said, smiling at the group.

"Agreed … General," Kalion spoke, swinging his leg over and landing on the ground, holding his reins as he also shook the general's arm.

"Where do you need us, sir?" Kikor gently spoke as she repeated the same thing, walking up to General Vana.

"You archers up to the ramparts … The rest … well, just rest and wait … Not much for the rest of us to do at the moment really!" Vana nodded to one of his men, who told him about the numbers of orcs outside.

Looking over as Dia slowly lowered himself to the ground, groaning, Vana ordered a few men to help the king to find some warmth and comfort inside when he noticed the empress' man walking up smiling.

"Ahhh, everyone … This is Quinor … He can help answer any questions … I have a wall to protect!" Vana nodded to Kikor and Kalion as they grabbed their bow staves and followed the man up the stairs to help out the Father Gate archers in defense.

"Are you the general's aid?" Amlora asked as she watched warriors of the empire disperse themselves and make themselves busy getting ready.

"Me? … No, no … I'm no aid. I'm Quinor … Guardian of the Empire!" His words made Meradoth turn around to stare at him as the rest of the group, slowly lowering themselves off their saddles, stopped and looked at each other in silence.

Bennak let out a small giggle but didn't speak as Whelor smiled as well, not knowing what to say to this man, when the area was covered in loud sound as Vana ordered the gate's horns to be blown.

Meradoth walked over, and looking at the smiling man, he whispered, "Who are you?"

* * *

The orcs tried their best to keep themselves moving in the cold. The morning sun was beaming down on their backs, but all they felt was cold as they watched icicles forming on their hoods. For a while, many walked faster or jumped upon the ground as the formation wound its way west towards the mountains ahead.

Many fell to the side and died in the snow, but the leaders of this ramble didn't stop and help. The last one that did was dead, and his spine was laying across the saddle of the dark figure leading the formation — Methnorick.

Behind the orc formation, the ice giants kept their eyes looking along the perimeter of the army. Not that they had anything to worry about, but orders came to them to keep watch for anything that might try to attack on their flanks.

Far ahead, another giant was put as point, with orders to find a track that would get them to the mountains. Methnorick and his armies in sight, the giant moved quickly ahead not stopping when he passed through a castle that had been built by men many cycles ago. Its walls had crumbled and fallen to the ground, but a tower still poked out of the snow.

As the giant got within a league of the base of the Forbidden Mountains, mountains that cut through the land, moving from the southeast towards the northern shores of the Cua Leas'a Ocean, he stopped to observe the movement of a group of snow wolves that were roaming.

For a few moments, he watched them not moving, even when one lifted its head to stare at him and then quick trot away, catching up with its pack. He smiled to himself as he felt a grumble in his stomach. He didn't have the time or the ability to catch them. Pulling himself up, he quickly he moved forward.

For him, it hadn't taken him that long to get to this point, as his feet were larger than a horse's or orc's feet, and his people had skill to almost run on top of the snow. Given their massive size and weight, it seemed almost impossible, but they almost looked like they did.

He got himself to a large boulder formation that he pulled himself up, grabbing the edges of one of the rocks until he got enough of himself up onto a ledge to look around. From where he was, he found he could clearly see the dark shapes of the army marching west. Looking north and south, he could see what used to be known as the Ice Road, a road that had been built by men and elves many cycles ago that connected the northern ocean to the southern reaches, but weather and the threats of his people and other beasts made it hard for them to use, so they left it. This was what he was looking for, for from there a smaller path branched west through the mountains that could get Methnorick's arm through the mountain, he was sure of it.

Almost there! he thought, looking up at the mountains and seeing fog rolling over its tops as it slowly moved passed them.

He looked back, catching the sight of his master slowly riding just ahead of the army. His dark figure sitting upon the horse even from this distance sent what was almost like a chill from the cold, but the giant's thoughts shot back to when he had seen Methnorick in one flash of movement kill an orc commander who questioned his marching orders. Even with his cycles of living upon the snow, the giant had never seen anything like it.

Find the road … Watch for enemies upon it … Keep it clear until I arrive! the giant thought, recalling Methnorick's haunting orders to him days ago. *I will do just that!* He swallowed as he moved his eyes up and down the road, seeing nothing but the cold wind moving the snow over it.

* * *

The light in Shermee's eyes lessened enough that she could see where she was standing. No horse in sight but standing, which she thought was curious.

Next to her were the two other warriors that had accompanied her, and she could see that they were as confused as she was, looking around to see where they all were.

"Empress … are you well?" Aamee whispered, stepping forward and placing a hand on Shermee's arm, checking

Shermee nodded back quickly that she was. "Fine, just fine!"

"Where are we?" Junack reached down, quickly patting her hip. "My sword … It's gone." Aamee quickly reached down and found that hers was gone as well.

"Your weapons and mounts are safe, Empress!" a voice rang from somewhere. The three women looked around for who was speaking when Junack saw who it was and pointed so the others would notice.

"Are we welcomed here?" Shermee swallowed when she finished, trying to act brave, believing that the women with her could sense that she was scared to death.

The women were scared as well, but they hid it well as they looked at their empress and then back to the being that was speaking to them: a woman, but not clothed in the same manner. This woman wore almost entirely white robes and a cloak covered with a gray fur and stood next to what looked like a throne.

"You are safe within my, realm Queen Shermee … Why have you come here?" The warriors were hearing words, but the three noticed this woman's mouth wasn't moving.

Shermee stepped forward, leaning her head slightly back as she pulled in a deep breath. "I have travelled from the capital … I need your help!"

Quickly, Shermee and her comrades were covering their ears, kneeling down in pain as the chamber erupted in the loudest shriek of laughter they had ever heard. Looking up as she covered her ears, she saw the woman staring at her still wasn't moving her lips nor showing signs of laughter.

She looked over at Aamee, who was clenching her head tightly. Shermee was wondering what to do when the laughter finally dissipated enough that they could let go of their ears to stand up.

"An empire that has abandoned us for glory and riches … an empire that sends no apology to its citizens that have been in pain … Your empire puts its own people in prison camps … an empire that only cares for MENNNNNNNNN!" The last word echoed, causing even the ground they stood on to shake.

* * *

Volkk swam over the area that once held the council for the great underwater city, which as now partly destroyed by the blue energy weapons. Floating next to the captain was Marn'azzi, who had not spoken since ordering the elf to send out word for those warriors that could still fight to gather along the northern perimeter and wait for Volkk.

Volkk's head gently shook, as he couldn't believe the devastation those things had done to his home. The blue and green glow that once shined high over the city now flickered. Those killed defending the city were slowly being picked up and taken to a place to be buried in the seabed that lay over a mile outside the city.

The carcasses of the beasts that lay everywhere were left where they lay for the time being. Volkk could sense that anger needed to be let out soon, as a few roaming bands of the young moved around, looking for any of the beasts or weird occupants that could be found and quickly dispatched in haste.

His eyes scanned the landscape of the city, noticing a few of the dolphins that had come to their aid also were taking their dead away, but many more were moving towards where Marn'azzi ordered them to gather with the elves.

"I know you want revenge, my child ... but now is not the time!" The soft words drifted into Volkk's mind as he looked over, noticing her looking directly at him.

"My people will want to do something soon," Volkk responded, moving a hand towards a group forming not far below the two at that moment. Both were feeling and could almost hear the sadness of the grieving as they hung in the water.

"I can feel the land up above waking up ... There has been ... death!" Volkk could sense from her words that she knew something that she was not sharing.

"Do you know ... these creatures that were inside these beasts?" Volkk floated to hang directly in front of her when, like a blast, Volkk was pushed back slightly as the wave from Marn'azzi slammed into him.

Volkk quickly recovered, but in looking back at her, his mind was suddenly filled with images that flashed across his eyes, making him grab his head, not from the pain, but trying to understand what he was seeing.

Land creatures ... flying ground horses ... cousins ... beings that look like elves ... and ... two beasts that almost look like Marn'azzi ... but smaller. Volkk closed his eyes tightly as the last image floated through his mind. Once the images stopped, he looked up at the surface as she floated there, seeing her arms wide open.

"Mother ... What is it? ... Why? ..."

"My children," she said, almost seeming to sigh, *"... come with me now!"* Marn'azzi turned, and quicker than he thought an elf could, shot off through the water to the north. Looking down at the city for a quick moment, Volkk could see that his people were doing their best in cleaning up ... *I'll be back soon,* he thought, and then, snapping his feet, he moved through the water, trying to catch Mother, still not understanding what he saw in his mind.

Chapter Thirty One

Volkk watched Marn'azzi float to the seabed as she rubbed her hands together, slowly at first and then speeding, turning the water around her like a whirlpool. Pushing himself so that the water rushing around didn't catch him, as he didn't have a clue what she was up to, the sea elf looked over the small coral mountain that separated the two from the elvish army gathered along with their allies, waiting.

When the rush of water began to roar, he looked back down and quickly brought his hands up to cover his face, as her hands glowed like that of the sun above. Trying to look, Volkk could just make out Marn'azzi lifting up her glowing hand as she stopped the movement and before he had a moment to think, in her next move she knelt down quickly and slammed her fists hard onto the sandy rock bed she was standing on.

"Godssss!" Volkk gasped as his ears heard the loud crack of rock that erupted under her hands. Lowering his hands, he watched the seabed almost shake and crack everywhere. He could see a wave of water high above their heads. His eyes caught the sight as one wave caught a mountain of coral, which instantly began to break up and fall into the sand, when he caught Marn'azzi looking at him.

"It is done!" he heard her speak, still catching the anger in her voice.

"What did you do?" Volkk gasped, cautiously wondering what she had just done to the seabed.

"There are things that I cannot explain without you seeing them for yourself, child … Come with me and let us bring the hammer down on those that brought sorrow to you and your people!" Marn'azzi smiled

as she rose up to look directly into his face.

The ground had stopped its movement, so whatever she did, he thought, it was now beyond his eyes and ears. But he trusted her. She was the mother of Marn, after all. Turning, he smiled back at her quickly, and together they moved over the ridge, where the elves and hundreds of thousands of their sea allies waited, ready.

* * *

You feel it, do you not? The words floated in the air like a whisper as a lone figure stood at the top of a rampart, looking towards the water and watching it hit the shoreline and rubble that used to be the massive port of Blath 'Na City.

The black-robed figure stood alone as it looked out from underneath its large hood. *How can she be alive, brothers!* Another whisper moved in the wind as the being stood, still letting the wind whip his robes around.

No need to worry, my brothers! The voice laughed in the wind, almost like thunder.

Encourage the cyclops and end this! another voice stated as the figure moved slowly to look back at the city that was burning and showing heavy activity from the thousands of orcs building machines.

Inside what had once been the city's main square, a group of orcs hard at work pulled the chains, trying to bring a massive block of stone onto a wheeled cart, when a flash made them stop and look around quickly. Seeing nothing except the wisp of smoke where something might have stood, unknown to the any of them, one of the masters had been standing, watching.

All along Blath 'Na, a sudden silence moved across the landscape as the masters gathered together, minus the one that had just left, moving and standing in a circle silently. Below, orcs and other dark creatures could feel that there was a sudden change in the air. Something was moving under their feet, or in the air, around them everywhere. None knew what it was.

Shermee looked at the face of the elf maiden standing not three feet from her — if she could call it a face, for the maiden's face was more a decaying piece of flesh that made it look like the elf was truly dead.

"I am not here to debate your mistreatment and deaths … I am here to ask your help, my lady!" Shermee whispered the statement now for the third time. Her head was still pounding from the maiden's laughter not long before. "Your people have suffered enough … I want to change that!" Shermee spoke the words but realized that she had no idea how that could be done.

"Change? … Change what?" The face again didn't move as the empress heard the words.

"I want to help you all return to the world … and live in peace!" Shermee was quickly thinking of what to do, but saying 'peace' only brought laughter that echoed loudly around her.

"I was murdered in a world I thought was all about peace …" Shermee swallowed, beginning to worry she had gone too far.

"I understand, my lady … I understand …"

"YOU UNDERSTAND NOTHING!" The echo made Shermee grab her head again.

"I … I want to!" Shermee grasped at the words as she stepped back, whimpering from the pain moving through her head.

"UNDERSTAND THIS!" Shermee looked up just as the maiden stepped up to lift a skeletal arm, placing it roughly on her forehead. Before she could stop the elf, her eyes rolled back as she began to see images and sounds move through her mind.

It was a gentle morning with the sun moving up over the mountains. To the right, a large column of riders slowly trotted down a well-travelled road. As the image slowly moved, Shermee began to understand that this column was elven maidens. Each was dressed in a gray cloak to cover themselves from the morning's chill. Many had theirs pulled up to cover their heads, but a few, the empress noticed, had them down, exposing their bright blond hair in the morning sun.

Shermee noticed that many were laughing and talking to each other as the image moved past one maiden that Shermee was sure had to be the maiden she was speaking to. Moving down, Shermee noticed that there were no escorts or guards in this column. She got the feeling that these maidens were traveling towards a place of worship.

The image continued moving as Shermee heard a gentle, high-pitched voice that almost whispered to her, "We were druids, clerics, maidens of great promise that our people hoped would bring peace over the lands … Our travels had brought us together to journey towards the northern city of God's Haven, where our people had built temples and places worship to contemplate life."

The image turned like the clouds above raining down, showing when the maidens noticed off in the distance silhouettes of riders — hundreds of them — at the top of a hill not far away, watching them.

Shrieks erupted all along the column as the maidens, fearing for themselves, quickly began urging their horses forward, riding hard down the road. Shermee could feel the fear they were experiencing. The mystery of who those riders were was quickly solved when they screamed out something that Shermee couldn't understand, but as one, rode forward and down the hill, charging towards the fleeing elves.

Shermee gasped as the scene turned violent before her. She couldn't even describe what she was seeing before her, but now she understood the hatred these maidens had.

"I understand now!" she whispered. "I … I understand, and I am sorry!" she repeated as tears formed on her face and slowly moved down her cheeks, causing her to close her eyes.

When the maiden pulled her hand away, Shermee gasped as the flash of images suddenly ended, causing her to fall forward slightly, looking up at the maiden standing over her.

"Your sorrow is not needed, but now you understand … No man is safe … They only bring death and destruction … and we are here to take it back!" Shermee pushed herself up to stand up as she noticed more of the maidens beginning to emerge out of the mist surrounding her.

She felt the presence of the two warriors that had accompanied her move slowly up next to her as she looked around, feeling the cold presence of the skeletal and decaying forms of the maidens around them.

Feeling a sense of urgency within her, Shermee breathed in a deep breath and spoke out with a raised voice. "Come with me and you can have enough deaths of men or male creatures to fulfill your need for revenge for many cycles … Help me end the destruction of a man that is bringing death in the north … With your help … this empire will be safe, a place where you all can live in peace!"

The faces hanging in the mists slowly turned and looked around at each other as the three women began to notice that many were not decayed as much as they had thought. *Clearly not far from being dead at all,* Shermee thought as each face emerged as a skull, turning itself into the face of a beautiful elven maiden. Each showed innocence and eagerness to see the world.

The three stood for what seemed hours of time as the faces gently looked towards them. Shermee looked at her two warriors, who returned nods, informing her they were well.

The silence was broken when the women heard a quiet rumble that sent a slight shake along the ground they stood on, making them look down. But it stopped as quickly as it had begun when they heard a single loud voice speak from the mist.

"Marn'azzi has awoken. Do you feel it, sisters?" The voice joyfully spoke as Shermee caught the sight of two bodies moving out of the mist, forming into two elvish maidens moving through the crowd to stand before them with their arms up as everyone around the three nodded with smiles.

"This is a sign from the goddess that she is the one …"

"We fight for the one they call Empress of the Empire …!" The words echoed, making the three smile brightly as Shermee took in the clothing on the maidens, which was almost like what she had seen in the images — soft gray and dark blue robes with cloaks hanging over soft dresses of unknown material — as they moved up to her.

"Where are we needed?" one of the maidens whispered, making Shermee blink quickly, seeing that she was moving her mouth to the words.

"In … in the north!" Shermee whispered, having to swallow quickly to get her voice back. "I do need to ask you, though … How do we get from here to there?" she asked, noticing their horses weren't around.

Made in the USA
Lexington, KY
11 March 2018